THE LETTER FROM ITALY

Mel Frances

First published in 2025 by Emby Books.

Copyright © 2025 by – Mel Frances – All Rights Reserved.
It is not legal to reproduce, duplicate, or transmit any part of this document in either electronic means or printed format. Recording of this publication is strictly prohibited.

The Letter From Italy is a work of fiction. The names, characters and incidents portrayed are entirely fictitious and purely a product of the author's imagination. Any similarities to places, and persons, living or dead is entirely coincidental.

For Dawn, miss you x

*'Many people will walk in and out of your life,
but only true friends leave footprints in your heart.'*
Eleanor Roosevelt.

1

Northern Italy, February 2020
A black Alfa Romeo Giulia Sport swept into the underground car park, and eased to a halt in bay twenty-six. The driver lifted a mobile phone from his jacket pocket and called his wife, fingers drumming on the steering wheel. Leo had many conversations with his wife, Verna, from his car, his office, and occasionally whilst taking a break during his daily run. Today was no exception.

'I wouldn't be surprised if this area is quarantined soon, fingers crossed I can get a flight home.'

Coronavirus was shutting down towns and cities as swiftly as motion-sensor lighting clicks off along a corridor; and northern Italy was bearing the brunt of the first European wave of infection.

'Hope you get out of there soon, and in one piece. It'll be great having you home, it's been a long stint this time.'

'Always good to work over here, and the team are excellent, but I can't wait to get back.' Leo yawned. 'How are the children?'

'All fine here, we've missed you. No doubt they'll be planning a warm welcome as usual.'

Leo sensed Verna's smile matched his at the thought of their children's homecoming plans. 'I'll let you know once I've booked a flight, and give the welcoming party a kiss each from me. Love you.'

'I will, love you too.' Verna ended the call.

Graziella inhaled the heady scent of citrus and woody vanilla, as afternoon sunshine illuminated the bougainvillea-strewn balcony. Twirling a thick strand of brunette hair around her forefinger, she watched bustling bodies in the narrow, cobbled street below. Residents of Lodi were going about their business before the inevitable lockdown. Barefoot, she padded across the spacious tiled floor to the kitchen, appreciating the smooth, cool sensation on the soles of her feet. As she stirred the risotto, Graziella recalled the first day Leo arrived at the car manufacturing headquarters six months ago. She was assigned as his P.A. for the duration of his contract. Their attraction was mutually explosive as they gazed at each other, and it was only days before she moved into his apartment.

In Graziella's mind, the looming pandemic meant Leo would have to stay in Italy, and those frequent trips to the UK, including visits to, the English family, would have to wait. Leo told her about his divorce and his children, but surely, once he heard her news, he would want to stay in his native land for good. She glanced at her watch, he would be home any minute, tonight would be extra special. Five minutes later she heard Leo's familiar, 'ciao, Bella,' as he entered the apartment. He walked up behind her and she glanced at his tanned, lean forearms around her waist as she prepared the finishing touches to dinner. As he swept the curtain of her plush hair aside, the thrill of his kiss tingled on the nape of her neck.

Leo changed out of his work clothes and emerged from the bedroom, noticing Graziella preening when he commented on the perfect dinner table setting. As the candlelight reflected in the gleaming white crockery, he asked, 'special occasion?' chewing on warm, fresh focaccia.

'Maybe,' she smiled across the table. 'What's the situation at work?'

'A meeting tomorrow,' Leo answered in-between gulps of the delicious pesto flavoured meal. He hadn't bothered with the salad starter, he was ravenous.

Her smile became a frown, 'you're not going in are you?'

'Not sure, will wait for a message or call to see if the offices and labs are being closed.'

'They must be!' Throwing her arms wide in disbelief, 'for goodness' sake, people are dying, yet the cars are more important.'

'Production has to continue. We don't know how long this virus will go on, weeks, perhaps even months, the company could lose a fortune if trade stops. I need to return to the UK soon to discuss what strategies my company needs to employ about the uncertainty ahead.'

'Why don't you consider moving here for good, my love,' Graziella pouted, 'it makes perfect sense, you can work from anywhere in the world, why England?'

'Not this again Graziella, you know my consultancy is based there and covers the whole of Europe, not only Italy. It's crucial I spend a significant amount of time in the UK. All this,' he said, fork in hand, gesturing around the luxurious apartment, 'doesn't come cheap, I need international contracts.'

'I know, I do appreciate it, but is there any rush to return?' then smugly, 'you probably can't for some time anyway as the airports are closing.' Leo stopped eating and tapped his mobile, then slid it to one side noticing Graziella's scowl.

They chatted over dinner, Leo picked up the wine bottle, 'where's your glass?'

'I'm not having any wine.'

Leo glanced up with raised eyebrows. 'Oh, you ok?'

'Yes,' a beautiful grin spread across Graziella's face.

He shrugged, filled his glass, then noticed her displeasure, something was odd.

'So … aren't you going to ask me why not?' she seemed frustrated.

'I guess you simply don't want wine tonight.' Leo thought it wouldn't be long before he didn't have to tolerate her playful banter, and immature guessing games about yet another anniversary milestone in their short relationship.

A shuddering dawning, rippled throughout his body as he looked into her deep brown eyes and gleeful face. Graziella placed a positive pregnancy test in front of him. With a squeal of delight, 'Papa!' she rushed over to him and flung her arms around his neck. Sitting on his knee trying to kiss him, she seemed disheartened at his blank response, so he put his arms around her.

Leo looked beyond the floating wisps of her luxurious hair, then beyond the gossamer drapes fluttering gently in the cool breeze from the balcony. His glazed eyes stared into the distant stars of the night sky, wishing he was anywhere else but here.

2

The morning after Graziella broke the news to Leo, the world had changed. Their town was designated a quarantine area along with several others in the Lombardy region. By 24 February 2020, police had cordoned off some towns as cases in the area were rising exponentially. In one town, two hundred and thirty people were admitted to hospital with Covid overnight and seven had died. Roadblocks were set up and a curfew meant the police could order residents to return home immediately, unless they were out for essential reasons.

Leo, blinking to fend off morning light, opened the shutters leading onto the balcony. Graziella breathed in, 'the bakery is still open,' as she joined him. Leo savoured the comforting aroma, noticing everything seemed different. He leaned over the balcony, to peer left, then right towards the town centre. Most of the buildings on their pretty street had their shutters closed as the sun streamed over rooftops. Apart from the echoing crystal-clear noise of a siren, with no other traffic to dampen its shrill effect, it was deathly silent. No people, no chatter and no footsteps on the pathway below.

'It's like a war-zone,' whispered Leo. Not only was he worried about the spread of the virus, he was more terrified of the prospect of becoming a father for the fourth time. A father to a child with a woman, he believed he was simply having an affair with. He cringed inside as he recalled telling Graziella he was divorced and certainly did not reveal when he returned to the UK, he was living a full and content family life with his wife and their three children. His phone showed two missed calls and a voicemail from Verna.

'You're surely not going into work.' He noticed Graziella's disdain as she glanced at his phone. 'We'll have plenty of time to plan ahead now you're going to be home for …' she shrugged and smiled, 'who knows how long?' She put her arms around his waist and her head on his chest. Leo rested an arm around her shoulders, depressed and nauseous, this nightmare was real. To his consternation, Graziella continued in rapid-fire Italian, explaining the development stage of the fetus, where they may buy a family home, and baby names they could consider. He looked at her, the poor kid, he thought, so excited. He needed time to sort out this mess. In a warped way, the pandemic may afford him time and excuses not to return to the UK yet, to his real life.

'I need to make a few calls.'

'Really! Work again?'

'No, Verna has asked me to call the kids because they are worried about me.' He watched her storm away with venom in her eyes. He would win her round later and the making-up would be incredible, it always was. The women Leo bedded were often unaware or dismissive of his marital status, it was easy. The situation was more complicated with Graziella, but he couldn't resist her. He suggested she left her job as his assistant, because he deemed it inappropriate for him to be romantically involved with an employee. Once she left, no one mentioned her, least of all him. His duplicity was all about planning, and he was a master at that; he was in full control, until now.

Leo looked at Graziella and thought, what the hell was she thinking, getting pregnant! They had never discussed it. She must have assumed this was a permanent relationship, forgetting birth control was also his responsibility. He watched her stomp from the bedroom into the bathroom. She often took a long bath when he was on the phone to, *"the English family."*

'How are things over there?' asked Verna, 'seems horrendous from news reports.'

'It really is horrific. The town is quarantined, so I have to stay here longer unfortunately until the situation settles down. The authorities have implemented a system whereby you can only go out for essential food shopping. I think the cleaning service is still in place here though, as they need to keep buildings sanitised.' He slid the precautionary lie into the conversation. 'I'll call the children this evening, but tell them I'm fine.'

Later, Graziella was watching her favourite TV drama, which conveniently coincided with the time he called home, always with his laptop facing away from the spare bedroom door. Leo was surprised when the precautionary lie became a necessity. Graziella inadvertently breezed into the spare bedroom, said his name, realised he was making and online call, and promptly left, not before a flick of anger crossed his face.

Leo's daughter asked, 'who was that, Daddy?'

'Just the maid service sweetheart.' He swiftly moved onto another subject, distracting her from any further questions. He was incensed on one occasion when Graziella posted an image of them on his company Instagram account, showing it to him triumphantly. He deleted the account immediately to cover his tracks, making damn sure there was no other incriminating evidence of him anywhere. He had to be scrupulously careful now.

By 9 March, Leo read Prime Minister Giuseppe Conte had imposed a national lockdown and the Citizens Protection Service needed the population to comply. On 10 March all flights to and from Italy were suspended, and unless passengers had explicit family or work reasons to travel, no one was going anywhere. Leo contacted Verna explaining he couldn't easily leave, and would rather wait until the situation was less risky, which played in his favour. For now, he was relatively safe from scrutiny. Graziella was in the early stages of pregnancy and her expectancy was not only for a baby, but for Leo to remain in Italy permanently to start their family.

3

Northumberland, February 2020

Twenty years ago, Leo met Verna at a vintage sports car rally, both admiring a pristinely renovated red 1960s MGB Roadster, when Leo struck up a conversation. The attraction was instantaneous. Her English rose beauty and his swarthy Italian looks were a perfect contrasting match. The three children they produced subsequently benefitted from the best genetics on offer. After studying in England, Leo worked his way up the ladder to a senior position at a leading car manufacturer in the north of England. They now ran an automotive software design consultancy, VLR Software, for prestigious car manufacturers.

Hannah, Verna's high school friend often said Leo's petrol head obsession with the high-octane world of prestigious fast cars had rubbed off on her too; as Verna had always desired fast, good-looking, powerful models, a metaphor perhaps. Hannah was Coronavirus doomscrolling, when Leo's handsome smiling face popped up on Instagram. 'How come middle-aged men with greying hair look distinguished, not old,' grumbled Hannah. Leo was standing with arms outstretched and hands resting on a rail behind him. The beautiful blue backdrop of Italian lake and jigsaw-blue sky was eclipsed by the stunning young woman in the foreground taking a selfie. Wow, thought Hannah, Bellissima!

There was no wording or hashtag underneath the picture, which was posted on his VLR Software Instagram account. Hannah tapped on the image and pinch-zoomed to scrutinise the girl, whose face was virtually obliterated by the biggest bug-eye designer sunglasses she'd ever seen. Bellissima was young, maybe early twenties, with a beautiful smile revealing toothpaste-ad, perfect white teeth. Hannah conjured up various scenarios; maybe Bellissima was a work colleague on a company trip or a young relative, a niece perhaps, though Hannah was sure Leo had no siblings. Maybe a random tourist had airdropped the photo to him, but who was he with at the restaurant? Or ... maybe he knew Bellissima ... and he knew her intimately. The image troubled Hannah. Alerted from her contemplation, she heard her son's voice. 'Is tea ready?' Ross shouted from his bedroom, 'I'm starving to death!'

Hannah yelled back, 'ah how awful, you poor thing, come down in five.' Hannah remembered the pizza and potato wedges were in the oven, and salvaged the meal in the nick of time as Ross wandered to pick up his plate. She messaged Evan, tea was ready, and heard rapid thumping down the stairs. In typical fourteen-year-old style, Bluetooth headphones slung around his neck, he took a drink and the piled-high plate, then walked away without a word. A sarcastic, 'thanks very much!' from Hannah, forced Evan to give her a sheepish grin as they looked into each other's blue-grey eyes. He hooked the kitchen door wide open with his foot, then headed upstairs. Hannah had long since lost the battle to have the three sit together for meals.

Ross was happy with his TV dinner in the former dining room, now teenage den. Hannah watched her little one trough, and thought, what an apt word. The man he would become was emerging in his eleven-year-old face. Hannah enjoyed a gigantic pizza slice, a bowl of wedges and garlic dip, forgetting all about the salad she had prepared to counter the fat-carb-fest. She put her arm around Ross and kissed his forehead, as he leaned in towards her, not once taking his eyes off the flickering screen.

Hannah returned to doom-scrolling, and refreshed the page, but Leo's image and the account was gone! She trawled Instagram, but extensive searches revealed nothing. She scrolled Leo's @VLRsoftware Twitter account and the same post appeared, but cropped to omit the girl. She used the translate function which revealed; Leo relaxing at the exclusive Ristorante Zai on Lake Iseo. There followed some technical blurb about the latest software innovation. Hannah concluded Bellissima must be a co-worker. But it was unsettling, Leo was married to her good friend Verna, should she say something? Hannah's brother Grant, was a whiz with IT systems, he spoke a different language, enthusing about the range of technical detail he worked with. She called him. 'Hey Grant, quick question,' anonymising the subject matter, 'can a disappearing image on Instagram be retrieved'?

'Short answer … no.'

The long answer, which she wasn't wholeheartedly interested in, began. She tried to follow Grant's verbal outpouring of techie data, which was interesting, but took her no further forward.

'Why do you want to know about an image that's been removed? Is it work-related?'

'Yeah, that's it.' As a Graphic Designer, Hannah's curiosity about a seemingly unimportant online image was easily dismissed.

The following day Hannah called her sister Ellie and ran the, Leo and Bellissima, scenario by her. She'd be over in the evening to discuss the issue. Ellie travelled to Hannah's suburban home, five miles west of Newcastle City to comfort her sister. 'Look what I have,' Ellie held out a bottle of purple gin, 'tastes like Parma Violets, remember them?'

'Yeh, disgusting. It'll be like drinking nanna's Yardley's lavender perfume.'

'It'll be fine after the first few.' Ellie poured drinks whilst Hannah found the Twitter image.

Hannah explained what she'd seen on Instagram and pointed out the cropped version. They analysed the possible explanations. Ellie concluded, 'hmm, difficult to say anything to Verna without any hard evidence. How much does she know about Leo's Italian lifestyle, maybe there's a young voluptuous female engineer working there he may have had his eye on.'

'I've been suspicious of him since I heard him talking with a, Julianne or Juliette, at one of their barbecues a year ago. It didn't sound like a business call as he seemed … you know … furtive, and instantly ended the call when I was nearby. There's something about him. Though I'm no one to cast aspersions, it was happening right under my nose and I didn't see it.'

'Hannah, really? Evan was nine and Ross was six, your life was a dearth of domesticity to say the least, and managing your career too. Considering Adrian worked in the financial sector, he left you in financial and emotional shreds.' Ellie paused. 'I like that you reverted to your maiden name, Hannah Kay sounds classy.'

'Adrian took his name when he left as far as I'm concerned and Geraldine is welcome to wear it as a badge of triumph.'

'I never knew what he saw in gorgeous ginger Gezza.'

'Erm it's Gerri if you don't mind,' simultaneous eye rolls. Hannah continued, 'Look, she's ten years younger than him, painfully vivacious, childless with an intact body, and he'll get all of her attention, he'll love that. I think she's jealous of his relationship with the boys though, and they haven't had any children. Shame really; would've been lovely to have some freckly, red-haired half siblings around.' Shrugging, Hannah poured another gin and raised her glass to her sister, who reciprocated. They both took a sip of the purple elixir, looked at each other, grimaced and said together … 'Yardleys!'

4

Hannah called Verna a day later suggesting they meet up as the country braced itself for lockdown. During the call, she asked surreptitiously if Verna had been to Leo's apartment and if she knew any of his colleagues.

'I met the business owner's family when Leo got the contract and visited the apartment. It's lovely, on a quiet street, not far from Lodi town centre and only an hour from Milan. I'd love to visit when all this is over, shopping in Milan is fabulous.'

Hannah could visualise Verna walking by prestigious boutiques, swinging exclusive shopping bags like Julia Roberts in *Pretty Woman*. 'Maybe you could visit when the contract ends, but who knows, with this horrendous situation.'

Verna mentioned Leo kept in touch with the children online and joked, 'Amara heard the maid, can you believe the cleaning service is still available in the apartment block, yet here I am looking after three kids on my own!'

'The cleaning service is still available?' Hannah repeated.

'Yes, why wouldn't it be?'

'Well ... I thought even relatives can't visit, so why would there be cleaners? Seems odd.'

'Strange thing to say. Why do you think it's odd?'

'No particular reason, I just do.'

Verna didn't let it go. 'Do you think there's something going on?'

Hannah was in two minds what to say and decided to get her misgivings out in the open, as there may be a plausible explanation. 'This may be absolutely nothing, but there was a photo on Instagram which looked as though a girl was taking a picture of Leo deliberately in the background of her selfie. But the post has disappeared and so has his account. The same picture was posted on his Twitter account, cropping the girl out, but it's probably a relative or work colleague.'

Verna laughed without conviction. 'He would've been out wining and dining clients, it's what he does.'

'You're absolutely right, I'm sure it's nothing at all.'

Verna seemed irritated. 'Do you think Leo is up to something?'

'Honestly, I don't know, but if you have a look on his Twitter account, you'll see the photo. He's wearing a yellow shirt, standing in front of a lake, but the girl in the foreground taking the selfie is missing. I wondered how he got the picture from her.'

'Maybe he asked her to take a photo, and she began fooling around. He gets loads of attention, you know that.'

'I did wonder, but you can see his mobile is in his shirt pocket, so it must be hers.'

'Sounds like your imagination is working overtime.'
'Probably ... forget it ... sorry.'
'Why don't you pop over before we go into lockdown, it would be good to catch up before that happens.'
'Sounds good, will let you know when I'm free.'
'Okay, see you.' Verna ended the call abruptly.

Hannah wished she'd never seen that bloody image, and kept her big mouth shut! As she filled the dishwasher, she wondered about any residual resentment from years ago. Leo asked if she would create some a new brand logo for his company. She paused from her dishwashing task recalling planning meetings she attended in her own time projecting a less than dynamic figure as her marriage was falling apart at the time. She used up her limited, frantic spare time in the early hours to work on the project. Her colleagues were preparing for her to announce she was going solo on the back of the lucrative contract, when she received a humiliating phone call from Verna to break the news, she hadn't got it. She slammed more crockery into the dishwasher. Leo didn't have the balls to tell her himself the contract was awarded to young, pretty Poppy Farquhar-fucking-Symington, or whoever she was! Still, Hannah had to question if this was a long-awaited vendetta? Dark guilty thoughts pervaded her mind, she couldn't rule out she'd seen what she wanted to in the lakeside image.

5

Hannah frowned as she placed a glittering gift bag on Verna's vast kitchen table. She sometimes didn't get it right with Verna, whose taste was impeccable. She was startled at the sound of crash metal guitar invading the peace.

'Keep it down!' Verna shouted upstairs as she closed the door. 'Marco's taken up electric guitar,' half-smiling, 'it's what thirteen-year-old's do.' She set about making a coffee with the latest upmarket gadgetry, the comforting roast-nut aroma filled the air.

'Evan went through that stage. He wanted lessons, but I couldn't really afford them …' trailed Hannah's sad admission, aggrieved she couldn't bestow unrestricted financial advantages for her two boys. Hannah glanced at the gift bag, she was on limited time and budget to pick up a peace-offering. The box of dusted truffles looked meagre, so she added the bottle of cheap Prosecco to make it seem more substantial. Hannah never got the hang of buying one classy item and leaving it at that, and accepted this as a flaw in her gift-giving psyche. Verna's last Christmas gift to her was a beautifully packaged de-luxe body care gift set, not too ostentatious, just right.

'Oh thanks,' Verna glanced at the gift bag whilst pouring the coffees.

Hannah hoped she didn't peek inside, saving them the embarrassment of faked appreciation. The potpourri and oil burner Christmas gift set from a bargain store was humiliating enough. Hannah was hard up then, because of her ex delaying the financial settlement during divorce proceedings. The expense of utilities, food and clothing alone for her growing boys nearly broke her. She inwardly cringed now, years later, at Verna's comment, *"you shouldn't go to any trouble, a nice bottle of red would do fine."*

Verna placed the coffee mugs down, 'still sticking with your accusations about Leo?'

A glance at Verna's crossed arms and serious face meant she wasn't messing around here. Hannah, looked into Verna's sapphire blue eyes and for the first time in their thirty-year friendship was stumped for words.

Verna continued, 'so, you believe my husband is having an affair in Italy, on the basis you saw a picture of him with a girl who had randomly taken a selfie.'

'All I was trying to do was understand, and find some sort of explanation. Maybe there isn't one.'

'I asked him and he said it was a waitress messing about when he was out with colleagues ages ago.'

Hannah was unconvinced, it looked like an exclusive restaurant where such behaviour from a member of staff wouldn't be tolerated.

Verna continued, 'we can't judge everyone by your ex's standards. Simply because Adrian ran off with someone, doesn't mean mine is capable of doing the same.'

'Do you truly believe I want you to suffer the way I did? This is the only reason I'm telling you what I saw.'

'What other information do you have that remotely leads you to believe Leo is unfaithful.'

'When we have spoken about Leo and his life over in Italy, you are quite vague and — '

'Well, you didn't have a clue! You're hardly the person to be giving me marital advice.'

Hannah took a breath. 'It's a pandemic, not even family is allowed in each other's homes, never mind a maid. I wasn't going to mention Instagram until that came up in our phone call. It doesn't sound right.'

'Shows how ill-informed you are. The accommodation is overseen by the company, they look after their people and would take measures to keep it sanitised.'

'Maybe in communal areas at a stretch, but individual apartments? Hey ... if Leo told Amara, it was a cleaner at 7 p.m. at night, fair enough. In fact, it would be 8 p.m. in Italy and isn't there a curfew? But maybe it *was* a maid service.' Hannah shrugged.

'They work different hours to the UK. You don't understand how things work in the business world. They still have riposo in Italy ... or siesta to you. Cleaners at 8 p.m. won't be unusual, but you wouldn't know that.'

'I am genuinely letting you know what I saw and what I feel about the situation. Don't you think it's strange he's not returned home yet?'

'He can't travel! The airports are closed. His town is quarantined, so he can't up and leave.'

'My sister Ellie's friend returned from a skiing holiday in the Italian Alps, and has to quarantine; so, I believe airports are open for limited flights so families can return home and for essential business.'

'So, you've checked! How suspicious are you? Honestly, you have no idea how my marriage is working … it's wonderful thank you very much.' Verna's defiant stare was fixed.

Frustration released Hannah's words, 'I have to be honest here. At your barbecue last spring, I heard Leo during a telephone call to someone called Juliette or Julianne, and it did not sound business-like at all. He shielded his phone and stopped the call abruptly when he realised I was nearby.'

'You've got to be kidding. Just because your life has fallen down around you and you haven't achieved a happy marriage, or got the financial rewards from the work you've put into your career. You can't even afford guitar lessons for your son, and you're running around in that ancient car which is almost being held together with paint from the look of it.'

'That's really underhand Verna. You've had everything on a plate and now something threatens your perfect world, you can't take it!'

'Okay … that's it, enough. Your accusations are ridiculous, you'll do anything to get back at Leo from years ago. Please go and take that with you!' Verna nodded at the gift bag, and walked to the sink to rinse out her coffee cup. Hannah picked up the gift bag, grabbed her coat and walked out of the kitchen.

Rocco, the Lhasa Apso, Ravassio family dog, looked up between the two humans with confusion. Hannah looked at the white fluffy creature bouncing alongside her in the hallway, with its caramel-coloured ears extending to eye patches. She was convinced his eyebrows were raised. As she walked out of the house, she muttered, 'even the bloody dog is a designer brand,' and continued to march down the driveway, not looking back.

Hannah got into her car, the one, 'being held together with paint,' repeating Verna's words. She was furious and fumbled starting the engine, which to her dismay, spluttered and stalled. Once it got going, she sped away. A little way up the road beyond the perimeter of the affluent estate, she came to a junction, and the car stalled again. She started it up, drove a little way, pulled into a passing place and sobbed. With a white-knuckle grab of the steering wheel, she yelled, 'fuucckk!' at the windscreen as the visceral hurt from Verna's condescending words filled her being. With a sneer she repeated Verna's words, 'you wouldn't know what happens in the business world,' then added her own words ... 'you poor pleb.' Hannah glared at her left-hand, her wedding ring was replaced with a neat silver dress ring. She took it off, threw it into the passenger footwell and it bounced off the pathetic gift bag. Hannah took off her glasses and flung them on the seat, rubbed her eyes, then habitually adjusted her bargain floral top, stretching it to create fabric folds to disguise her expanding midriff. Hannah despised herself, she had upset one of the best friends she had ever known and they may never come back from this.

In her kitchen Verna rinsed out the cups with fervour, opened the kitchen door to the increased volume of guitar and shouted, 'for goodness' sake Marco, keep the bloody noise down!'

Ten-year-old Amara popped her head through the French doors. 'What's the matter Mum?' she asked with a concerned frown, narrowing her deep brown eyes.

'It's okay honey, Mummy's got a headache.'

'Can Izzy have some juice please, she said she's hungry, but she means thirsty.' Big sister Amara rolled her eyes at the common occurrence of her little sister getting her feelings confused.

Verna looked into the cavernous American-style fridge crammed with food and drinks. 'Of course sweetheart.' She handed two bottles of fruit drinks and snack packs to Amara, who darted away, then stopped, standing by the French doors,

'Is everything okay with Aunty Hannah?'

'Amara, there's nothing wrong, everything's fine.' The practiced easy smile appeared as she went over to hug her daughter. She's an astute little thing, Verna thought about her middle child. At least she wasn't the one who was the cause of the stretch marks and caesarean scarring on her stomach, she could thank Izabella for that, and the awful pregnancy and birth. She was a last-minute decision, as Leo had desperately wanted another child. Izzy was stunning, like a renaissance painting with sumptuous ringleted blond hair, striking blue eyes and a full mouth, the image of her mother.

Verna opened the fridge to gather ingredients for

dinner, and reflected on the contrast from the paltry upmarket offerings in her affluent childhood home. All she wanted was the comfort of beans or cheese on toast, a fried egg sandwich or tomato soup, like Hannah's family had. She remembered the laughter, the haphazard happiness of staying at Hannah's. The time they wanted to try out a new sandwich toaster and kept getting random foods out of the cupboard and fridge. *"Let's try a combo of cheese and marmalade toasties!"* said the eldest brother, grabbing food as the others looked on laughing.

"Hey, no ... stop, don't make a mess and waste food." Hannah's mother was powerless to stop her four children, and joined in with the hilarity. The cheese and marmalade toasties were good, Verna smiled at the memory; the smell of toast, the sweet and savoury taste all washed down with cheap lemonade. Verna wiped her eyes and sniffed away those reminiscences of Hannah's joyful Geordie family.

Verna's perspective changed, under her breath she said, 'who the hell does she think she is accusing Leo, because of some random picture.' Verna made another coffee, and headed for the conservatory to diminish the screeching guitar. She held up a perfectly manicured hand, Verna had been the proprietor of a successful chain of beauty salons pre-children and knew how to look after herself, so why would Leo have an affair? Of course, she didn't know his every movement, though she recognised the name Julianne or Juliette, and Leo was delayed returning from Germany, or was it France, a few times? She'd always accepted his explanations and put it down to the demands of running an elite business.

A guilt pang struck Verna, Hannah was a genuine friend, she had been her rock helping out when the children were younger. Her gaze fell upon an old family photo on the sill, Verna scoffed, 'you were no bloody help at all were you, Lena?' at her stunning, yet bizarre mother. Verna dearly wished she had been more patient and rational. Instead, her cherished friend Hannah had left her house under a dark foreboding cloud.

6

Hannah spent the next day feeling wretched when she thought about Verna. She called Ellie, her confidant and shoulder to cry on.

'What's up? You sound upset.'

Hannah's words tumbled out with sniffs and sobs. 'Me and Verna spoke about Leo and the photo, and the maid thing. She did not take it well, it … it ended on bad terms, she asked me to leave … accused me of jealousy, wanting her marriage to fail like mine … so I stormed off.'

'Really! I'll be over this evening after work, half six okay? What's this about a maid anyway?'

By this time Hannah was in floods of tears and could only manage to squeak, 'okay.'

Ellie arrived later that evening, long plaited hair, in her usual attire of loose yoga pants and slouchy top, looking relaxed but concerned. There was a familial look between the sisters. Hannah tried her best to recount the telephone and kitchen conversations verbatim. The sisters were ensconced in the modest conservatory, Hannah's peaceful thinking space.

'I cannot believe she would speak to you like that, but she was probably hurt too, I guess.' Ellie could always see both sides of an argument.

'It was awful for us both. It's made me feel bad about myself, about my life. I'm a failure as a mother, as a wife, a friend ... everything.'

Ellie put her arms around her. 'You are an amazing mother and the best sister anyone could have. You have a successful career, you're hilarious, intelligent, kind, talented, beautiful and ... okay ... enough.' Hannah smiled at her sister's concern and kind words, and her jovial manner was grounding.

Ellie continued. 'Let's face it, Verna's life has been fortunate, she's been given everything on a plate. She's never had to work, apart from her beauty salon empire, funded by her parents of course. She even had a nanny after she gave up work. Remember, when the three of them were younger as she couldn't cope with Izzy.'

'True, but she had little support, her mother was useless and Leo was away a lot,' she paused. 'What shall we have, I think a glass of red will do the trick for me.'

'Agreed.'

'There's something about Verna's reaction.' Hannah was still, glass in hand, 'I wonder if she has suspicions, and that's why she was so defensive with me. Maybe I hit the nail on the head?'

'Some women do know, but are prepared to put up with it for the lifestyle. Maybe you've always tried too hard with Verna, and she doesn't like it, now you've told her some home truths.'

'Possibly, but I feel so desperately sad about it all.'

Ellie said, 'people and relationships change over time. Remember the girl I knew in college? All she did was take, take, take from me, draining every ounce of my patience and energy. It was always about her. I spent my life trying to make her feel good about herself. I empathised with her disappointment, and dropped everything to support her when she was stressed. I wasted time and money going on weekend trips and nights out I couldn't afford, because of some sort of duty to console and entertain her, but it wasn't a friendship worth having.'

'I do remember her, wasn't she your first girlfriend too, to add further complication.' Hannah knew about Ellie's bisexuality, many didn't, and she supported her sister through the exploratory teenage years. 'I've known Verna over thirty years, it's an awfully long time to break up a friendship. It feels inconceivable I may never see her again, but I wouldn't know what to say if I called her. We both need to cool off for a while perhaps. It's a shame about the boys too, her boy Marco does look up to Evan and I don't want to stop their friendship.'

'Don't worry, they'll stay in touch online if they want to. You will need to grieve over her if there's no going back, like the loss of any relationship.'

Hannah said, 'well, I certainly know how to do that.'

'You were far too good for Adrian.' Ellie had a sudden recall. 'Ah now! That Cameron chap, he's a bit of all right. What's happening with the lovely Cam?'

'We're still in touch and we've met for a couple of coffees. He wants to take me out on a proper date, but it's going to be difficult with lockdown looming. I don't know, he came across as a tad immature, no depth. I don't want to end up looking after another man-child.'

'Give him a chance. Maybe what you need is a frivolous romp with someone with no ties. He seemed a lovely guy … I think, I was possibly fairly hammered the night we met him.'

'Dating in your forties is a disaster. I don't know what men want, apart from the obvious.'

'You're always considering the other person. Try shifting your thinking to what you want instead?'

'Dunno, I tried those dating websites and there was the work colleague, but my heart wasn't in it. The thought of introducing the boys to another man would have been strange, too much effort. Who would want me? Been single for years … the state I'm in,' Hannah looked down at herself, 'with two teenagers in tow as well.'

'Lots of men would! And you are allowed a life.'

'Remember David, dated him for a few months, but after the awkward romp when the boys were at their dad's, it fizzled out.'

'He was a pleasant enough guy, quite nice looking I seem to remember.'

'Hmm yes … pleasant … exactly. Not much in common, he wanted to impress me with his sports car, his knowledge of world cuisine, and he bored me to death at times recounting tales of working as an extra on telly. God knows how many times he told me he was in, *Vera,* and reckoned he got along great with Brenda Blethyn.'

'Ha! Yeah right.'

'I know, the conceited git, he was more interested in talking about himself than anyone else. I'd never have introduced him to my boys, he wasn't interested. Plus, I had far too much shopping, washing and housework to catch up on at weekends than to have the time and energy to be someone's fuck-buddy.'

Ellie laughed. 'No, you never seemed impressed with his upmarket evenings of fine dining with the perfect accompanying wine, in the most expensive place whether it was any good or not.'

'It's just not me, the day he said he was working away, I knew he wasn't, I closed the front door and blocked his number before he drove away. Couldn't wait to be on the sofa in my jamas chilling out, watching a dark Scandi brutal murder, not having to suppress breaking wind. Reminds me of a woman I worked with in a bar during the Edinburgh Festival when I was at Uni,' said Hannah, 'she apparently had never farted in front of her husband. Wore rather busy makeup, turquoise shimmer eyeshadow, sugar-pink lippy, and shaved her eyebrows, with fake ones pencilled in. Always wore a seventies maxi crocheted mustard cardigan, the bell sleeves kept dripping in the drinks … odd woman. Surely a lifetime of trapped wind isn't a good recipe for a harmonious relationship?'

Another few glasses of wine and the evening descended into reminiscing about their childhood and adolescent adventures.

'Do you remember The Kaylahs, what a brilliant band they were.' Ellie laughed.

'We were excellent, I'll have you know. My posh-school

violin lessons were so worth it, weren't they? Me and Verna practising sounded like screechy cats. Thought we were going to make it big, like The Corrs. That big charity concert was exciting though, when the slimy talent scout said he'd get us a recording deal.'

Ellie sneered, 'ew, imagine the casting couch, yuk!'

'Not sure posh school has done me much good. Though I do love my job and Edinburgh Uni was fantastic, I do wonder what I've achieved at times, and now I've buggered things up with my lovely friend?' Hannah wandered down memory lane in her mind.

A few moments passed, then Ellie said softly, 'I know when you were first arranging nights out with Verna, you got yourself in a right tizzy thinking about what to wear or how to do your hair. I know you'd buy new designer clothes which you could ill-afford because you felt inadequate.'

Hannah looked at her sister, the honesty was unbearable, but acceptable. 'True, but that was about me, not her. I had to curb the spending on lavish nights out, weekends away and birthday gifts. I used the phrase; time is a more valuable gift than anything we could buy. I rehearsed the line to make it sound spontaneous, how pathetic.'

Ellie suggested, 'maybe it's time for Verna to get off your bus?'

Hannah nodded solemnly, recognising their often-used phrase, and repeated it, 'life is like a bus journey, you may travel with someone for a lifetime, or it may only be a day; but at some point, it's the right stop for them to get off your bus. Maybe Verna got off at the last stop?'

'It also means there are many stops ahead for new

people to get on.' Ellie sat bolt upright, slouchy top dropping down her arm, she picked up Hannah's phone and offered it to her. 'Message Cam and arrange a date. I'll stay with my nephews while you go out. Come on Hannah, time you had some fun. He seemed really sweet … and keen. Remember, the only things you regret in life, are the things you didn't do.'

Hannah winced, 'where on earth did that nugget of wisdom come from?' She sent a message to Cam, and the response was instantaneous, *anytime!* Hannah and Ellie worked on an agreed date and that was it, all arranged, she'd meet Cam at the same bar where they'd originally met

7

The Bridges Bar, Newcastle, December 2019

Hannah was enjoying a mulled cider, she was also enjoying the company of her brother and sister, and really enjoying the music of a new local indie rock band, *Altradias*, at The Bridges Bar in Newcastle's Ouseburn Valley. It was approaching the Christmas break and everyone was switched to party mode. The atmosphere was vibrant, but the bar was rammed. In the break the clatter, chatter, laughter and shouting, was at an unbelievable level, but it was wonderful. Hannah was being jostled and crushed at the bar trying to get served, being constantly overlooked when a man behind her asked if he could get her a drink.

'It's okay, I'm in a round, but thanks.'

'It's going to take you ages to get served, what do you want?'

Hannah told him the order and he yelled over the top of the heads in front of him. A young inexperienced member of the bar staff responded immediately and served his drinks. Hannah usually disliked that kind of attitude, however, on this occasion she was quite happy to get the speedy drinks. He wouldn't take the cash offered. She noticed his dark eyes and the crinkling at the sides when he smiled. They had surreptitious glances at each other during the evening across the crowded bar. He approached her at the end of the night, introduced himself, and offered his telephone number. She was going to say, no thanks, when Ellie butted in and gave Cam her number.

Cam looked at Hannah and asked sincerely, 'is it okay if I give you a call?'

'Yes, of course.' She smiled, she liked him and those twinkling brown eyes. When Cam contacted Hannah the following evening, she was quite taken aback. She had swapped numbers on occasion years ago with men she met on nights out, but nothing ever came of it. She agreed to meet for a coffee after New Year. Hannah left work early and after a cosmetic freshenup, she tentatively set off. She wore her favourite coat, which she didn't remove during their date as it hid a multitude of sins. They kept in touch with another two coffee dates, friendly phone calls, texts and humorous posts over the next few weeks, Cam asked a few times if she'd like to go for a drink, but she always used the excuse of needing childcare. Hannah questioned, what was she scared of? Now a date was arranged, she was alone with her damn insecurity demons. Anxiety crept over her at the thought of a proper night-time date, what would she wear? She smiled at her brother's comments about her *"still rockin' the rock-chick look."* She decided to wear the same outfit as when she met Cam. Contact lenses instead of the jam-jar bottom glasses she needed at work of course, and her beloved coat and ankle boots.

Hannah had fallen in love at first sight with the soft leather, burgundy ankle boots in Fenwick's department store. She'd stared at them during shopping trips hoping they'd go into the sale, alas they never did. They were way out of her usual price range, so she scrupulously saved for months, because money should never stand in the way of true love. She hugged the box when she finally purchased them. Hannah had never been a glittery, glitzy girl, and chose understated jewellery to top the outfit. She tried on the ensemble and was relatively pleased with the result, it was too late to lose those few pounds now anyway.

Hannah approached the table in the Bridges Bar, Cam stood, he was warm and welcoming. 'Great to see you,' he gently hugged her and gave a gentle kiss on her cheek, 'at night too, I was beginning to think you were avoiding me,' he jibed gently, with a crinkle-eyed smile.

'I'm usually in bed by half-nine.' Hannah said truthfully.

Their first evening date was great, the conversation was easy, and Cam had a well-paid steady job, Hannah was relieved to hear. She was cautiously thrilled as they mutually agreed to meet again and the lingering goodnight kiss was indeed pleasing. They enjoyed another night out, and watched a movie with takeaway and wine at Cam's home. His modest two-bed house was in a decent area on the outskirts of the city. They chatted easily during the evening, and he proudly showed Hannah his six-year-old daughter, Sara's bedroom, which was full of colourful unicorn bedding, L.O.L. dolls and Peppa Pig soft toys. There were pictures of Sara at various ages all around the house.

'She's your double,' remarked Hannah, 'gorgeous.'

'Like her dad then, huh?' Crinkly smile. 'Sara was only a toddler when me and her mother separated, and she moved back to Leeds. We get along well and her partner is a great guy. They recently had a baby, so she's thrilled to have a little sister. I see Sara as often as I can.' Cam asked Hannah, 'would you run through your family again, there's a few of you isn't there? You were with your brother and sister on the night we met?'

'That's right, and we're a close lot. There's four of us, with only a year or two between us in age; Jake, Ellie, me, then Grant. I'll start from the top, mother is Martha, father is Tommy. Oldest brother Jake is married to Megan. They met in the army and started a family very young. They have four adult kids, and he's quite the Victorian Dad; no TV, encouraged into other pursuits, yomping up mountains, wild swimming, camping and survival skills. They all play musical instruments, and have careers ranging from falconry to marine biology. Ellie, is my big sister, though we're only eleven months apart … I know,' she glanced at Cam's questioning expression, 'what were my parents thinking?'

'Don't think they were thinking actually.' Cam smiled.

'Ellie is married to Geoff, a widower. She inherited two step-children, now adults, both lovely. Ellie is quite the non-conformist in the family, travelled all over the world, she's great fun. Then, me and my two gorgeous boys, Evan, fourteen and, Ross is eleven, I had with Adrian. Finally, Grant, who is married to Shona, she's Brazilian. Quite the ambitious couple, no children, great jobs and love the high life.'

Cam repeated; 'Martha and Tommy are mam and dad,

Jake and Megan have four adult children. Ellie and Geoff, she has two adult step-children. You with Evan and Ross, then there's Grant and Shona.'

'Not many people can remember them all in one go.' Hannah enjoyed Cam's attentiveness. He was genuinely curious. She didn't get the impression he was feigning interest for her benefit. Hannah entertained Cam with tales of her childhood and the manic household they were brought up in. She modestly explained how she achieved a scholarship to Eastfield, an independent girls' high school.

'My brothers and their friends mercilessly took the micky out of me in my old-fashioned school uniform, particularly the bottle-green felt hat I had to wear. I stuffed it in my bag the second I was out of the school gates. They would put it on and mimic a posh accent and the amount of St Trinian's jokes … well, you can imagine.'

'Private education, eh? Was it a good experience?'

'I hung around with my brothers and sister outside of school, so I didn't miss out on anything. The fact there were no boys in school probably helped me concentrate on lessons. I got good qualifications and went to Edinburgh Uni to study, my first choice, so … yeh it was positive.'

'Set you up for a good career. Gorgeous and clever, what more can I ask for.'

Hannah's face flushed. This was ridiculous she thought, she was forty-two and blushing like a debutante at the compliment. She snuggled down to hide her face from him. 'Flattery will get you everywhere.'

'Great,' said Cam, 'you are the most beautiful, intelligent woman I've ever met in my whole life.'

On the next occasion they went out, Ellie offered to stay over with the boys, saying to her beloved sister, 'it's been a few years Hannah, you must be gagging for it by now?' As her gorgeous, rampant laugh rang out.

'You,' Hannah said pointing at Ellie, 'are a terrible person, but a wonderful sister. Thanks for the childcare hon, and yeah, can't wait to get my rocks off.' Hannah found some provocative underwear from years ago when sex was still dynamic with Adrian, but slung it out. She invested in some new lingerie, carefully choosing from the sexy-for-forty-year-olds range. She was pleased with how her new underwear looked, she wanted to feel as confident as she could on her first night with a man for years.

After a lovely evening, a few drinks and sensual kissing on the sofa, they got into bed. Hannah snuggled into Cam, and he wrapped himself around her. He was of rather a chunky build, which Hannah was grateful for, as she may have been intimidated if she was sleeping with someone with a super fit, toned body, after her six-year hiatus. They took their time throughout the night indulging in each other's bodily pleasures. Hannah enjoyed the feel of Cam's hands caressing her, his breath on her neck, his sensual kisses, and she could see and feel he was equally excited by her touch. She was so ready for him as they made love. The feel of their bodies joining in pulsating passion swept over Hannah's being, it was breathlessly thrilling. Throughout the night they had fun together as well as mutual satisfaction. They both agreed happy sex was much more fulfilling than feeling the pressure to perform and look perfect. Eventually, they fell into a satisfied sleep, snuggled into each other.

Hannah and Cam woke in the morning and after the familiarity of being together overnight, they engaged in an energetic and satisfying lovemaking session. They were both incredibly content. The eye contact, gentle touches and togetherness over coffee in the morning was lovely, she didn't want to leave. They made promises to meet again really soon.

8

The Kay family got together in the limited space they had called home as children, and Hannah wondered how on earth they all fitted in the modest three bedroomed house. She shared with Ellie in the box bedroom, Grant shared with Jake, until he left to join the army, and they all somehow squeezed into the tiny kitchen for meals most evenings. They never thought it overcrowded, to them it was, and still is … home. It was a nervy fraught evening, a far cry from their usual buoyant, noisy gatherings. Hannah was terrified her parents, or any of her siblings would meet their demise from the deadly virus that would inevitably be rampaging the country. Their conversations centred around whether it was only the elderly who would be affected, however concluded it could be anyone, as younger people were also dying. They watched the government briefing on 16 March 2020 outlining the plan to fight the virus.

'If it's so bad like Italy, why aren't they locking down now?' was Megan's panicky question. She was ashen and trembling.

Jake put his arm around his anxious wife. 'We'll keep

the family safe Meg. If it means we can't visit for a while, so be it.' He turned to his parents mustering all of his authority, 'you are not to leave this house, if you need anything, ring any one of us and we'll sort it.' Hannah hadn't seen her older brother looking so stern. Despite their protestations, the parents were outnumbered by their children, all vowing to ensure their shopping, medical and other needs would be met.

'So, what you're saying is, I can't even walk to the paper shop every morning like I always do?' asked a bewildered Tommy.

'You could die if you catch it!' Despite her military experience and keeping cool under pressure, Megan was prone to histrionics when it came to family. However, she only expressed all of their inner trepidation.

The family huddled, glued to the news footage from Italy, casting flickering lights over their disbelieving faces. Devastating images of distraught health workers appeared, looking determined but bewildered, powerless to stop the onslaught of Covid's exponential spread. The unmitigated onslaught of death and misery, they all knew would arrive soon on British shores, provoked fearful tears.

After the broadcast and discussion of what may come, Hannah's mother Martha returned from pottering in the kitchen with a tray full of assorted mugs surrounding the large bulbous, Brown Betty tea-pot, all survivors from the 1970s. The perfectly brewed tea in familiar mugs was a comfort to all. Megan had brought along her signature muffins of varying flavours and decoration, which offered a much-needed treat. The Kay family gathering ended with extended warm hugs all around as they went their separate ways. Hannah knew her parents were being brave, reassuring their children they would be fine and it would be over soon, but the look on their faces as she drove off brought her to tears.

Hannah was feeling low as she arrived home to two hungry baby birds. Both boys, beaks yapping, asking when tea would be ready. It never ended with Evan and Ross, some days she couldn't fill them up, they were desperate for slabs of pie and a mountain of chips. Hannah discovered a huge family Lasagna and some garlic bread in the freezer which she put on to cook, explaining it would be forty-five minutes before it was ready, to their moans and groans. She hadn't taken off her coat as she poured a glass of wine. Not the solution to everything, but, it had been her solace during the marriage break up, temporarily dampening the pain. At times she wondered how on earth she managed to keep working and looking after the boys after frequently downing a bottle a night. Smiling, she looked at the comforting glass of ruby liquid and answered her own question, 'my wonderful family held me up when I needed them most.'

The smooth Merlot tasted good, and though it didn't happen often these days, sitting in the corner of the conservatory with wine dredged up heart-breaking, humiliating memories. After eleven years of marriage, she had no idea it was in jeopardy. Adrian got up one Saturday morning six years ago, having arranged for the boys to stay over at his parents and revealed the stinging words; he was leaving. He'd planned the whole thing. Hannah was incredulous.

They had made love the previous night, which was routinely satisfying. Hannah was tired a lot of the time, genuinely tired, it wasn't that she didn't love Adrian. Their passion had ebbed from the young hormonal desires in their twenties; but with children, shopping, domestics, and work demands, it wasn't something Hannah needed to put on the family calendar, or maybe she should have? Meanwhile Adrian was enjoying lunchtime sex sessions at Geraldine's flat.

'Is it ready yet?' Hannah was startled as Ross appeared by stealth at her side. He chuckled as she jumped.

'Been playing, *Resident Evil* again? You shouldn't be playing that, nearly scared me to death! It's nearly ready, come and give me a hand setting the table.'

His shoulders drooped, he was trapped, he had to help out. Ross could be conciliatory a lot of the time, he hadn't reached the dismissive stage of his elder brother as yet. Hannah messaged Evan, if you want food, join us in the kitchen. Then smiled at his response. Hannah needed this. Sitting with her boys close to her, she enjoyed their banter and even their arguments. She looked into their faces with such affection, feeling a deep warmth inside. Everything would be okay, she convinced herself. She let them go without clearing up, a rare treat, so they dashed away in case she changed her mind.

After clearing the kitchen devastation, Hannah sat in the same place as all those years ago, recalling her emotional trauma. Sitting in stunned silence as Adrian explained how it was going to work out; the money, the house, the contact with the children. He was moving in with Geraldine, a woman Hannah had met briefly at a work Christmas dinner the previous year. Adrian reassured Hannah she would be okay financially, but she was not. The settlement was way less than she expected, as Adrian had surreptitiously hived away and transferred funds from their savings, and there was nothing she could do except make a claim for child maintenance from him. At least she kept a roof over their heads, by demanding to transfer the house into her name, which only increased mortgage payments with the buyout.

Hannah sipped her wine and a few tears rolled down her cheeks, it was inevitable when she recounted explaining to her innocent, bright eyed boys why daddy wouldn't be living with them any longer. It was as if she needed to exorcise the divorce devil again. Adrian left a trail of emotional baggage behind, enough to fill a large suitcase and two small ones. Her mind wandered to Verna, she had been a good friend to her during those depressing weeks and months after the separation. She helped her out until she got back on her feet, she picked up the children from school when Hannah had to work late. She offered reassuring, calm companionship too.

Hannah placed her glass aside and picked up her phone. She was on the verge of ringing Verna … but, in silent stillness, thought of the accusations she had made. Verna may never want to speak to her again.

9

Verna, February 2020

'It's going to be here soon, isn't it?' Verna asked Leo during a call. He was sitting on a wall in his usual quiet spot, half-way through his run. Exercise once a day was allowed in his town, and although the police weren't as active on the streets, they were still moving people on.

'For sure, it's going to be everywhere and things aren't improving here, hundreds of deaths each day. I'm trying to arrange a flight home, so I'll let you know how I get on.'

'It'll be good to have you home. I can tell the children are worried about you, Marco is putting on a brave face. I don't have the news updates from Italy on TV any longer.'

'I am really missing you all,' it was genuine, Leo would rather be anywhere else than Italy for more reasons than the pandemic. 'Soon as I can book a flight, I'll let you know. Love to the kids and … thanks Verna for taking care of them while I'm away, it can't be easy for you.'

'Got no choice, have I? Hopefully you'll be back soon.'

It was a strange comment from Leo, he rarely praised her, especially on motherhood; he took it for granted she would expedite the role competently. He often complimented her previously, and was the most romantic man she'd ever known. Pre-children, they would fly off to luxurious exotic island hideaways, or for exclusive city breaks, and he'd arrange for the best bespoke service wherever they went. She was showered with gifts, and was indeed his princess. The memories faded, those days were long gone. Maybe he was doing that with someone else? Verna couldn't get the adulterous thoughts out of her mind and cursed Hannah again for putting them there. She was torn, because Hannah didn't have a malicious bone in her body, and wouldn't make accusations unless she thought something wasn't right.

'Mummy! Izzy's got stuck again and she's crying,' said Amara.

'Izzy, sweetheart, why do you keep doing this?' Verna had to stand on a chair then onto the high dresser in the master bedroom to help Izzy down off the top of the wardrobe. It was a strange habit she had started; this was the third time this last fortnight. The dresser was too heavy to move for Verna, even with Marco's help, to prevent Izzy from repeating the activity. Verna gently eased her daughter's rigid body out of the gap, just deep enough for a six-year-old child to crawl into. She wiped the tear-stained face and cradled her until she reached the floor.

Marco emerged from his room, 'what's all this about? Why does she do it?' He couldn't help but smile, having had to perform the extraction himself the last time.

'I'm not sure Marco?' Turning to Izzy, still cradling her. 'Please darling, don't climb up there.' Verna was concerned her children may be picking up on her own recent anxieties, thinking with irritation, Leo better get himself home soon.

Once Izzy calmed down and Amara's worried look left her face, she invited Izzy into her bedroom. 'Let's play Harry Potter!' She was obsessively reading the books. Amara pointed her wand at the bedroom door, 'Alohomora!' and shoved the door open with her foot. 'See Izzy,' with outstretched arms, 'it's magic.' She was brilliant at distracting her little sister who skipped along after her. Amara looked so cute in the fake, Harry, spectacles.

The glasses reminded Verna of Hannah when they first met at Eastfield School for Girls when they were eleven. Hannah wore circular national health glasses and looked drab with her dark brown hair, stunned expression and darting eyes. Verna approached Hannah on their first day, and took her under her wing. From that day on they were inseparable. Hannah was unique, she was from a different background to the other girls. She was so funny and easily the brightest girl in their class. Verna recalled the last time they met, before the kitchen argument, sharing a raucous belly laugh at old school photos of the ridiculous uniform and games kit they had to wear. They played Lacrosse, for goodness' sake she thought, shaking her head, which was hilarious as they were both desperately hopeless, flailing about and creasing in two with laughter at each other's efforts. She smiled at the memories, she poured a glass of wine and held it into her chest, she really missed Hannah.

Verna placed her glass aside and picked up her phone. She was on the verge of ringing Hannah … but, in silent stillness, thought of the way she'd spoken to her. Hannah may never forgive her for saying those cruel things.

10

Italy, February 2020

Leo watched Graziella trudge from the bathroom after completing her daily bout of morning nausea and wearily sit at the table. She shook her head to his offer of coffee. He stood behind her massaging her shoulders. 'It seems the UK will be following Italy in lockdown soon. I need to make a short trip to expedite some work strategies with my UK team,' then warily, 'and to see my children, as who knows how long it will be until I can travel again.'

A bitter argument erupted, however Graziella was extremely fatigued and hadn't the strength to challenge this decision and quickly calmed. Leo suggested she arranged to go and stay with her parents as early pregnancy was taking its toll. She agreed and contacted her health services to arrange for special dispensation to move in, as she would not manage alone.

Leo relaxed as soon as he dropped Graziella off with her parents, then within an hour, he was at the airport. His intention was to explain to Graziella he was moving permanently back to the UK in May, and would end their relationship.

Asking Graziella to consider a termination had been out of the question. She belonged to a close, loving Italian family, where babies were revered as gifts from God.

Wearing a mask for the two-hour flight to Heathrow was not a problem as he sank into the roomy premier class seating and dozed off. His connecting flight to Newcastle also went without a hitch and he was greeted enthusiastically by the children and Verna waiting at the front door. Leo offered his usual, 'ciao familia!' with outstretched arms as the children gathered to him.

Verna looked pleased to see him and they managed a generous hug once the children had dispersed. 'Were you working on the plane?' Verna asked as he slung his laptop and flight bag on the floor. She couldn't have been more wrong; in between naps on the flight, Leo was consumed with how he was going to manage his complex situation. He called Graziella in the taxi from the airport and hoped she wouldn't try to call him that night. He wasn't sure if she knew his home contact details, but she could find out the information from ex-work colleagues.

The family shared a sumptuous dinner; Verna had prepared his favourite dishes. An entertaining evening ensued, with the children excitedly catching their father up about the last few months.

Marco implored, 'Dad come and play on my new PS4 game, please!'

'Dad needs to rest up tonight Marco,' Verna interjected.

'Tomorrow son, I promise, your mother's right, I could do with a rest tonight.'

When the children were settled, Verna asked, 'have you

considered reducing the amount of travel, or coming home permanently. There must be options for you to be more UK based with the pandemic?'

Leo noticed an earnest expression on her face. It wasn't a passing comment. 'I am getting weary of the constant travelling and being away from the children ... and you.' Verna was standing beside him as he remained seated at the table. He put his arm around her waist as she leaned into him to kiss his mouth. His body responded to her touch, but he was so weary and hoped she wasn't intent on a night of passion, as was their usual homecoming ritual.

Verna intended making it a special night with her husband. She took a scented bath, scrubbed, polished and moisturised her skin, it looked and felt like smooth alabaster. She climbed into bed and lay beside him wrapping her arm around his waist, resting her head on his shoulder, kissing his neck and placing her soft smooth leg over his thigh, expecting to feel his inevitable rising urge. The powerful familiar impulse to make love to her husband kicked in, Verna had missed him. However, Leo was distracted by his phone.

'Are you going to try and relax?' she asked.

He replied with a tirade of issues about how difficult it was trying to keep up with the demands of working at home, relying on zoom calls, which compromised his effectiveness and he was under pressure. He seemed exasperated as he placed the phone on the bedside table. Verna sensed tension between them, but he put his arm around her and gently rested his chin on top of her head. He gave her a peck of a kiss on her forehead, slid down the bed, rolled over, away from her, closed his eyes, yawned luxuriously and said, 'God I'm so tired,' and was asleep within seconds.

Okay, Verna thought, he's tired, it must've been stressful living in those disturbing deadly circumstances. He was obviously under extra pressure to get work completed in an unorthodox manner. However, he had never, in all the years before and after they were married, ever refused sex, especially on returning from abroad. Verna looked at her smooth arms atop the new sumptuous duvet she'd bought online; the gossamer touch of her violet, satin chemise draped between her legs, and the bubbling frustration of her unmet sexual desires raged. Yet, the overriding feeling was of uneasiness. She wanted to make Leo's homecoming as wonderful as possible, but it was one big anti-climax.

Verna lay awake for a long time, as adulterous suspicions crept into her mind. Leo was an intelligent, astute man; he would know she was fishing for information if she questioned him, but she needed to elicit detail without it sounding suspicious. He would deny an extra marital affair of course, but with close observation, she may be able to get a sense of his honesty. Verna was torn because for all she knew, Leo was working hard to provide his family with the trappings an increased income provides, and a serious accusation of infidelity would sound incredibly crass. She looked at him, the rise and fall of his regular breaths brushed against her. She leaned over to kiss his shoulder gently, so as not to wake him, and inhaled the cedarwood, neroli scent of his cologne, one of her favourites. Verna couldn't conceive Leo would ever do anything to hurt her or their children.

Leo took Rocco out for an early walk each morning, Verna noticed he would make a call before he left the end of the cul-de-sac. Italy was an hour ahead; it would be 8 a.m. probably a work call, but just maybe ... Verna dismissed the notion, reassured in their relationship as Leo had returned to the virile, fun-loving, romantic husband she loved and their sex life was as vibrant as ever. One morning as they were enjoying a freshly squeezed orange juice, Verna repeated, 'it would be good if you didn't have to travel so much, or work from home permanently, especially under current circumstances.'

'We couldn't have this lifestyle if I didn't put the hours in where I'm needed.' Leo seemed irritated.

'That's true, but you've seemed more stressed lately, I guess the pandemic hasn't helped anyone's mental health.'

'Definitely, it's bloody awful over there and it's going to be as bad here really soon.'

11

Leo spent time playing games with Marco on his console, after a run around the garden with the girls, and Rocco after breakfast. His children were growing and he was missing it all. Verna popped her head around Marco's bedroom door and grabbed his dirty laundry bag. 'I'm having a coffee if you fancy one?' Leo leaned over to Verna and hugged her.

'Thanks, I do appreciate everything you do.' She looked great in a fitted NYC grey sweatshirt, capri jeans and pink pumps. What was he thinking hooking up with Graziella? Verna was a wonderful wife and mother and fabulous for her age, he did love her. He pushed thoughts of his lover and their unborn child away, but the stress of having to secure some privacy to make secret calls to Italy remained a constant worry. Downstairs after they finished their coffees, Verna put her jacket and trainers on and went out to the garden to play with the children. Even Marco had dragged himself away from his console to play with Rocco on the lawn.

Rocco was excited and barked his delight at the

boy-human, he was faster than the two girl-humans, but Rocco always got to the ball first.

The lively laughter rang through the French doors as Verna ran around with the children. It seemed idyllic, while the rest of the world was in turmoil. Leo had his own personal turmoil as he regarded the blissful scene. He rested his head in his hands and whispered, 'what a bloody mess.' His brain whirred with clicks and clunks as the cogs joined and separated like clockwork, but he was no nearer solving his life puzzle. A compulsion to confess everything gripped him, but he could lose everything and a tear dripped onto the table. He galvanised himself. He had to stop this self-pitying thought process and take decisive action; he was a solutions guy after all. He didn't have to worry about Verna and the kids for the time being as this life, his real life, was rolling along smoothly.

Leo was playing on, *Minecraft*, after dinner with Marco, and somehow the images of building blocks in the game put a thought into his head. 'The apartment!'

'What?' asked Marco turning to him.

'Nothing son, had an idea.'

Leo and Verna had purchased an apartment on Newcastle's prestigious Quayside as an investment. It was waiting for re-decoration before they rented it out or sold it, neither of which would happen during the pandemic. Leo could make it a fake work base. He could contact Graziella from there regularly, as it would appear to her, he was living on his own. Leo suggested the plan to Verna about him using it as an office, as he needed peace and quiet for a few hours a day to connect with colleagues in Italy. Verna agreed it would be ideal. It bought Leo time and space.

Leo took Rocco out for his long evening walk and called Graziella. Rocco looked up at his master, who was fast-barking into the small box. He whimpered for attention, but to no avail.

Leo explained to Graziella, 'the situation in the UK has deteriorated, and it's uncertain when I'm able to return due to travel restrictions.' He held the phone away from his ear at the barrage of Italian angst that exploded. Leo took control, 'I'll ring twice a day darling, and your family will take good care of you until I can return.'

Once Graziella had calmed, she agreed it was best to stay with her parents. Leo knew she would be distracted in the evenings with her family, therefore less reliant upon him to respond to incessant pregnancy-related chat. 'Mamma and Pappa are so excited, but so sorry the wedding will have to now be after baby is born.'

'Oh, right.' Leo gave a nervous laugh and thought, fucking hell … wedding! He hadn't conceived that idea; he was already fucking married. The reality of this situation terrified him. The call ended peacefully with loving, reassuring words. Leo loved Graziella in his way, but wasn't truly in love with her. His well-practiced art of make-believe romance was finely tuned. She reminded him of being young and carefree. They had lots of fun together. He enjoyed spending time with her; she was a warm, adventurous, sexy, humorous young woman, who took good care of him with a warm meal and a warm bed. She was everything Verna had been when she was younger and vivacious.

Rocco, gasping, with tongue lolling, was puzzled as to why his master took him around the same block five times.

He dived head-first into his water bowl when they returned to quench his raging thirst.

Leo spent the following days at the, now, Quayside office. He called Graziella twice a day as agreed, and they spoke for an age, her mother often joined in too. This arrangement was working well, he manipulated missing weekend calls, saying he was caring for his children and would be busy overnight. Both Graziella and Verna believed Leo was working hard, but he was bored out of his mind, sitting alone in the apartment missing time with his children. He would play games and listen to music, or read, but he certainly didn't have work to do; production had closed down and though there was always some ongoing development, it was tedious. His days became shorter, he'd love to give up the subterfuge, but simply could not.

Everything was closed, there was nowhere to go, except for a walk through the eerily empty streets of a silent city. Leo often stopped and looked up to take in the grand detailed stonework of Georgian buildings he had never noticed before. He absorbed the wonderful architecture of the Theatre Royal, and Lord Grey's Monument standing forty metres high, majestically overlooking the elegant curve of Grey Street, which was free of parked vehicles and people. There was no hustle, no bustle, no traffic noise and few other human beings about. It seemed apocalyptic. He could smell early spring flowers instead of vehicle fumes. As he walked along the Quayside, the vibrant blue sky was crystal clear; he could hear the river lapping, and noticed a faint smell of salty air as it flowed towards the sea. The sound of birds chirping resonated in the pristine air, without traffic and aircraft disturbance. It would have been unique and glorious to share the experience, if the pretence wasn't so utterly soul destroying.

After several days of family life, interspersed with dragging days at the apartment, Leo returned to Italy prior to the UK legal lockdown on 26 March, under the guise of finishing his contract. He was devastated having to return as he and Verna had reconnected their emotionally strong bond, and with genuine sadness in his eyes at the vision of his children waving at the door, he got into a taxi and left for the airport.

On the flight to Milan, Leo wasn't enamoured at having to feign delight at Graziella's growing abdomen. However, after a few contented days with her, he was beginning to form an attachment with his unborn child. He had longed for another baby after Izzy. He was fulfilled as a father, in contrast with the relationship he had with his own estranged father, who lived not far from him currently, but had not made contact. More planning time was available for Leo to arrange his permanent departure, but he wondered what he really wanted.

12

Hannah, March 2020

On 23 March 2020 the UK population was ordered to stay at home, three days later lockdown measures legally came into force. The national mantra was everywhere; *Stay Home - Protect the NHS - Save Lives*. Hannah spent another two nights at Cam's until restrictions forbade their meetings. With sadness they parted on the last day, knowing it would be some time before they could meet up. They both deeply respected the plans in place and agreed if people worked together and stuck with it, hopefully the virus would diminish sooner rather than later.

'At least the regulations advising contact between children and separated parents means I can travel to see Sara. We've decided I'll travel once a month to spend a little time outdoors with my precious girl.' There was no sparkle in Cam's eyes today.

'It's something I guess,' Hannah tried to express a positive take, 'I'd love to meet her when we're done with all this.'

A few days after their parting, Hannah was sitting working from home at her laptop thinking about Cam, about his kindness, his relaxed demeanour, his crinkly brown eyes, mischievous personality, reassuring hugs, and his sexiness. She decided to use the forced separation time to introduce the concept of a boyfriend to her sons.

'Course you should get a boyfriend, Dad's been with Gezza for ages,' was Evan's response. Knowing she should correct Evan from using the family nick-name to her preferred, Gerri, she chose not to. In her mind's eye, she could see the signatures in her handwriting on gifts and cards for the boys, *from Dad and Gerri*. Omitting - love from, and would it hurt her to add kisses to the greeting? Stuff that! Evan can call her what he likes.

Hannah looked at Ross, waited, then as she was busying in the kitchen said, 'Ross, what do you think?' Sitting in the adjacent teenage den, he was silent, pretending he hadn't heard. He firmly held onto the game controller, not taking his eyes off the TV, obviously at a crucial point on FIFA. At least she had sown the seed and had Evan's blessing; a decent start. The lovely tulips in ombre shades of gold and damson, and the Mother's Day card caught her eye. She delighted in the memory there were still chocolates left from a gratefully received gift from her lovely sons.

Working from home meant Hannah missed going into, BlueSea Graphics in Tynemouth, on the north east coast, for a catch up, and sharing innovative ideas on a variety of projects with her colleagues. When the company website appeared online, there was a sense of pride as she'd created a seahorse design for the letter, S, when they renewed their branding logo. She was considering moving towards freelance work and had submitted a design for branding of a major new local tourist and leisure venture. She had high hopes as she was advised her work was shortlisted. However, she didn't fool herself, the competition was immense.

'How's the online school work going?' she asked, whilst she had Evan's attention.

'Okay, a bit crap really because you don't see your mates,' he shrugged.

'I'm now part of your teaching team, so you'd better knuckle down when home schooling begins.' Her comment was met with a sarcastic eye roll. Recently, Hannah turned a blind eye to Evan's noisy online gaming with his friends often into the early hours. Why create another area of inevitable conflict. Choose your battles, was one of the best pieces of parenting advice she knew. Evan and Ross being stuck together at home did not make for harmonious family life sometimes. She was overjoyed when they would sit together playing games or watching TV, they had to, there were no other same-aged people to interact with in person.

Ross took his older brother's jibes well and tried not to respond to the goading as Evan inevitably won most games and arguments. Ross took great pleasure when he got one over on his big brother, leaping about and yelling right at him, *"in your face!"* He always looked to Hannah to reaffirm these rare achievements which she duly gave, with an obligatory smirk to Evan. Though sibling cabin-fever would raise its ugly head, and she missed her family and Cam, some aspects of lockdown were okay. Hannah loved the frequent movie nights with her sons with snacks or takeaway. Being grateful for small mercies, and counting blessings became part of a nation's voice.

13

Verna, April 2020

Verna and the children were reconciled to the fact Leo would return home for good as soon as he could, which was some compensation for the tearful parting. Over the following days, Verna focused on keeping the house and garden in order, and enjoyed witnessing the first buds of April's spring flowers surfacing. Trowelling the flower beds, she had to overcome her irritation of destruction to patches of worn-out lawn in front of Marco's football nets and where the girl's played badminton. A piercing, crack! interrupted the still air, Marco had blasted his football smashing one of the large terracotta pots, spreading compost carnage all over the patio. 'Marco, for goodness' sake!' She was livid, but the shock on his sweet face reminded her of her own mother's terrifying outbursts, she instantly calmed down, hugging him. Both were in tears and Amara came out in sympathy. Izzy seemed oblivious and laughed at the mess.

Rocco was alerted to the mayhem and trotted over sniffing each of them, to check they were all okay.

After clearing the mess, Verna contentedly watched the children play, sipping a coffee, sitting on the patio steps leading onto the not so pristine lawn. She hoped for a future where the family could travel again and she could spend quality time with Leo. A realisation struck her; they had been reliant upon Hannah's support in the past. Hannah would come and stay over and look after all five children to give her and Leo some time out. Verna kept having the guilt pangs of taking advantage of a good person, who at the time, was struggling with her own relationship, but would always be there for her.

Marco had asked about contacting Evan recently, he hero-worshipped him. Verna recognised Marco suffered in the absence of adult males with his father working away; his uncle Simon living in Bournemouth, plus a grandfather who had little interest in his grandchildren, now living in Spain with his third wife. Verna suggested Marco contacted Evan directly online, which he had, to no reply. He suggested she could ask Aunty Hannah to tell Evan to get in touch. Verna was desolate, she hadn't realised what a huge hole Hannah and her family had left in her life. Hannah would be agreeable to contact, if it concerned the children, but what would she say. She could start with an apology for the things she said, but … Hannah had made those unfounded accusations about Leo which still vexed her.

Later, Verna was compelled to look at the image on the @VLRsoftware Twitter post, to remove any doubts about Leo. He appeared, looking his usual stylish self, relaxed in his linen yellow shirt and, yes, his phone was in his pocket, with no one in the foreground. She tapped the picture, and pinch zoomed to extreme magnification. Her heart sank, there was a tiny glimpse of the corner of a pair of sunglasses with strands of dark wisping hair, but then, that only confirmed Hannah's description, nothing more. Verna's furrowed brow was the only visible expression of innermost doubts. Who was taking the selfie, was Leo intimate with the girl taking it? Would there be a maid service in a pandemic? Then there was Julianne, if she was brutally honest, Verna had suspicions. She had been so busy with the children, she preferred to sweep uncertainties aside, and Leo having an affair may have passed her by.

An overwhelming sense of isolation shrouded Verna, her family were absent, there was no chatter at the school gates or popping in for coffees with other mothers, no fitness classes, no wining and dining with her husband or any social life. Her neighbours were kind, but she wouldn't confide personal details to them. Life was gloomy and lonely. She heard recent murmurings, through the Megan grapevine of mutual friends, Hannah was seeing a lovely guy. She raised her glass of gin and tonic, 'good for you Hannah. I hope he makes you happy,' then she curled up on the sofa and broke her heart at the loss of her best friend.

14

'Mummy, mummy!' Verna was alerted by Amara's voice. She was making the bed, feeling shabby after several drinks and falling asleep on the sofa, then rolling into bed in the early hours fully clothed. She darted into the hallway, where Amara was in clear distress, 'I can't wake Marco!'

'What do you mean?'

'He's sleeping and won't wake up, Mum please.' Amara was in floods of tears.

Verna rushed into Marco's room, with the dreadful weight of fear in her brain, quaking throughout her body, with simultaneous thoughts that he'd died in his sleep. There was no greater fear for any parent. Marco was lying on his back, ghostly grey.

'Marco wake up!' before she knew it she was shaking him quite severely, and he stirred. In an instant her fears began to subside.

'Baby, what is it, what's wrong?'

Marco could only muster a croaked response, 'feel terrible.'

Verna felt his forehead, it was a furnace, she drew his

duvet cover back and the bed was soaked in sweat. Amara was stunned looking on from the bedroom door. 'Amara.' She didn't or couldn't move, 'Amara! Get some ice from downstairs and a towel.'

Switched into action, Amara fled downstairs as if her life depended on it, and returned within minutes with a huge bowl of ice and a bath towel. Verna wrapped the ice in the towel and gently drew it over Marco's stomach and chest. 'Amara, come here, keep doing this, and talk to him, don't let him fall asleep.'

By this time Izzy had arrived in the doorway and suggested, 'I can sing to him.' She began singing dramatically in a loud tone.

'That should do it,' said Verna as she sped to the main bathroom for the thermometer, and paracetamol which may help to bring his temperature down, but what the hell was wrong with her beautiful boy? She was in a panic, what was the regular temperature for children, how could she be so stupid not to remember, she simply could not focus.

In the bedroom, Marco was shivering, she stopped Amara using the ice-towel. His teeth were chattering but clenched, and Verna was worried he was going to have a convulsion. 'Marco,' she spoke gently but firmly, and encouraged him to accept the thermometer in his mouth. After a short spell, it read a little over 39°C.

Marco croaked, 'my head Mum, my head.'

It took all of Verna's will to not burst into tears. 'You're going to be okay son,' she was keeping it together, only just. 'Amara get my phone, quickly.' Verna made a call to health services for advice, she was terrified Marco had a bad bout of Covid, she'd read some children had died, or it could be meningitis. She was advised to monitor him, for increasing severe headache, vomiting, rash and breathing difficulty, also ensure hydration and give paracetamol. Throughout that night, Verna lay on the floor in Marco's bedroom and her mind whirled with fear as he wasn't improving. She'd tried to help him get up to go to the toilet, but he was too weak, so to his shame she helped him as he lay on his side to pee into the bowl Amara had brought the ice in. They were both crying. He slumped back in bed and could not move or hardly speak. She was on high alert, sitting cross-legged, straining to hear his breaths, watching his chest move with each inhale.

As morning dawned, there was little change, she knew she needed to call the medics and was terrified her baby would be whisked off to hospital and end up on a ventilator. She'd sent Leo a number of texts and some photos, knowing they'd concern him. But he should be here, helping her with their children. It gradually became lighter and she took a moment to call Leo, they had a heated debate. A fleeting resentment flooded her mind, Leo should be here for his family! Verna called Leo again and left a voicemail. He called back within twenty minutes and said, 'how the hell could this happen Verna?' There was impatience in his voice.

'You have no idea how demanding it is with three children on my own at home during a pandemic, with no help whatsoever. I was making the beds, and guess what Leo, I can't stop a virus or whatever it is floating into our house! It's not the time for arguments, Marco is very poorly, I have to look after him.' She ended the call, later her phone showed a voicemail, it was Leo humbly thanking Verna for taking charge of the situation. He would let her know how the journey was going as he was on his way to departures. His voice cracked as she heard, *"love you Verna, I'm so sorry."*

Verna called health services again, advising there was no change, and was told paramedics would arrive as Marco's temperature was not improving. Verna needed someone, anyone, Leo wasn't here, her mother had always been useless, her father lived in Spain, her brother was in Bournemouth, and the one person who could offer some comfort was, Hannah, but she'd ordered her out of the house accusing her of envy and said many cruel things. Verna sent a message to Joyce, her neighbour, telling her of the situation, to ask if she'd keep an eye on the girls.

'Amara get Izzy ready and have a snack bar then go and play out in the garden so Joyce can look after you when the medics arrive.' Amara dutifully did as she was told, within ten minutes Verna could hear joyful words as Joyce and husband Nigel entertained the girls with badminton. Verna was so grateful for this adult support.

Rocco was thrilled, he liked the new big human playing with them. He had a really loud bark!

The paramedics arrived, masked, the epitome of calm efficiency. Marco was woozy, as he tried to reply to their questions, as they completed the examination. Whilst they couldn't identify if it was Covid, Marco was certainly suffering from a severe virus and the worry was it could become bacterial, and his oxygen levels were low. They were reluctant to take him to hospital and offered sound advice regarding any changes.

'I don't want you to take him either,' whispered Verna.

'You'll be able to take care of him here, but we advise no close contact with anyone else for now. Only you in this room and stay masked as a precaution. Please call again if anything changes. He's a big strong lad, got a good chance of shaking this off.' There was a reassuring smile beneath the mask. The medics left, and Verna wondered how she was going to keep the house running, care for the children and Rocco, he needed regular walks. Joyce and Nigel stood in like troupers, they were a blessing. She could hear Joyce soothing Amara calming her anxiety as Nigel distracted Izzy with Rocco, though Izzy had got over the trauma rather quickly. Verna at the top of the stairs and Joyce at the bottom had a conversation and put a plan together until Leo returned. Amara's bewildered little face appeared beside Joyce.

Joyce said, 'come and help me with dinner, and we'll watch a Disney movie afterwards.' Looking at Verna, 'we're around anytime you need us, don't you worry.' Joyce and Nigel were heaven sent. Verna kept her vigil, she avoided coming into close contact, and remained masked in close proximity to them.

Leo had arrived home and was distressed to witness his boy lying in bed as weak as a kitten. It was four days before Marco was sufficiently recovered to eat a little and sit up in bed watching movies. He would soon be able to continue schoolwork online, much to his consternation. Amara was intuitive to his needs, and recovered board games she found tucked away they hadn't played for years. Marco was dismayed when Izzy would wander into his room with a toy stethoscope around her neck and her plastic medicine kit. She put her soft toys on his bed in a disciplined line, 'let's play hopsittles, I need to 'xamin you.' She put the stethoscope on his chest, 'how is the patient today?' He had to oblige as she took his temperature with her thermometer and ordered him back to bed as it wasn't right. He was half way through a game, but nurse Izzy wouldn't take no for an answer. Marco bought into the whole act, he had no choice!

15

May was approaching as Leo returned to England to help Verna with the children, and two weeks had flown by. His phone often buzzed which was dismissed as, 'work-related.' He was dismayed each time Graziella's number displayed. The family were in the middle of dinner, so he switched it off. He made an excuse, 'going up into the study to check something out.' No one paid any attention to him as he left the room, they were all tucking into a fresh fruit salad with cream.

'Not so much cream Izzy!' he heard Verna say as he went upstairs.

He switched his mobile on in the privacy of the study and heard Graziella's voice. She was outside somewhere. The message kept cutting in and out, however he ascertained from her rapid Italian, she was at an airport. An airport? Where? In Milan? Where was she? His heart sank and he called back, it went to voicemail. He tried again, voicemail again. Christ! Was she here, did she know his home address; could she be in a taxi on her way? It would take twenty minutes for a cab to arrive from the airport. Shit! He could walk to the end of the road and divert her somehow, maybe to the flat and he'd meet her there. Jesus, he hadn't imagined she would get a flight over. Leo was really panicking, he could feel the blood surging around his veins, his heart was thumping in his chest, in rhythm with the pulse in his temples.

Fleeting visions flashed through his mind of a pregnant Graziella turning up on the doorstep, as Verna and the children looked on, not understanding ultra-fast Italian speech. He was already making excuses; he could say he was being stalked and the mad woman had tracked him down, but Verna would ring the police. No, not a good idea. He looked at his phone anxiously waiting for it to ring. Even in desperation, he could rationalise it was not fair on Graziella, an innocent party in all of this. Verna was an innocent party too. His children were. Graziella's family were all innocent, his unborn child was too, everyone was, except him. Nausea overcame him with guilt, and his stomach heaved.

'Do you want dessert Leo?' came a shout from downstairs.

He was startled at the voice, which shook him out of his trance. He was having palpitations, but said calmly, 'no, I'm fine.' A prickling sensation crept up the back of his neck and head that he was going to pass out. He managed to keep his voice clear and shouted downstairs, 'an urgent situation has arisen; I'll be up here sorting out the mess for a while.'

'Okay, there's plenty for later anyway.'

He hardly heard the last comment. Normal life was playing out in his home downstairs, yet the terror in this room was palpable. He tried Graziella's number yet again, it was ringing! She answered, 'Ciao Papa Leo!' in a light cheerful tone.

'Where on earth are you?' he asked in controlled panic. She was enjoying a takeaway coffee at Newcastle airport waiting for him to pick her up, didn't he get the message? She told him she was feeling well and energetic now she had left the first trimester of her pregnancy, and thought she'd surprise him.

'I'm on my way,' he spluttered and ended the call. Okay, thinking quickly, he'd go to the flat. He had to make it look as though he lived there. If he packed a case, it would seem strange to Verna. He shoved as many things as he could into his backpack. His mind raced, were there any clothes hangers, or a toothbrush, or cutlery, or anything at the apartment? He always got takeaway food. With relief he knew one of the beds had been made up. Unless … he could book a hotel room … but in lockdown, it was unlikely without prior arrangement and Graziella would rightly question why wouldn't he take her to his home?

Calming down as he knew she wasn't going anywhere 'til he picked her up. His brain's floodlight searched for plausible explanations; he would say the flat was sparse in preparation for returning to Italy, he had put stuff in storage, maybe she'd buy that? His mind was whirling, he was light-headed. What the fuck was she doing, coming to England? What the fuck was her family thinking, letting her travel, at almost five months pregnant, in a pandemic? Leo shouted downstairs as he frantically crammed more items into the backpack. 'Verna, I need to go to the flat!'

He didn't want Verna to see the abject fear in his eyes, wildly searching the room for obvious things to take. His wash-bag, where the hell was it?

She appeared at the bedroom door, 'you okay Leo, must be something serious?'

'I'm going to be up all night sorting out the bloody mess going on over there.'

'Really? Isn't it something you can communicate online from here?'

'No, it's a full system crash. I've got plans for the circuitry at the apartment, it's a complete cock-up.' The irony of Leo's words was completely lost on him. 'I'll take some clothes in case it turns into an all-nighter. Where's my wash-bag?' Verna retrieved it from the spare room and handed it to him, which he squashed into the backpack.

'Sorry honey, see you tomorrow or whenever this gets sorted.' Leo hooked the bag over his shoulder, galloped down the stairs and left the house without a goodbye to the kids. In seconds he was back, almost tripped over Rocco, who was wondering why his master was dashing off? Leo, made full use of his long limbs, bounding upstairs three at a time to retrieve his laptop, he nearly forgot it, which would've been a major erroneous giveaway of the subterfuge.

Verna, was standing at the bottom of the stairs and said meekly, 'Okay, bye, see you later, or tomorrow?'

Leo walked straight by her, without a word and no kiss, totally preoccupied with the momentous event unfolding before him. Verna was in ignorant bliss Leo was going to meet the woman he had been having an affair with for several months and who was carrying his unborn baby. A baby which was a genetic half sibling to their three children Marco, Amara and Izzy.

Leo arrived at Newcastle airport, where Graziella emerged from the revolving door into the cool northern air, inadequately dressed in only a light cardigan for warmth. She was trailing a cabin bag behind her and waved frantically to him with a beaming smile. Leo's heart sank as she got into the car, threw her arms around him, jabbering away in Italian. He made pleasant small talk, feigning surprise and delight at her arrival. Graziella looked as though she had expanded rapidly since he left Italy.

It was a twenty-minute drive to the flat on the Quayside. He parked the car and they both ascended in the lift to the apartment on the fifth floor. Graziella loved the open river view of the illuminated Newcastle and Gateshead bridges from the apartment. She looked around at the sparse furnishings and emptiness of the place. Leo immediately explained, furnishings were in storage as it was waiting to be decorated, however because of the pandemic he was unable to get anyone to do it. This was, at least, a half-truth.

Leo took the bag full of essential shopping he picked up at a convenience store on his way to the airport into the kitchen, and filled the cupboards with the basic groceries. Graziella was astounded at the lack of food. Leo laughed, and passed it off as a man living alone who relied on fast-food and takeaways. All plausible lies. Graziella said things would have to change and they should go shopping the next day to buy ingredients to make some healthy home-cooked Italian food. Whilst that sounded brilliant as she was an excellent cook, Leo was utterly dismayed at the position he was in. At least he had maybe twenty-four hours to message Verna to say the work situation was dire, which bought him a bit of time.

'How long had you intended to stay Graziella, you really shouldn't be travelling in your condition during the pandemic.'

'I checked with my midwife. I'm healthy and able to travel, there were no problems at all. I took the safety precautions at the airport, and used the business account to travel premier class, for me and baby.' A radiant smile erupted as she rubbed her small bump. She looked beautiful.

Leo tried to sound nonchalant, 'I was going to ring you this evening to tell you I was making my way back in a day or two because Marco is recovering well.'

Graziella suggested, 'we can travel back together, but I thought it would be nice to come and have a look around your city.'

Leo planned to book the next available flights back to Milan. He would need to create a plausible story about the business being in dire need of him returning for Verna's sake. The following morning, they walked along the Quayside and he showed Graziella some of the historic features of the city. They called into a small supermarket in the city centre and bought some products for Graziella to make a meal that evening. Leo was distracted, wondering how he could find an excuse to leave the apartment and return to his house. He messaged Verna; *Things are bad, staying overnight here, but I'm needed back in Italy. Going to end contract soon as I can xx*

Verna replied; *It's for the best, Marco really needs you here. Be good to have you home for good. See you soon x*

Graziella accepted Leo must say goodbye to his children, so he left after their homecooked meal. He explained to the children he had to return to Italy urgently. Marco looked away wiping his eyes, which upset them all, and tears flowed.

Rocco looked up at the humans. They all had water coming out of their faces, and made strange noises.

Leo told Verna his flight was leaving in the early hours, another lie. He hoped to hell she didn't check the flight times from Newcastle airport. He was of course offered to stay for dinner, but refused stating he needed to sleep before getting the flight. He arranged to put the apartment keys in the post box in the communal area and would sort everything out when he returned. It was an emotional goodbye. If he could delete the last several months, he would remain in the safety and security of his loving family.

He was gone for less than two hours. Whilst Graziella was full of many types of hormones, her sexual drive was raging and she desperately wanted to make love to Leo. This hadn't happened many times, but Leo was not up to the task. Graziella was curious but she didn't seem to dwell on it and said to him it must be because he was emotionally struggling. Leo agreed, and fell into a fitful sleep.

16

Hannah, April 2020

A month after their last date, Hannah and Cam had online calls, it was difficult for him as he wasn't seeing Sara and expressed his concern, 'I hope she doesn't forget who her daddy is, she's distracted during online calls, mostly her new baby sister. I'm really bored too, so I've taken up running again and with not going out drinking with the lads, I'm getting really fit. I played cricket and trained for the North Run every year, apart from last year when I lost the motivation. It'll be a while before gyms reopen, so I've bought a new bike and made the most of getting out on it while I'm furloughed.'

'Well done you, I've been a complete slob. No motivation, I definitely need your inspiration to get off my fat arse.'

At one point, during the call Cam stood, took his top off and in action-hero pose, revealed well defined pecs and biceps, one adorned with his Celtic band tattoo. He then patted his toned stomach as his jeans slipped down his hips. His face had thinned and his hair had grown in. The vision of his face, body and the waistband of his

Calvin Klein's actually gave Hannah quite a thrill between her legs. It was an exciting memorable vision of the toned up, boho version of Cameron Wallace. One she would save for later.

Hannah was gaining weight in the weeks since lockdown with her sedentary lifestyle. Chomping on donated chocolate and inner goodies from the boys' easter eggs hadn't done her any favours. Hannah noticed silver strands sparkling amongst her brunette hairline as she brushed her shoulder length hair, which desperately needed a trim. Her cruel insecurity demons decided to dance around her mind and play havoc with her self-esteem. Cam was almost three years her junior and she convinced herself, he'd drift away with a childless, fit, thirty-odd year old when everyone was released back into society.

Hannah had completed a few charity runs and decided to dig out her old, squished, Mizuno trainers from the musky smelling under-stairs cupboard, with the intention of going for a run. She messaged Ellie and Megan, they may fancy a jog at some point, Ellie responded with, WTAF! Then an online call from Ellie alerted her screen. Hannah explained she needed to get fitter after seeing her younger boyfriend's buff physique. 'Why hasn't someone come up with a decent word to describe a person in a mature relationship to replace, boyfriend or companion for fuck's sake. It makes you sound either eight or eighty? Is Cam merely a friend, or man-friend, or lover. He isn't my partner, yet. The terminology sounds ridiculous, I mean; significant other or life partner … yuk.' Maybe she should have known better than to ask Ellie.

Ellie suggested, 'Totty, Arm-Candy, Love-Muffin, Snuggle-Butt, Tiger, Stud,' and variations of, 'My Boo, Boyf and Boopkin.'

'You've completely made those up,' accused Hannah.

Ellie countered, 'I haven't, I think the introductory phrase, I'd like you to meet Cam, my snuggle-butt, is perfectly acceptable.'

A chat with Ellie always cheered Hannah up. They agreed a time and place for a socially distanced jog with their sister-in-law Megan, well, a walk to begin with; she must do something about her weight gain and apathy. Whenever Hannah mentioned Cam, Evan was fine, approaching fifteen, he had many other things on his plate; the absence of friends and the ever-changing situations with schoolwork. Ross however, fell silent if Cam was mentioned. He was at the awkward eleven-year-old stage of figuring out if he was still a little boy or whether he should be more grown-up. He didn't ask any questions or comment at all. One evening the three were enjoying chilli and rice, when Hannah looked at Ross and asked directly, 'are you okay if we meet with Cam when lockdown is eased?' He shrugged, got up, walked away with his chilli filled bowl, didn't make eye contact and went into the other room.

'That went well,' said Evan with a wry smile. 'He'll be fine Mam, everything's a bit strange right now.'

An element of resentment rose within, so it was okay for Adrian to have buggered off and shacked up with, Ginger Gezza, while they were still married; yet here she was, years later, still single and feeling guilty about introducing someone new to her boys. Ross would be fine, she'd take Evan's reassurance. Evan asked to see a picture of Cam and remarked. 'Aye, he looks great, bit younger than you is he?'

Her cruel insecurity demons were having an absolute riot! Hannah contacted Cam, and suggested he meets with the boys when restrictions permitted, which he agreed. She couldn't wait to get her hands on his daughter Sara too and imagined her sweet little face tucked up beneath her colourful unicorn-adorned duvet.

'By the way, we need to discuss contraception next time we're together, I had a recent scare and wondered if it may have been a pre-menopause thing, though I'm still a bit young for that.'

'If we had a baby, it would be beautiful if it was anything like it's mother.'

'What a lovely thing to say, you after brownie points?'

'But … when you bake a beautiful cake, you tend to complement the chef not the oven.'

'I'm not having that you cheeky sod.'

'Sorry,' he said, still grinning.

Hannah knew Cam was missing the banter with his mates. They had virtual bar nights and online quizzes enjoying conversation and a few drinks, but it wasn't the same. She had good feelings about Cam despite her insecurities; he had a lot of qualities and she totally fancied his pants off. They discovered many things in common, food and music, they would make plans about which groups they would see when things were back to normal; Biffy Clyro, Nothing But Thieves, and Foo Fighters were at the top of their list. Hannah had seen the latter three times and confessed to being in love with, Dave Grohl, Cam admitted he was too.

The lockdown situation, although incredibly frustrating, prevented Hannah taking things too quickly with Cam. Her feelings were reaffirmed whenever they spoke, and she thought about him constantly. Absence was making her heart grow fonder, she was falling for him, big time.

17

Italy, April 2020

Leo and Graziella returned to the apartment in Lodi after a trouble-free journey. Whilst Leo was terrified of telling Graziella he was leaving her, he knew he had to do it, but not today. He would choose his moment carefully. His guilt was reinforced when he looked into her sweet face as she said, 'we're home Papa, now we can start to make plans.'

His heart was torn into pieces, then he thought about his beautiful children in England, particularly the bond he had with Marco, and knew where he wanted to be. The moment came when he had to tell Graziella the next morning, he couldn't delay any longer. He ensured there were no sharp or heavy objects she could grab nearby. Leo made coffee, Graziella wanted fruit juice. The anticipation of the calm ambience being blown away by an Italian hurricane, scared Leo to his core. His coffee cup rattled as he tried to steady its landing on the table, he took a breath, looked at her and said, 'Graziella I have something serious to tell you. I'm so sorry, but I'm leaving to return to England. My children need me, and, I ... well, we believe the children deserve us making another go of it.'

Graziella looked at him with a blank expression. He studied her face she had not processed the information. 'Do you understand what I am saying Graziella?'

Graziella nodded. Then staring beyond him, she spoke in a monotone voice, surprisingly in English and repeated, 'you are leaving me to return to your family in England.'

'Yes, that's right.' The tension was palpable, broken only by the sound of muttering outside as people passed by. It was a living nightmare. 'I am so sorry. I want you to know I have truly loved you, and I will support everything you and the baby need.' It was unnerving. Graziella did not fly into a rage. Her behaviour was unexpected. She looked at him and said, again in English, 'so, this is how it ends.' She got up and walked into the bedroom.

Leo couldn't believe how calm she was taking this and her speaking in English was bizarre. He tried to overhear her phone conversation, but struggled to keep up with the pace of whispered, rapid colloquial Italian.

He stood in the doorway. 'Graziella, please can we discuss this, what about the baby?' He moved to the sofa as Graziella did not respond to his request for dialogue. The edgy silence between them was excruciating. Leo fidgeted, wringing his hands, trying to catch her eye to engage conversation.

Fifteen minutes later the apartment door opened, two men walked into the room, Leo's vulnerability filled his being, but he was invisible to them. Graziella emerged from the bedroom and greeted her older brother and her cousin, who embraced her as she wept. She had crammed items into her flight bag, which was still half packed from the previous day. Graziella walked towards Leo, who was standing, and looked directly into his eyes, she slapped his face so hard, it stung like scalding water was thrown in his face. She said nothing, picked up the unfinished glass of juice and dropped it at Leo's feet. The shattering orange explosion resonated, as shards of glass pierced his bare shins. She turned and walked out of the door with the two men following. The door closed and everything fell silent. Leo was utterly mystified about the scene that had played out in front of him. He sent a message to Graziella, asking her how she wanted to make arrangements for the baby, or if there was anything else she needed. No reply.

In the evening, once he cleared up as much sticky orange glass as he could, Leo rested in bed, but could not sleep. His shins stung where the glass had cut his skin, fortunately there wasn't much bleeding. He had tried to eat but was sick to his stomach. It couldn't possibly be over like this, he thought, there was no plan for the child. He got out of bed completely disorientated at the strangest event that had ever happened in his whole life. The adrenalin rush hadn't left his body from the expected onslaught from Graziella. He was bereft he would never see her again, as a million thoughts pervaded his mind; had she known? Maybe she wasn't as easily duped as he had thought. Maybe she was waiting for this to happen. Had she discovered what was really going on with his family in England? Did she know he'd lied about being divorced, but hoped he would stay with her because she was pregnant? He was exhausted and eventually dozed off on the sofa.

Leo heard shuffling at the door, it opened with a key and he assumed Graziella had returned to talk with him. He lifted his head from the sofa and recognised the outline of the same two men in the dim light. The door clicked shut, and not a word was spoken. Graziella's cousin, a man-mountain, pulled Leo up off the sofa and held his arms behind his back. He was facing her brother, whose black eyes burned like a devil.

'Hey! What—' Fireworks exploded in Leo's head, as a loud crunch, and immense pain overwhelmed him. Bludgeoning bony knuckles hit his face. His lower lip burst open as he crumpled forward, with blood pooling onto the floor. The warm gelatinous liquid spread across his cheek as he slumped into it. Successive sharp, rapid kicks into his torso seared into him, accompanied by grunts of exertion with every kick from his assailants.

Man-mountain dragged Leo upright like a rag doll and pulled his hair back so he was a few centimetres from devil-eyes. Leo smelled alcohol as devil-eyes whispered with dark menace, 'if you ever go near Graziella again, you will die.' He head-butted Leo as man-mountain released his grip and dropped him onto the tiles with remnants of sticky shattered glass. Leo saw a blurred vision of two shadows walking out of the door. He heard the mechanism softly click as the door closed. He sucked in air, but couldn't move. As the sound of a car engine faded away, he drifted into unconsciousness.

Leo woke, stunned and confused. The sound of his

laboured breathing rasped in the stillness. He tried to focus on his swollen left hand resting on the floor in front of his face. His middle finger was broken, deliberately perhaps, but he couldn't recall it happening with any clarity. His blurred vision and the excruciating pain in his head scared him; was this the point at which he died alone in the apartment from head wounds or internal injuries. His mouth seemed full of dry cotton wool. He noticed a spider, motionless, underneath the sofa, and used his native tongue to whisper, 'ragno,' as he floated into another unconscious slumber.

Leo awoke with clearer vision. The spider was gone. His body felt like a jumble of fluids and bones being held together in a delicate bag of skin. Nothing seemed to feel in the right place. He slowly looked down at his blood-stained, glass encrusted legs, and circled his ankles. He gently bent both his legs; nothing was broken. He raised himself onto his right elbow and caught sight of his blue shirt, now soaked red. He eased towards the sofa and propped himself up against it. His brain was slopping around like washing in a machine, and he could hear a pulsating whooshing noise as blood pumped around his temples.

After some minutes, he tried to stand using the sofa as a prop, but couldn't and rolled onto his knees instead, as glass shards further pierced his lower legs. With his arms resting on the sofa in front of him, he held his head up with his intact right hand. At least his neck wasn't broken, he had to be thankful for that. He was worried in case there were damaging effects from concussion. He had no idea how long it was since the assault, or how long he was knocked out. The small gold crucifix his mother gave him, which he always wore, had been wrenched off his neck and lay on the sofa in front of him. He held it and said a prayer. Leo was from a religious family and praying was engrained within him. He had denied his faith in adult life, which was the cause of angst between him and his father, who was a devout practising Catholic.

Leo managed to pull himself up into a sitting position on the sofa. He froze at the sound of a car engine, terrified if Graziella's family had come back to finish the job, he couldn't defend himself. He sluggishly eased into a standing position, swayed, then made three cautious steps towards the large dining table that dominated the room. He used the table to steady himself, like being heavily sedated, his inner balance was not doing its level best. He used the table to propel himself to the bedroom door. Once inside, Leo looked into the mirror as he rested his elbows on the drawers and couldn't believe what he saw. He took in the detail of the monster face staring back at him.

The unrecognisable reflection was a face swollen to half the size again. One of his eyes was closed and the other, which he could vaguely see out of, was engorged with blood and puffed up. He tentatively touched his nose, which seemed intact, but one cheek was inflamed with deep purple bruising; his cheekbone was fractured. He slowly turned his head, the congealed blood beside his ear concerned him, although it could be from the injury to his mouth or cuts from his eyes. He opened his mouth slightly and realised one of his teeth was missing. There was a hole in his lip where it had ripped through the flesh, he winced as he touched the tender spot.

He lay on the bed knowing he required medical attention, however did not want to alert the authorities to the assault. He recalled with irony, Graziella's cousin was Polizia. Maybe he was skilled in torture techniques of a human body without killing it. The repercussions of any further connection with the Italian family would be dire. He had been ruthlessly kicked in the stomach and although he had pulled his knees up instinctively to protect his groin and shield some of the blows, they had hit home. Leo huffed with pain at the effort to remove his shirt. His moans were from a deep place within, as he had never experienced such agony. He spent the night dozing off, propped up with pillows to prevent sliding sideways and choking. His breathing was impaired by his swollen mouth and throat.

'Go away! Go away!' He woke with a horrific sharp shock that someone was leaning over him. His heart raced as he stiffened, then realised it was a nightmare. The blazing morning light stretched across the room. Bruising appeared on his torso, like the land masses on a map of the world. There were scratches and scrapes from their boots, which he knew would have no trace of him on them by now. He looked at the clock on the far wall, it was 5 a.m. or maybe 5 p.m. Below the clock, Leo noticed the spider, motionless, watching him. He fell asleep again.

The next time Leo woke, the spider was gone, every inch of his body ached and he couldn't stop crying. All he wanted was to return to England; to Verna, to his children, to his home and his true life, wishing none of this had ever happened. He had no clue what time it was, but it was daylight, and he guessed two days had passed by. He shuffled, with a stooped gait, to retrieve his mobile phone. There were several missed calls and voicemails from Verna, since his last message to say he had arrived safely. His fingers were tender however, he typed a brief message; *Hi sorry for late reply. Advised senior exec ending contract. Planning return. Hope you and children good. Can't wait to see you all xx*

For two days, Leo lived under the threat of someone turning up and taking out more retribution upon him. Waiting for the demon in a horror movie to suddenly attack without warning, only increased Leo's anxious trauma. He locked the windows and shutters and wedged a chair under the handle of the front door. He was terrified of going out to shop, wanting to avoid stares and questions about his injuries. He had to eat and forced himself to consume some dry cereal and breadsticks. He made coffee, but the stench of sour milk from the fridge disgusted him and he painfully retched into the sink as he poured the sickening glugs of lumpy milk down the plug. His hands shook, there was no strength in them as he tried to squash the empty carton in the bin. Leo spotted the spider, motionless, on the floor, mocking him.

Overnight, Leo's shredded nerves conjured up shadows across the bedroom walls which freaked him out, so he went to lay on the sofa. He noticed the spider was missing. He looked at his hands, 'not again,' they were shaking uncontrollably, it was happening every few hours. The door of the apartment across the hall banged shut, he flinched, staring at his door. He held his breath, wishing his heart wouldn't thump so loudly, any invader would sense it. He scoured the apartment for places to hide, and figured he could lock himself in the bathroom if anyone broke in. His phone was always charged, always in his pocket at all times; he'd ring for help next time.

His battered body was weak, as was his fragile mind, he had to conjure up another lie to explain his injuries to Verna, he did everything to diminish them with cool baths and ice compresses. Another day passed as he kept up the pretence of work to her. He found some cosmetics Graziella had left and used it to disguise the worst bruising on his face. One of his eyes was healing well, however the other was bloodshot with a deep purple colour around the socket. The swelling around his mouth had reduced significantly but still hurt like hell and felt lacerated inside. The congealed lump of blood where his tooth was punched out was slimy and disgusting, his breath stank despite cleaning his teeth with toothpaste on his finger and trying to rinse with mouthwash.

Leo looked in the mirror at his face, concealed with cosmetics, and he rehearsed a few sentences that he may say to Verna on the phone, he wanted to avoid a lengthy online call. He took a photograph of his face in the mirror and sent it to her with a message saying how stupid he was to have drank grappa before taking a shower, and had slipped on the tiled floor banging his face onto the side of the bath. He noticed the spider, motionless, above the mirror, it knew he was a liar.

Leo ignored the spider's mockery. He wasn't sure how he was going to explain the extensive bruising to his torso and legs, which were fortunately fading with the constant applications of ice wrapped in a towel. The puckering on his lip didn't look too bad externally, but inside it had set as a hard lumpy mass. Leo had practiced trying to verbalise properly, and watched a video of himself in an interview to compare if he sounded vastly different. His phone rang, he recoiled at the shrill echo breaking the silence, Verna's name appeared, he held the screen some distance away and answered. He'd chosen a long-sleeved crew-neck top so no visible bruising would show. He willed for calmness in his voice. 'Hey, hi, how are you and the kids?'

'We're fine, but you're obviously not.'

'Honestly, I'm good now, but it hurt like hell when I slipped.'

'Shouldn't you see a doctor and get checked if it's a head injury?'

'I'm fine, honestly. I called the surgery and they gave me the okay, they're limiting face-to-face visits, and it wasn't an emergency, I didn't lose consciousness or anything.'

The lies were racking up again. Leo confirmed he had finished the contract and would return home permanently soon. A relieved smile crossed his face after the call. He contacted the housing agent to stop the lease on the apartment and finalised payments. He hired a maid service to clean up, momentarily regretting the memory of the, plausible lie, to his daughter. He sent an email to the senior production manager at the company to tell him he was moving back to the UK. An immense warm sense of calm flooded through his mind and body as he booked his final flight home.

Leo scrolled through the contacts in his phone and deleted any relating to his time in Italy. He hesitated as

Graziella's number appeared. He deleted it, along with all texts, emails and images. He hoped he could keep the birth of the child a secret from Verna. He knew Graziella's family weren't affluent, so he'd expect financial requests would be made at some point. With any luck, he could make a gigantic payment and that would be the end of it. Whilst he regretted, he would never see the child he would have with Graziella, it was for the best all ties were severed now, and it never came to light again. All the lies and excuses he made, all the affairs and one-night stands he had over the years were shameful to him now. He was sickened by the deceit and vowed it was time to stop.

He spotted the spider, motionless, under the dining table and said, 'the place is all yours now, I'm going home.'

18

Verna, May 2020

The Ravassio children were fascinated with their dad's bloodshot eye and his missing pre molar tooth. The gap was visible when he smiled, which he wasn't doing much. It was never found and Leo assumed he may have swallowed it. Verna had tried not to reveal her shock as Leo explained he wanted to wait for dental treatment in England. He had waited three weeks before he returned, under the pretence he was still working, however it was, in reality, so his injuries would heal.

Rocco sensed change. His master was back. Different. Doesn't bark. Doesn't run. Rocco raised his head smelling the scent of his mistress. She put food in his bowl and scratched behind his ear. Rocco rested his chin on his paws, looked up soulfully, but wasn't hungry.

Leo asked Verna, 'would you like a drink?' stumbling a little walking towards the fridge and steadying himself with a hand on the back of her chair. He rubbed his ear with irritation.

'Sure, a gin would be nice.' Leo was standing looking

into the fridge. 'The tonic water is on the right at the bottom,' directed Verna. She recognised Leo struggled to concentrate and also seemed overwhelmed at the noise from the children.

'Daddy!' Leo spun around and dropped the bottle of tonic at the sound of Izzy's voice.

Verna got off the seat to see what Izzy wanted and picked up the bottle, placing it in the sink as it fizzled beneath the partially opened cap, 'You ok?' she asked him. He nodded and returned to his seat, sitting in silence. 'You don't seem to have much energy these days, even a walk with Rocco or a short game of badminton or football in the garden wipes you out.' Leo nodded, but said nothing. Verna worried there was something more significant than the after-effects of the fall. 'How's your stomach been, still getting cramps?'

'A little now and then, but I don't feel like eating.'

'Unusual for you to lose your appetite, maybe you should get checked out.'

'I'm fine, it's been the stress of work, great to be home resting.' His weak smile didn't convince her. Most worrying for Verna was he had lost his libido. She observed him looking at her when she was naked, however didn't take the opportunity to touch her. He was having night terrors too.

Verna was awakened, squinting from the bright illumination of garden security lights through the half open blinds. She stretched her hand out, Leo wasn't in bed. Looking out of the window, he was sitting on the patio steps. She put on a warm robe and joined him.

It was 3 a.m. on a cool, May morning. 'Can't sleep?' she

asked in a whisper, rubbing his back. His skin was cold to touch, the thin t-shirt and his boxer shorts weren't offering much warmth. She grabbed one of the fake-fur throws from inside and draped it around his shoulders. Rocco was snuggled beside him.

'No, I can't, but I thought there was someone in the garden.'

Startled, 'should we ring the police?' Verna looked around the silent garden.

'No,' then with a glazed expression he said, 'it was more I sensed someone was out here … know what I mean?'

'Not really, did you hear something?'

'No, but I could … sort of feel there was a presence outside … like, my brain knew it and told me to go and check.'

Verna was becoming spooked by Leo's odd response. 'You must've been dreaming; they can seem realistic. If there was a noise or movement, the security lights would come on, and I know this little thing,' stroking Rocco, 'is a bit useless, but he would definitely bark if he heard something, was he alerted when you came downstairs?'

'No.' Leo's vacant stare remained.

Verna noticed Marco's cricket bat behind him. 'Come back inside, I'm sure it was simply a vivid dream. Your mind can play tricks on you, especially when you're fatigued.'

Leo stood mechanically and shuffled back into the kitchen with the throw still around his shoulders, then made his way upstairs. Verna was shivering, unsure whether it was from the cool air, or Leo's disassociation from reality. She picked up Rocco and soothed him so he wouldn't bark, and placed him back in his basket. She ensured doors and windows were locked, then spied the cricket bat, but she wasn't going back out to retrieve it. The motion-sensor lights in the garden clicked off. Instantly her pale, ghostly figure was reflected in the glass door, against the blackness outside. The silence was unnerving. Rocco snuffled! She spun around, then scooted upstairs taking them two at a time.

The following day, Leo appeared subdued. He hadn't been sleeping well, so she put the events of the early hours down to extreme fatigue, but it continued to worry her. She had googled symptoms of stress, depression and anxiety and Leo was displaying classic signs. 'Leo, I know there is something not quite right with you since you returned from Italy. Our brains can conjure up weird things from sleep deprivation, but sometimes you're like a different person. Maybe we should go to couples counselling or something?'

Verna was of course thinking about his lack of desire and the loss of the fun, vibrant conversations that were an intrinsic part of their relationship. She noticed his bodyshape had changed too; he slumped when he walked, he had lost his toned, lean look and was gaining weight around his middle. He wasn't motivated to take the morning run, as was his routine as long as she'd known him. He lacked interest in healthy food and often lay in bed all morning. Characteristics which were markedly different for her husband.

'I was wondering, about the fall you had, maybe you've suffered more injuries than you thought.' With no response she continued, 'or, it's possible you may have had the virus. You could be suffering from Long Covid, it affects normal functioning, even if you had none of the classic signs at the time; fatigue, headaches, muscle pain, and lack of concentration are all symptoms.'

'I've been thinking of seeing a doctor to be honest, I know I'm not feeling well, but it could be simply overwork and fatigue.'

In the early hours Leo awoke, lying in bed looking at his beautiful wife. Her soft skin and her neat body; he drank her in. She was so supportive, and his immeasurable guilt arose, how could he have treated her so badly all these years. It took him all of his resolve not to break down in tears. Leo didn't allow Verna to see the extent of the physical and emotional pain he was in. He slipped quietly out of bed, to let her sleep and made an appointment with the GP as soon as the surgery opened. His truthful comments about experiencing insomnia and self-destructive thoughts gave the receptionist no alternative than to offer him a video call appointment that day.

During the video consultation, which he took in the study, whilst Verna and the children were out walking Rocco, he unexpectedly wept describing what happened to him in Italy. He'd had no release from everything locked inside for months. The youthful doctor was incredibly sympathetic to the shattered soul he was witnessing crumble in front of his eyes. Leo said his wife knew nothing of the, random assault, as he put it, because he didn't want to worry her. Whatever suspicions the doctor may have had about his testimony, Leo was reassured the information would remain confidential on his record. When Leo was more composed, he described the head whooshing sensation, light sensitivity and piercing tinnitus among other complaints.

The doctor completed as full a consultation as he could via a screen and said, 'you've received some significant knocks, fortunately they seem to be mostly superficial bumps and bruises, including a possible fractured rib from your description. Keep vigilant about any latent concussion symptoms you may experience and get back in touch if anything changes or deteriorates, especially with hearing or eyesight.'

They discussed the emotional impact of such an event and the doctor prescribed pain relief medication and antidepressants, which should help him sleep, he also made a referral for counselling, but advised the waiting list was extensive. Leo was given some helpline contact numbers in case he experienced a panic attack, or wished to talk through his anxieties, but was encouraged to share his condition fully with his wife. Leo picked up the medication as prescribed, and sat for some minutes, looking at the white paper bag on the car seat full of chemical products with the chemist name printed in green. He thought wryly, he hadn't required more than over the counter pain relief medication in his whole life, purely to counter the effects of over-indulgence. How his life had changed through his own selfishness.

Verna was, as always, supportive, as he explained the outcome of his medical appointment. 'Not sure what to do about continuing the business, but I need income.' Leo looked around the vast kitchen. 'If you want to be a key player in this field, you have to keep up your profile and be in constant circulation with major manufacturers. But I've had enough of being abroad, I don't have the energy right now. Maybe I could look into smaller contractual work, I still have contacts in the business.' Leo had anxieties of Graziella or a representative approaching him for money, but he would deal with that when it happened.

Leo was perched on a high stool at the breakfast bar, Verna put her arms around him, standing between his legs and said, 'take it easy for now. We need to get you back to the healthy guy you've always been.' She moved closer and kissed him. The familiarity for Leo caused stirring sensations in his groin. Verna felt them too against her stomach. They looked into each other's eyes, she smiled and said, 'well, it's a start.'

One morning, following a sensual, if brief, sexual encounter, Leo and Verna continued conversations about how they should progress with their financial situation. At least Verna did, she hadn't wanted to put pressure on Leo as she could see he was struggling and the depression did not seem to be lifting. There were some glimmers of hope when he seemed less anxious, however he avoided conversations every time finances were mentioned.

19

It was now high summer in June 2020, and a pragmatic Verna took an empathetic approach to their situation, but she needed to pin Leo down. Over coffee one morning she said, 'we're in this together, if we do need to make major adjustments to our lifestyle, so be it.'

'But what if it means we have to sell this house,' Leo suggested.

Verna was horrified at his comment, but did not reveal her anxieties. This was the home she had always dreamed of. This home, her three children and a wonderful husband was the perfect secure life she desired since childhood.

'I can take a look at the books, I used to run the finances for VLR Software when you first started out, and I already have access to the business accounts. I never had time once the children came along, maybe now it's my time to work. Once the children return to school, and we see the end of the pandemic, there is no reason why I couldn't start up my own business again.'

Verna ran a successful upmarket hairdressing and beauty business and was in the process of opening a third premises in the affluent Northumberland area, when she fell pregnant with Marco. By the time she had Izzy, she stopped trading and sold the business, making a decent profit, all of which was ploughed into their dream home.

Verna offered, 'I could build up my own beauty business again, it wouldn't bring in as much money as VLR Software, but in time, when you get back on your feet, you may feel like doing some more contracts.'

Leo nodded, 'I feel like an empty shell and my brain is scrambled. But, yeah, I may feel more able getting back into the game at some point.'

'Okay. We have a plan,' she took Leo's hand and kissed him gently on his cheek, 'I'll come up with a budgeting strategy to see us through the next six months. We'll have to cut back, no holidays even when travel is permitted, and no other high expenditure.'

Verna set to work without hesitation that morning, whilst Leo prepared breakfast for the children. Verna had been an extremely organised, financially astute manager, and would have some form of a plan within the week. Life was potentially going to change drastically for the Ravassio family. During the course of her investigations, Verna discovered recent inaccuracies within the company finances. There was no trace of any incoming payments for three months from March to May. She scoured the online accounts and wondered whether the company had not paid yet because of the disruption from Covid. Verna asked Leo about consultancy payments for the last few months of his contract, and he was dumbfounded. He really didn't know what to say, however, to distract this anomaly away from

Verna, he suggested he would make contact with the company to ascertain what had gone wrong, but he knew for sure the contract was suspended in March.

The prospect of the task he had been assigned, sent Leo into a tailspin. He was tired from looking after the children all day, and wasn't sure if it was the medication or simply brain fog, but he couldn't think straight. Prior to his relationship with Graziella he had always been meticulous in his financial planning.

Leo accessed his online business account, and his eyes flickered across a list of incoming and outgoing transactions. He blinked a few times as a freakish thing happened. The black numbers against the white background seemed to be crawling randomly around the screen. He rubbed his eyes, put on his reading glasses, and looked at the screen. He could make some sense of the information, but within a few seconds the digits began to ant-crawl again. He rigidly held onto the desk, rubbed both eyes and focused on the screen, willing the figures to settle, they didn't. He closed his eyes, looked away to focus on something else, then went back to the screen. This time the numbers were quivering, so whilst he could read them, it was impossible to look at them for long.

Leo came out of the study and went into the master bedroom, lay on the bed and recalled he had deleted the company CEO, Fabrizio's, number. He wondered what time it would be in Italy now. He experienced distress at having to check his watch, constantly forgetting the time of day. He looked at his phone screen with a furrowed brow, questioning whether he would be able to sustain a conversation fluently in Italian. There was a block in his brain where his Italian speaking skills had left him. The phone went dead, he'd forgotten to charge it.

'Did you manage to contact Fabrizio?' Verna popped her head around the bedroom door as she went into the bathroom, which startled him.

'Not yet, I'll keep trying.'

Verna came out of the bathroom, looked at Leo, crossed her arms and said, 'well they aren't going to get away with not paying you. You had to travel to and from Italy when the horrendous system crash occurred? They should at least give you an hourly rate for the time you spent working on it.' She told him dinner would be ready soon and returned downstairs.

Leo had a moment of inspiration, he held a private bank account with spare money, maybe he could transfer it over. He glanced through to the study, but couldn't face trying to access online accounts. He was being drawn back into a web of lies and deceit. It was a web of his own making, only this time he was the fly, well and truly trapped.

During the night Leo lay awake in bed, the medication did not seem to be dampening his anxieties, maybe it hadn't fully kicked in yet. He needed to get up as he couldn't lie still any longer. He slid out of the bed trying not to wake Verna. He could see lights flickering under Marco's bedroom door as he crept along the hall, he silently stepped downstairs, and sat in the conservatory. He was alarmed to see two dark shadowy figures standing near the big oak. Transfixed, he watched as they slid silently behind the playhouse. He shook his head and rubbed his eyes, believing he'd imagined the vision. Then one of them crawled up onto the playhouse roof and turned towards him. Illuminated, unblinking eyes opened and stared into him from the mask-like face. He could hear a low, murmured echoing voice in his head.

'If you go near her, we will kill you.' The figure slid down the side of the playhouse and both of them, spider-scuttled across the lawn, eyes darting, then returned to the tree. He heard their whispers, 'do it now, do it now, do it. Now!' Leo was glued to the chair. He wanted to leap up, but his leaden body could not move. He was panicking inside, he needed to run away as fast as he could. Panting rapidly, he saw the figures lift off the ground, then float up the tree trunk, transforming into two huge ravens at the top of the oak tree, then they flapped away. Sheer terror fixed Leo to the chair, his breathing came in short gasps. He could still hear the shadows' distant voices in demonic whispers, 'we will return, we will return.'

20

Verna assumed Leo had taken Rocco out for an early walk as she called out for him and for Rocco as she stepped downstairs, but neither responded. There was no sign Leo had made the children's breakfast or packed lunches. It wasn't such a bad thing if he'd gone for an early walk, maybe even a run. Verna glanced at her watch and pelted upstairs, 'time to get up girls! Marco are you ready?' busying around gathering school bags and picking up school uniforms off the floor, encouraging the two girls to get up and get ready. Marco bleary-eyed came out of his room wondering at the commotion. He told Verna he was on a study day and wasn't required in school.

Verna piled the girls in the car, like many parents, ever grateful schools had re-opened. They were a little late, causing Amara anxiety. Verna held her hand and took her to the school gates, whilst Izzy skipped alongside. One of the new teachers in a funky-print face mask waved and beckoned the girls over. Verna thought she looked like a university student in her contemporary outfit, poker straight glossy hair, and fresh-faced skin. 'Thank you so much Miss Collins, sorry we're late, bit of a hiccup this morning.'

'Absolutely no problem.' Miss Collins turned to the girls, and directed them inside reminding them to follow the socially distanced arrows along the floor.

Verna returned home and shouted for Leo. Nothing had changed, nothing had moved, still no Leo. She took orange juice up to Marco who was now alert and logged into the school study guide. She looked in every room, even checked the playhouse. She was starting to become anxious, with no idea how long Leo had been out of the house. She called him, it clicked to voicemail, on her way to the bathroom she spotted his phone on the bedside table. Verna plugged in the charger and in a few seconds, her missed calls appeared. A look of consternation sculpted her face as she stood there for a few moments; it was odd for Leo to forget to charge his phone and especially not take it with him.

'What do I do now,' looking around as if some solution was going to appear before her; she went into the study and it looked like there'd been a burglary, as if someone had been rifling through the drawers. An absolute mess of documents were strewn around the floor. 'What on earth has he been doing?' It was eerily quiet as she went downstairs. Verna got into the car and decided to do a trawl of the surrounding streets and local area. Their home backed onto open Northumberland countryside, so he could be anywhere. She wept, eyes wildly searching the roads and pathways for any sign. Had he met with an accident? Should she ring the police? Maybe first talk with her neighbours, Nigel and Joyce, they were her surrogate parents and she was reliant upon their support. She pulled up in her driveway and thought, this was another occasion where she wanted to ring Hannah, to hear the reassuring, rational voice. She knocked next door, her distress was evident, 'what's wrong, what's happened,' asked Joyce, 'are the children okay?'

'Yes, they are, Marco is in his bedroom doing school work and the girls are in school.' Verna burst out, 'but I can't find Leo anywhere! He's taken Rocco for a walk, but he's been gone for over two hours and he left his phone.' Then words frantically tumbled, 'um, Leo … Leo's behaviour has been erratic lately, and he's … um, taking medication for depression and not sleeping.' With wide eyes. 'Will that impair his thinking? I don't know. What if he's depressed and … and done something?'

'There's nearly always a simple explanation for most things Verna.' Nigel said calmly and donned his coat, 'I'll take a walk around the local tracks and paths.' He set off with purposeful strides.

Joyce invited Verna inside, 'I'll pop and check on Marco, be back soon.' Marco was hungry and he asked where dad was. 'He's taken Rocco out for a walk; he'll be home soon.' Verna tried to act nonchalantly.

'Bit of a long walk.' Marco turned in his swivel chair, 'I'm not stupid. Dad has been acting really strangely. We learn about mental health at school, I know about depression and I know you don't want to say anything in front of Amara and Izzy, but I can tell there's something going on with him.'

Verna looked at her son, at nearly fourteen he would become a man soon enough. 'You're right sweetheart, dad's not too well right now, Nigel is looking around the local pathways to see if anything has happened, like he's sprained his ankle or something. He forgot his phone, but I'm sure he will be safe somewhere. He may even have gone to the doctor's surgery if he wasn't … you know … feeling well.'

Marco's face crumpled and his chin was quivering, his eyes filled up as she hugged him. 'Please don't worry Marco, we'll get him back to normal soon … I promise,' changing the subject swiftly, 'are you on a break from your schoolwork?' he nodded. 'Okay I'll get you something to eat to keep you going, what do you want?'

'Panini,' as she left the room she heard, 'and crisps and a biscuit … please.'

'Okay,' a brief smile crossed Verna's face, 'some things never change, no matter what.' Verna took a brimming tray of food and drinks upstairs and stood behind Marco as he sat at his desk. She put her hands on his shoulders, 'I'm going next door and we are going to find dad.' She gave him a reassuring pat, 'please try to concentrate on your lessons.' She kissed the top of his head. His hair smelled of men's hair products, signs he was growing up, but he was still her little boy.

Verna returned to Joyce's and she suggested contacting the doctor's surgery, in case Leo had gone there, then the police.

'If there had been an accident,' Nigel gently placed a hand on Verna's shoulder, 'you may already have been informed by now. I'll have a drive up around, Bolam Lake area see if there's any signs there.'

Verna called the local police service, and explained the situation. After an anxious hour, with no signs of Leo from Nigel's further search, two police officers arrived at Verna's front door. During the interview, conducted in staccato-style mask conversation, they discussed Leo's mental state, one of the officers asked if they could have a look around which included any loft space. This was agreed, one police officer headed upstairs as Marco, ashen-faced, emerged from his room. The officer reassured him they were simply checking things out in line with procedures. Verna let the officer look around at his own free will and popped her head into Marco's room with a reassuring smile. Information was relayed to the control room and officers were assigned to search the area. Because of Leo's recent mental health situation, they deemed it enough of a risk to put resources into an immediate search for a missing person.

Joyce and Verna sat together in the front room whilst Nigel was outside chatting with the police officers. Verna noticed a red car pull up beside the police car, and a young couple were talking to the officer. She went outside to hear a perplexed young man, 'we saw this guy, in his forties maybe, wandering around the small row of shops, about five miles away. We asked him if he was okay as he was sat in the middle of the pavement. He wouldn't give his name and said he was waiting for his wife to pick him up because the shadows were following him.' Then he shrugged, 'he spoke some foreign words to, Spanish or Italian maybe.'

The young woman continued, 'he said he couldn't remember his address, but then gave us some directions, so we thought it was this estate, as we live nearby. We offered him a lift but he refused to get in the car. So, we said we'd try to find his wife and headed home.'

The young man said urgently, 'we didn't just leave him, an older chap said he'd stay with him. When we spotted the police car, we wondered if there was a link.'

The young woman said sympathetically, 'he seemed out of it, like spaced-out, and he was all muddy.' She looked down, Verna knew the young woman recognised she was probably the man's distraught wife. From the description, it must be Leo, Verna thought, but no dog was mentioned. The officer radioed through the exact location and Verna heard a car was dispatched. Would you come with me the officer said, to identify him and we'll take it from there, then asked her to wear a face mask. Verna got a mask from the house and put it on. It was now 11.40 a.m. she was getting into the car and hesitated. Joyce told her to go, but to ring school to authorise Joyce to pick the girls up if needed.

As the police car pulled up at the shops, a female officer crouched in front of Leo, using soft reassuring words and he seemed to be responding. The relief was immense, Verna's heart was pumping like a steam train. Another officer was trying to disperse the small jumble of onlookers. Verna walked up to Leo, he looked into her eyes and said, 'Where have you been!' He was incandescent.

'Are you okay Leo?'

'No, I've been waiting here forever!' Leo had never spoken so sharply to Verna, and she reacted by staying silent.

The female police officer calmed the situation with reassuring words. Verna asked about Rocco, but Leo didn't reply. The female officer spoke with Verna suggesting they transport him and her to the nearest appropriate resource for mental health support. Verna mentioned Rocco and gave a description to the officer, who seemed more distraught about the dog.

'We'll look for him, is he chipped and does he have a collar?' Verna affirmed this. The officer was concerned as a dog like Rocco would be a real prize if someone nefarious found him.

Leo was compliant sitting in the police vehicle. He looked at Verna, almost through her. 'Where's your car? Why are the cops giving us a lift?'

'I must've got the wrong place to meet you Leo,' she said softly, 'I was worried, that's all.'

This seemed to appease him. His senses seemed numb, maybe from the medication and there was no spark in his eyes at all. His face looked gaunt and he hadn't shaved for a number of days. As they headed for the destination, he closed his eyes and seemed to fall into a slumber. Verna couldn't believe the change in her husband since he returned from Italy, and wondered what the hell had happened to him.

21

Leo was admitted for Mental Health triage at Northumberland General Hospital for assessment. There was no requirement for any legal section under the Mental Health Act, as Leo agreed to stay voluntarily. A Covid test was completed, he was clear, and didn't resist appearing physically wiped out. During the meeting with two workers, all masked, sitting two metres apart, Verna was astonished when Leo kept referring to insects crawling in his computer, also shadows following and threatening him. 'Even as they were flying away,' he fluttered his hands in the air, 'I could still hear them saying they would be back to kill me,' he said in matter-of-fact tone.

Verna had entered a portal into a surreal world, watching and listening to her husband recount what he believed he had seen, in a perfectly normal way, though he would keep looking around when he mentioned the shadows. She was able to describe Leo's sudden deteriorating behaviour to the team, and understood he had a psychotic episode, triggered possibly by an event or extreme stress when he was in Italy. The team would monitor his progress and review his medication. They would need consent to access his medical records which Leo had given and Verna supported. Verna told him to get some rest. He was unresponsive. As she left, Leo said, 'I'll ring the police to ensure the guards are in place overnight to protect you and the kids, I'll be safe here.' It was so bizarre how Leo could rationalise the events as a reality. Verna was a lost, bewildered woman standing outside the unit waiting for a taxi.

There was a voicemail from an unknown number. A woman from the Local Authority left a message asking whether she was the owner of a Lhasa Apso called Rocco. 'Oh my God, Rocco!' she had forgotten about him. She called the number immediately and was informed a police officer had found the dog and alerted them to take care of him. As Rocco had a collar and was chipped it was easy to identify the owners.

The woman advised, 'he required a little medical attention from scratches and needed a few stitches. The Veterinary Service will keep him overnight as he was sedated and they'll contact you in the morning to pick him up.' Verna sniffed and wiped her eyes, she took the details and contacted the surgery identifying herself as Rocco's owner. A man's voice answered and reassured her, he would recover. He asked, 'how did Rocco get the injuries?'

She had no idea, but improvised, 'oh, my husband took him for a walk and said he suddenly ran off and must've got lost or caught up somewhere as he couldn't find him anywhere. It was really unusual though, he's such a loyal little thing,' her voice cracked.

'Ah yes, they will do that if they see something interesting. Please don't worry, he'll be fine. We'll be in touch in the morning and you can pick him up. He's a lovely little beast, you're lucky he was found by a police officer.'

'Was it a female officer?'

'Yes, a young blonde woman.' Verna knew it was the same one, who was probably more concerned with Rocco than Leo, so was she in this moment. She wondered what on earth Rocco had been through. She called Joyce to say she'd be back in time for the girls. On the journey home she formulated what she would tell the children and how truthful she would be with Marco. The girls would assume it was a physical complaint as their concept of mental health issues would be sketchy.

Verna managed a quiet word with Marco. 'Dad had a mental health assessment and is suffering from extreme exhaustion and stress, which has led to depression.' She omitted the delusional episodes. 'He has to stay in hospital so they can sort out the right medication and he can rest.' Sadness was evident in his eyes, he was trying to be brave. 'It is something he can recover from honey, don't worry. It'll take time.' He nodded. She would have an ally in Marco but it was a heavy burden for her boy to manage, and she worried about any shame and anger he may feel towards his father. Verna collected the girls from school as normal and settled them together with Marco, to tell them about Leo, explaining the doctor wanted to be sure daddy was okay after he hit his head. She said it was nothing serious to worry about, and he needed rest. Marco acknowledged this explanation with a nod, and half smiled at Verna when Amara asked, 'so, will they examine his head?'

There was a little tap on the front door and Joyce's voice was heard. 'Hallo, only me, your friendly neighbourhood bubble-buddy!' The concept of, support bubbles, had been introduced to alleviate social isolation, and Joyce appointed herself bubble-buddy to the Ravassios. She walked in and presented some freshly baked scones, 'wondered if you could all do with a little treat?'

'Yummy!' shouted Izzy. Amara looked on, waiting for Verna to admonish Izzy for devouring the goodies. Verna let her defenses down allowing Izzy to enjoy the delicious warm crumbly offerings, lathered in melting butter and jam. The smell was divine and so comforting. Verna smiled at Amara and mouthed, it's okay. Amara responded with the sweetest smile, sat next to her sister enjoying the scones.

'I've made sweet and savoury. Marco, do you want one of each?' Joyce asked.

'Absolutely! Cheers Joyce.'

This woman is an angel, Verna thought. When the children were settled, Verna offered a glass of wine to Joyce, which she eagerly accepted and looked earnestly at Verna. 'Can I help you with the children's meal tonight, you must be worn out.'

Verna looked at the scones, 'they'll be fine Joyce, thank you,' and they sat in the conservatory as the children indulged in scone heaven.

'I've wondered whether to say anything … if it helps … but … Nigel suffered from PTSD. He had to be pensioned off from the Army. He's on medication for anxiety even now. But we have a life. I wish he would travel abroad, as that's something we haven't quite been able to do yet.' She offered a sorrowful smile.

'Ah Joyce, the poor guy,' said Verna sincerely, 'that can't have been easy.'

'No, we had some awful years, times when he was scared of his own shadow.'

The word sent a shiver through Verna and her eyes darted to the garden.

Joyce noticed the flinch. 'Something similar may be happening with Leo. Anxiety can be brought on by lots of different things.' She walloped her wine down.

'Let's have another,' suggested Verna

Joyce was thrilled, 'we don't keep alcohol in the house either, it was another trigger for Nigel,' she said rolling her eyes, knowing she had a confidant in Verna.

'Well, there's always loads in this house, anytime,' said Verna, 'and I'm going to be needing regular medication myself,' as she emptied the rest of the bottle into the glasses. Joyce amused Verna with humorous tales of Nigel's more bizarre episodes. They had a good laugh, it was exactly what Verna needed, normalization, and she suggested Joyce should suck a mint before she went back home or she'd be rumbled for afternoon drinking.

Joyce got up and tottered to the front door, with an exuberant, 'byeee!' to the children. She'll be snoring and drooling in her armchair in minutes, mused Verna.

Verna arrived at the Veterinary Centre the following morning to pick up Rocco after dropping the girls at school. She laugh-cried at his little face as he eagerly shuffled towards her from the vet assistant's hands. He offered a tiny, hello, bark and snuffled into her as she held him. It was the same man she'd spoken to the previous day. He explained the treatment and showed her how to manage aftercare of the shaven patch where they had treated the wound on his side. Rocco weakly licked her face as she carried him to the car, placed him carefully on the front seat and wrapped him in the blanket from his bed.

Throughout the journey, Verna could hear his whimpers and whines as he dreamed. 'Master. Long walk. Running water. Lie down boy. Here boy. Run. Hide. Jump. Hide. Run fast. Houses. Humans. Bark, bark, bark! Ouch. Tired. Sleep.' Rocco looked up at Verna, gave a faint growl as he heard her soft calming voice, enjoyed her gently stroking around his ears, and he fell asleep.

Verna looked adoringly at the little panting body beside her. 'Ah Rocco, if only you could tell me what happened.'

The children were delighted to have Rocco back home. They showed curiosity about his injury and Verna had to reprimand them for playing too robustly with him, 'he's not a toy and he must rest.'

When the children were settled in bed, the dead-weight of having to mask the exhaustion and trauma she felt inside overwhelmed her. Verna wished for her husband to come home, but not the Leo she left at hospital. She wished for the Leo she knew intimately. She wished for the man she had married to return to her, with his charismatic, romantic style, his handsome face, stunning smile and strong, lean body. No one could ever make her feel the way Leo did. That was the Leo she now missed terribly and would always love. Verna wanted her life back, to spend time with her friends. Verna would dearly love to talk through the intricacies of her challenging situation. Her automatic default was Hannah ... Hannah would understand what to do and they would find humour in the situation. Hannah may have blocked her number, and would she dare to leave a voicemail, what if Hannah simply cut the call?

Verna went into the kitchen, opened the cavernous fridge and selected another chilled bottle of Pino Grigio. She opened it, poured herself a large glass and sat in the conservatory; she took a sip, savouring the ice-cold, sharp liquid on its way down. If only Verna knew her good friend Hannah was doing exactly the same thing, at exactly the same moment. But neither woman knew about the changing fortunes in each other's lives.

22

Hannah, May 2020

The wheels of commerce were still in motion during Covid. Mick Lynwood, head of the joint leisure venture from the Borough Council called Hannah to congratulate her on the success of her submission. The board had reached their final decision for her brand guide and logo design for the, Riverside Quays, leisure development. Hannah's simple line drawing design combined two iconic images of the arch of the Tyne Bridge and the curved steel dome of the Sage Music and Culture Centre, which fused industrial heritage and contemporary arts of the North East riverside area. This was going to change her working life. Hannah called everyone and whilst she enjoyed the adulation, a sense of dejection overtook her later in the evening. This event would usually result in a boisterous Kay family gathering of fun, lots of celebratory drinks, and much laughter, but restrictions didn't allow such gatherings. She celebrated in her own way with a bottle of champagne shared with Evan and Ross. Evan wanted another glass but Ross's face looked like he was sucking a lemon, 'urgh, that's pants.'

'It's not worth me resigning as I'm still furloughed,' she said to Cam online, 'but I am excited about a different future when life resumes,' sipping her champagne, 'I wish you could join me in a celebratory drink.'

'Hold on.' Cam returned to the screen, 'a JD and coke fits the bill,' he raised his glass towards the screen, and appreciating Hannah's upbeat demeanour said, 'you are an amazing woman. You can't have had it easy on your own with the boys and now this, it's brilliant. I'm proud of you Hannah, and will be bragging to my family and friends about your achievement.' Cam's words brought tears to Hannah's eyes. Of course, her parents were proud of her academic qualifications, and assumed she'd succeed no matter what she did; but to be told by Cam he was proud of her, was wonderful. They looked into each other's eyes via screens, both with a desperate longing to touch each other.

'All this is crippling me,' Cam said without constraint as his eyes filled up. 'It's been weeks since I saw anyone. I miss you so much, and Sara, my family and my mates … everyone. How long is all this going to go on?'

'It's bloody awful and all the time we are staying at home trying to keep people safe, thousands are still dying. I feel so guilty enjoying this moment when I know some people have lost so much. Have you seen the pictures of the faces of the people who have died in care homes and retired medics who have gone back to help out and lost their lives.'

He nodded, 'it's terrible. Those daily briefings make you want to put your foot through the TV screen, when you see what their mates are getting away with, failed contracts worth millions and driving to test your eyesight,' Cam's frustration was brutally evident, 'for fuck's sake.' Shaking his head, 'it's the transport workers, retail staff, the support workers and the health staff who are the real heroes.'

Hannah agreed. 'It's like the population is a traumatised child and those in power are neglectful parents, they can't offer security or reassurance in a situation running out of control, it feels so unsafe, helpless and hopeless. All you can do is sit there watching it unfold, it's devastating.' Hannah touched the screen and felt tears prickling, 'I'm really missing you. Wish I could see you, and feel you close to me.'

Cam touched the screen, 'I miss you too, it's rotten right now, but don't forget your success. We'll celebrate as soon as we can.'

Hannah heard Evan shout, 'can we order pizza now?'

'Come in here Evan,' beckoning him.

Evan appeared in the conservatory and she encouraged an introduction to Cam. Cam asked what pizza he would order. They had a chat about their favourite pizzas, and the call came to a natural end when Cam suggested, 'you should get the takeaway ordered, those lads will be famished.' Evan smiled and left the room so Hannah and Cam could bid their goodbyes. Evan repeated Cam seemed a nice guy and it would be good to meet him.

In the following days Hannah had a number of online meetings, about how the Riverside Quays project would be expedited, but for now, they had put the brakes on progress until such a time they could get rolling again. The exposure, prospective contracts and inflated fees going into Hannah's bank would be a real boost.

On 13 May restrictions had eased in England for two people from different households to meet outside and stay two metres apart. Cam, Hannah and the boys met in the park, but it was tough as nails for the lovers to get through. Hannah's excitement bubbled within as she recognised Cam's familiar walk from a distance as he approached them. With a broad grin, he introduced himself to the boys. She was able to appreciate his new found physique and athleticism as he had a kick about with Evan and Ross; also happy he didn't wince at the sight of her immensity, and in fact, complimented that she looked great. They stayed for an hour, had a walk around the pond, and the old Victorian bandstand before they left for home. Every ounce of resistance was needed to combat the magnetic pull between Cam and Hannah. It was awful, but necessary. She wondered if she would have weakened into a quick hug and kiss if the boys weren't there. She would never allow them to see her break rules. Good job they were there, Cam was irresistible! They met again on a few occasions and by June the stay-at-home Covid restrictions eased; schools and non-essential shops reopened and people got back into work.

The extended Kay family remained fiercely protective of each other and their parents. Dad was now allowed to resume his morning walk to go for his newspaper, which pleased him immensely. Evan and Ross had saved some pocket money and contacted Aunty Ellie to order a bath gift set from them to be delivered for Hannah's birthday and to celebrate her work success. She arranged for Hannah's favourite brand and said there was enough for flowers too, there wasn't, but that was fine. When the gifts arrived, Hannah burst into tears, the boys understood they were happy tears. I'm going to run a lovely bath with my new products and pamper myself. It's a gorgeous gift, thank you both so much.' She hugged them for far too long which they tolerated, but were equally comforted by their mother's warmth. 'You'll make your future girlfriends very happy.'

'You mean boyfriend in Ross's case.' Evan said shoving his younger brother onto the sofa.

'Tell him to shut his dish!' Ross retaliated.

Hannah quelled any ensuing argument and aggression from the testosterone-filled situation, by appealing to their better natures, saying she wanted a nice peaceful night and they'd get yet another takeaway later. 'Wouldn't bother me who you bring home, as long as they're good people and you're happy, is all that ever matters to me.' Hannah looked at the lovely bath gift set, her favourite, which reminded her of Verna's last Christmas gift. A sadness sank into her, and she wished she could share this joy with Verna, who would love to hear all about Cam. It would seem strange to call Verna out of the blue, and she still worried about an unfavourable response, Verna may have blocked her number, and would she dare to leave a voicemail, what if Verna simply cut the call?

Hannah decided to take a glass of wine up to the bathroom and prepare a soothing luxurious bath. She selected a chilled bottle of Pino Grigio, opened it, poured herself a large glass, took a sip, savouring the ice-cold, sharp liquid on its way down. If only Hannah knew her good friend Verna was doing exactly the same thing, at exactly the same moment. But neither woman knew about the changing fortunes in each other's lives.

23

Evan announced, 'I'm wearing a mask in school as I'd hate to bring the virus home and make you ill.'

'Is that because you think I'm old and vulnerable?' jibed Hannah.

'Well no, but, you know … who would do the shopping and make all the food if you became ill?' Evan held a bowl full of snacks to keep him going until tea time. 'Is Cam coming over,' laughing, 'he's good fun, but rubbish at FIFA.'

'No, he's off to see Sara this weekend in Leeds, but I'm hoping he'll be around more often, it's good having him here. He's in our social bubble now, so he can visit regularly.' Further Covid restrictions were lifted in July, and Cam gradually moved in with Hannah over a period of a few weeks, as there was no point him staying at his own house alone.

Hannah said, 'your sister Jayne has done you a great big favour, offering to support your parents so you can be our bubble-buddy.'

'She's good in a crisis, was brilliant when me and Julia separated, got a lovely relationship with Sara too, they love each other to bits.'

'Can't wait to meet them both, Sara is a little peach.' Cam had air-dropped recent photos of his last visit to her and preened at Hannah's comment.

'With a serious expression he said, 'it's good my bubble status allows me to stay overnight to prevent me from becoming socially isolated.'

'That right?'

'Yes, to support my mental health,' he slid his arms around her waist as she was reaching for dinner plates, and nuzzled into the nape her neck.

'Down boy.'

Cam smiled as he took the plates to the table, it was great having him around.

The next morning Hannah was jubilant, 'at last! I can get my hair done.'

'Don't know what the fuss is all about.'

'Just because you prefer the windswept and interesting look …' Hannah noticed Cam run his fingers through his lengthy hair.

'You taking the pee or what?'

'You could do with a trim, I'll do it if you like!' she said with glee.

'No chance! I'd better get to the barbers.'

Hannah felt wonderful after a visit to the salon. There was something so cheerful about doing an ordinary thing, sitting in the chair, with layered foils sprouting around her head, the only difference was chatting whilst wearing a mask, but a small price to pay for the pamper. Summer holiday destinations were off the agenda this year. She decided to have a few lighter tones to blend in with the encroaching hairline grey. She admired the new subtle sun-kissed look when she got home, as did Cam. She then scrutinised her skin in the magnifying mirror, and decided she was in pretty good condition with few wrinkles, pleased she had inherited her mother's youthful trait. Hannah had been out on a few gentle runs, well she had to use the new trainers after all, and was generally more active since lockdown was easing, so altogether she was happier in her skin.

The household eased into becoming a family of four and the current guidelines meant they could meet two other adults. In conversations with family and friends there were various interpretations of what people believed was allowed in designated county tiers. The overall message was clear, stay two metres apart, wear masks, and use sanitiser was the norm. Hannah and Cam had taken the boys out to an upmarket tapas restaurant for an indulgent evening in the city, where Covid protocols were in place. It was a lovely evening however it naturally wasn't as relaxed as a pre-lockdown experience. They signed up to the track-and-trace system to scan themselves into venues with doubts about the efficacy of the system from recent reports, but it was the right thing to do.

Hannah had a lovely, cocktail-fuelled evening out at a new wine bar with five of her closest colleagues from BlueSea Graphics. She decided it was time to leave the company as her freelance contracts increased. It was awful for the friends not to be able to have a huge group hug at the end of the evening, but a paltry wet-lettuce wave had to suffice, however they made drunken promises to never lose touch and have many more nights out when they could.

She was rather shabby the following morning when Cam, who was busying about in the kitchen sorting the recycling, asked, 'shall we bother with, eat-out-to-help-out this month?' in relation to the latest scheme to keep the hospitality industry afloat.

'To be honest, I'm not bothered, happy to socialise in gardens. I get the whole premise of the scheme, but fear it will increase transmissions, when you see crowds of people in the city queuing to get into venues.' Hannah could imagine the minuscule spiky virus gleefully sailing airborne from one nose or mouth to another, or perched on a handrail waiting to cling onto the next human skin that brushed by. 'It was an eye-opener last night when I drove by, the First Avenue restaurant on the Quayside, and the doorman was shaking hands with a customer. Was he kidding, great example to set, not.'

Cam followed Hannah with ice-clinking drinks to the garden chairs. The August breeze floated around them bringing the scent of Freesia, Iris and Sweet Pea from the various glazed pots which they enjoyed creating together. The white-hot sunny brightness enriched the colour of the flowers and warmed their skin as the sound of bird-chirps lifted their spirits. Hannah was mesmerised, watching a tiny dark orange ladybird making its way along the arm of her chair. In an instant it's brightly spotted back lifted, flitting into the air on tiny gossamer wings.

The summer scent reminded Cam of a recent garden visit to Hannah's sister Ellie and Geoff's home. 'I was smashed at Ellie's, wasn't I? Did I make an arse of myself H? I'm really sorry showing you up in front of your family.

Think her husband Geoff thought I was an idiot, when I tripped and trampled the flower beds and spilled my drink,' Cam facepalmed, 'still feel so stupid thinking of it now, how embarrassing. It was such a lovely sunny day and the cold beers were going down far too easily.'

'Nah! Don't worry, ol' Geoffrey needs livening up, if I'm honest, I'm not sure what the attraction is for Ellie. He's a good bit older, and comes across as … maybe … a little dull at times, but what do I know?' Hannah wondered if there was still an element of dissatisfaction in her sister's relationship, but she seemed happy and content with her life.

'Dry sense of humour though, clever, and quick-witted,' added Cam.

'He's quite a brilliant academic actually. He's had medical papers published and all sorts. I'm always a bit wary of a Consultant Psychiatrist though, analysing everything you say,' she smiled.

'Well, it wouldn't take him long to figure out I'm a bit of a dick,' laughed Cam.

'You are not,' retorted Hannah laughing, 'Ellie was highly amused, she loves you to bits. I do wonder if she gets bored with Geoff sometimes? His kids are brilliant actually, think they're a kind of gifted family if you will, all highly qualified. His daughter is an international airline pilot, and his son is a geologist, turned nature cameraman. He travels the world examining rocks from volcanoes and studies earthquakes, it's fascinating. He's done a few TV documentaries and it's always a thrill to see his name on the credits.'

'Bet Ellie's a great step-mam, didn't she want to have kids?'

Hannah recalled Ellie's varied partners in her younger years. She knew her sister sometimes didn't fit in anywhere, mainly because she couldn't conform to what everyone wanted or expected from her. 'Ellie has always been a one-off and done her own thing, never seemed to settle at anything until her mid-thirties. She was arty like me and had a career in fashion design, earned a fortune, got disillusioned with the whole industry and simply packed it in one day. She turned to selling her own artwork, which is brilliant. In her late twenties, she sold her house and took off to Indonesia, Australia and New Zealand for eighteen months, travelling and working; she finally ended up returning home after a jaunt around China. She now restores artworks and is a curator at the Northern Museum. Geoff already had the children when they met, so she probably was content enough bringing them up. Tragic actually, his wife took her own life, which is why I believe he transferred his medical skills from general practice to psychiatry.'

'Mmm, yeah there is a melancholy air about him. But if anyone is good for the soul it's your Ellie, she's hilarious and super-bright. Maybe the intelligence is part of the attraction? Sorry you landed yourself with a bit of a thicko here H,' mused Cam.

'You are most definitely not that Mr Wallace. We wouldn't be together if you were, it's not your mind I'm interested in anyway.' She slid her hand under the sleeve of his t-shirt to stroke his bare bicep, leaned over and gave him a sensual, sweet little kiss. A fleeting contact in case the boys appeared. They were now used to seeing the pair holding hands and the regular but not over-the-top kisses.

It had taken several weeks before the boys were comfortable with their mother's attention being directed away from them. At times, either or both of them placed themselves in-between the couple at first. Cam noticed they stopped doing it, they seemed to trust him now.

Life rolled along without drama all summer and into autumn as Hannah and Cam's routine ran with practiced precision. Cam was back at work on site, he had originally trained as an electrical engineer, however retrained in joinery which he preferred. Cam could turn his hand to different trades, he had a good reputation as a skilled worker and was never out of employment. The boys were pleased to be in school, adapting well to wearing masks, sanitising, studying in bubbles, and using one-way systems.

Hannah was content apart from the underlying anxiety for everyone to remain healthy. She enjoyed her role as the matriarch; the homemaker, the comforter, the provider of huge healthy meals and freshly laundered clothing for the small, medium and large males in her family. Hannah cleared and renewed everything she could in their home, from teaspoons to tables, and whilst she wasn't a slave to Feng-shui, decluttering was incredibly cleansing. The home had a thorough make-over with a minimalist, contemporary style. Looking around the transformed living room with a satisfied smile, Hannah wondered if she might enjoy interior design, maybe another string she could add to her bow, who knows. She found it surprisingly fulfilling and understood how Verna may enjoy the role of home-maker, but gosh it was mind-numbing at times and day-time TV was an absolute no-no! Hannah set up her laptop, clicked the Bose on, and as the gentle rhythmic background music filled the air, she sipped a comforting herbal tea, looking out over the garden.

She was finally overcoming her association with imposter syndrome, believing now she was actually good enough. Her smart watch timer buzzed, 'time for a break.' Hannah had the luxury of adopting healthy time-management, and not overworking it as she had in the past. After an invigorating sunny walk, and lunch, she indulged in online browsing, searching for smart, contemporary workwear. Hannah also perused the list of local guitar tutors, selected a few and would have a chat with Evan about whether he was serious about taking lessons. She could afford it now; recalling Verna's hurtful words, though she did wonder what was going on in her life.

Cam appeared interrupting Hannah's reverie, 'Julia has suggested we meet Sara with your boys.' Hannah was thrilled, an outdoor meeting was arranged that weekend halfway between Newcastle and Leeds at Richmond in North Yorkshire.

Julia and her partner Niall had settled in a sunny spot by the river. A wave of adoration swept over Hannah at the tiny, Cam carbon-copy in little girl form. She was so sweet, really pretty and Hannah had tears in her eyes when she leapt into Cam's arms for the biggest hug and gave him a thousand kisses. Hannah wanted to grab her and squeeze the daylights out of her petite little body, but to Sara, she was a stranger. Julia and Niall were a lovely couple too, much younger than her and Cam. Hannah appreciated the attraction for Cam; Julia had a bubbly personality; an hourglass figure, currently enhanced from baby weight, a round pretty face with clear skin, huge blue eyes, adorned with winged eye-liner, and full lips. Her tinted rich-plum hair gave a leaning towards goth.

Sara performed a few dances she had been learning at her online classes and she sang and flung herself about doing gymnastics too. It was a truly lovely day. Once the ice-creams were had after a few hours of fun, Sara whispered something into her mother's ear and Julia said she'd ask if it was okay. She wanted to give Hannah a hug, which simply couldn't be refused. Hannah absorbed every notion of the fairy-like little princess who coyly walked towards her, big brown eyes gleaming, with her arms stretched out wide. She smelled like fresh peaches and the warm skin on her pale arms was as soft as marshmallow around Hannah's neck. The breeze brushed wisps of her dark brown hair across Hanna's face like silken strands. It was a fleeting moment and Hannah was overcome with an urge to devour her.

Sara then turned and flew at top speed, leaping into Cam's arms yelling 'Daddeee!' as he crouched, nearly knocking him over. He brushed her hair aside and was whispering reassuring words as she became a little upset because they had to go. He encouraged her to return home as baby Melody needed her bath and bed. The distraction was instant as she rushed over to the buggy to check on her baby sister. Hannah recognised Cam's innate parenting ability and caring nature, as did her ovaries who were calling to her from within, but she suppressed their wicked intentions. The afternoon had worn thin for Evan and Ross and they couldn't wait to get back to their online cliques.

They'd done a great job of fussing over Sara, patiently playing piggy-in-the-middle with her. On the return journey, the boys were plugged into their iPhones.

'Can't wait for a time when Sara can sleepover, but we'll need a bigger house.' Hannah turned to Cam.

'True.' Cam was pensive. 'Your lads were brilliant with her, I will thank them when they're back in the real world,' nodding to the phone-obsessed in the rear seats. 'Six-year-old girls can be so annoying, but they were really patient.'

'It's the way they've been brought up of course! Sara is so wonderful, you have a lovely relationship, no worries about that precious little princess forgetting about her lovely daddy.' She squeezed Cam's knee, 'she's so beautiful … though you dare mention chefs and ovens!'

24

Cam was online with his sister Jayne, and introduced her to Hannah.

'Hi Hannah, lovely to meet you … virtually at least.' Jayne smiled. She didn't look much like Cam with her blue eyes, and only the slightest resemblance around the shape of her mouth would suggest they were siblings. Her fair hair was cut into a sleek geometric bob.

'Hi, great to meet you too Jayne. Thank you for supporting this whole social bubble thing with Cam, it's much appreciated.'

'How are you all getting along? Is he behaving and pulling his weight? Don't let him get away with anything.'

Cam clicked his tongue and rolled his eyes, then turning to Hannah, 'Jayne tells me our old aunt in Scotland has died and her funeral needs arranging.'

Jayne continued, 'Great Aunt Marie was our dad's aunty, her brother was our grandad, he died before Cam was born and I don't remember him. Dad has been left to sort everything as she had no children and there's no other surviving relatives. It's a bit of a mess, as Marie lived a quiet single lifestyle in her rambling old house, and little is known of her associates, if there are any.'

'I remember going to visit her, she was a canny old thing,' said Cam, 'in the true sense of the word, sharp as a tack.'

Jayne said, 'Martin and I visited her when we travelled to Scotland. Miss Marie Lorna Wallace, by all accounts, was a tough old thing; she'd been all over the world as a young woman, quite the pioneer. She wrote a non-fiction book about the Wallace Clan, and was an historical research assistant at the university. I'm sure she'd been an archaeologist of some sort up in the Highlands, but women weren't allowed to claim it as a profession then, but good to have a feminist ancestry.'

Hannah knew instantly she and Jayne would get along, she bid her online goodbye, then left to get on with the washing. There was Jayne looking great, while Hannah resembled, Medusa, unwashed hair, unruly straggly bits sprouting all over, no make-up, wearing her mankiest old top.

The following day Cam was leaving for Scotland with Jayne and announced, 'need to pick up ma kilt on the way.'

'Okay, Braveheart, are you going to paint your face blue, and go commando under your kilt?' Hannah asked.

'Aye, I'll do that bonnie lassie.' In contemplation, he said, 'shame, dad is the only one left from three brothers. One took a heart attack in his fifties, and the other died not long afterwards in an industrial accident at a forge where he worked.'

'How awful, poor Fraser. I'd love to know more about

your family history and meet your parents, and Jayne, not via a screen either.'

'I haven't met all of your lot yet. I'm looking forward to meeting the rest of the Kays … has a ring of The Krays, doesn't it?'

'We're not that bad!'

Hannah hadn't seen Cam so animated when he returned after several days in Scotland. 'It's absolutely stunning up there, the place is amazing. I appreciated it when we were kids playing in the huge garden and running around the big house like mad things, great for hide and seek. But as teenagers I didn't think it important to visit old relatives, shame, from all the information we now know about Aunt Marie, she was quite a character. Turns out Marie was a hundred and two, born at the end of, World War Two. She was an avid writer and there are memoir-type journals around, be really interesting to read them.' Cam smiled, 'we spoke with her GP and in his words, *she simply expired in her sleep.*'

'So, were you strutting around like the Laird of the Manor, in your kilt?'

He laughed. 'Jayne always wanted to move back to Scotland, the house is miles away from civilisation in the Galway Forest area. There's a dark sky observatory, some beautiful falls and walking tours in the hills, and guess where it's near … Loch Doon!

Hannah revelled in Cam's enthusiasm about the trip and understood his deep regret at not spending more time with Aunt Marie. 'It's a life lesson,' hugging him, 'you realise how important family and friends are.'

'It does make you think more about keeping in touch with people, especially through this pandemic situation. Bit of a cliché, but life is short, even at a hundred and two years old.'

'It's so sad, an independent, fully-lived life ended with the grocery delivery man raising concerns when she didn't answer the door,' said Hannah ruefully.

'True, but Aunt Marie was a trouper, apparently, she kept a loaded hunting rifle in the kitchen, for rabbits and game until she became too infirm to hunt for her own food. An eccentric recluse it seems, you wouldn't mess with her.'

Hannah raised her glass of wine to Cam and clinked his beer bottle. 'In memory of, and with every respect to, your Great Aunt Marie.'

During a garden visit the next day, Cam's parents, Fraser and Eileen agreed with a plan to convert the property into a small guest house. Fraser commented, 'I'm chuffed to bits the house will remain in the family, it's our Scottish heritage,' he puffed out his chest and his slight Scots accent became more pronounced. 'The house dates back to 1730, and our family is one of tragedy, Marie's father died of kidney failure after the war, Black Water Fever it was, from Malaria. Then his wife, Marie's mother, died of pneumonia. The kids were only eleven and thirteen, so they moved into the big house with their grandparents. Marie inherited everything, she never moved home and she's outlived everyone apart from me.'

After discussion, the Wallaces chose a name, Laurel Tree House, as it reflected Marie's middle name, Lorna. Cam's mother Eileen said, 'I read the name Lorna was originally created by R.D. Blackmore in his novel, *Lorna Doon,* and it was adopted as a Scottish girls' name, which represents the laurel tree. It's symbolic of honour and victory, so we thought it a fitting tribute.'

Cam was appointed project manager to lead renovations. He was happy to leave his employment, stating he'd done his time and it would be good to move on. He turned to Hannah. 'It means I'll be spending time away from home.'

'Too good an opportunity to pass by.'

Time marched on, an early autumn breeze swirled around the garden, whipping up loose leaves. Another difficult parting ensued, no hugs were forthcoming. That night Hannah lay in bed listening to Cam's gentle snores. She reflected that within several months, she'd risen from the depths of despair, sobbing in her car, full of self-loathing following the argument in Verna's kitchen; to achieving a fulfilling career. She was ever-grateful for her family's health, plus she could look forward to a financially secure future with a man she truly loved.

25

The renovation work at Laurel Trees began. Cam knew enough people in the industry to put together a good team. Lots of trusted friends had lost their jobs in the trade, it offered opportunity to earn. One Monday morning he said to Hannah, 'off I go again, it's great up there, loads of fresh air and there's plenty of space to work safely, but I do miss you H.'

Hannah grabbed his arm as he got out of bed and pulled him towards her.

'No time unfortunately,' he leaned over to kiss her. 'My lift will arrive soon. Good job we make the most of our weekends.'

They smiled at each other, sharing a mutual moment thinking about the joy of the previous evening's carnal pleasures. The residual ambience in the bedroom was of pure lust. 'It's not forever and it's for family, but I miss you too,' said Hannah.

'It'll all be worth it in the end, the house is amazing, wish you could see it.'

Hannah appreciated Cam's rear view as he walked

towards the ensuite. When he was showered and dressed, he joined her in the kitchen for a 6 a.m. coffee. They hugged and kissed at the sound of the van pulling up, 'see you Friday.'

Hannah made a bowl-size mug of coffee and checked the, Hexagon Development Group, website; a new design proposal had come her way. If she was going to travel to London to discuss the proposals of branding for their new retail complex, she wanted to ensure it was worth the trip. At first, she was reluctant to travel, however on balance she determined flying was the safest option. Like many, Hannah longed for the freedom from masks, but the constant intrinsic fear of passing on Covid infection was greater.

Hannah ensured she was suitably made-up and wearing smart executive clothing for the initial online meeting with the management team. She wondered whether others on the call were in their smart-upper, pyjama-bottom combo. She, however, made the effort and enjoyed pairing her new work wardrobe for potential live meetings in the future. Her duck-egg blue soft shirt, brought out the blue-grey in her eyes, thankfully her eye-bags of tedium had long-since faded. Hannah ensured the boys, who had returned from school, were well out of the way and loaded with grub, so they wouldn't burst in asking for a cheese sarnie. The online meeting was productive, they invited her for a face-to-face consultation at the development head office in London. She knew they would be interviewing other designers, so took nothing for granted.

Two days later Hannah took a, masked Covid-restricted flight, from Newcastle to Heathrow, she was met at the airport by a helpful, smartly dressed young woman who transported her to the meeting. As she walked into the ultra-modern, window-walled meeting room, full of young casual executives; she gulped, suppressing her rising impostor syndrome, inwardly saying, you're a skilled professional, you look the part and repeated her internal mantra - you deserve to be here.

Hannah instantly recognised Graeme's face, the guy she had a couple of dates with at BlueSea Graphics. They gave each other a nod of recognition and he said, 'I wondered if it was, *the*, Hannah Kay.' Others in the room looked at him. Explanations would come later. There could be no accusations of nepotism as she knew nothing about him working here. Hannah greeted him warmly, minimising the jolt inside. She was pleased they parted on good terms and had not had any form of deep romantic or sexual interaction. They had enjoyed each other's company, more in a professional light. The team were impressed with Hannah's confidence and creative free-thinking ideas. She had learnt to be adaptable to the client's needs. She was good at this. She remained positive throughout, took notes, asked exploratory questions and used humour when appropriate, ensuring they were fully informed of her extensive skill set and experience.

'Do you fancy a drink or coffee before your flight. There are a few places open, be lovely to catch up.' Graeme asked.

'That would be great, it was good to see a familiar face when I walked into that room.'

'Feels intimidating doesn't it. I remember when I came

for an interview. It's a great company and they're a good bunch.'

Hannah was happy to accept the invitation and realised these sorts of events would become part of her working life. She was truly thrilled and although money had not yet been clearly identified during the meeting, she knew this contract would be gainful, should she secure it. It was great catching up with Graeme, he was a good link for her and would act as a personal referee to the company and sing her praises.

Hannah called Cam that night after an exhausting day, and excitedly told him about her time in London, however the reaction she got was unexpected. Cam was clearly not impressed and dismissive; unusual for him. She wondered if he was simply tired; his monosyllabic, dull responses indicated so. He did not express any happiness or support for the wonderful progress she'd made. Over the following two days the text messages she received from Cam were short and to the point. They omitted any reference to the usual loving or amusing remarks with suggestive emojis. Hannah was disappointed and less than impressed with Cam's responses.

Cam arrived home that Friday evening and Hannah greeted him warmly, with a hug and kiss, she had been looking forward to seeing him and enjoyed the masculine whiff of, wooden-shed and hard work. He didn't really respond. 'Why is your face tripping you up?' She was going to say, like a slapped arse, but thought better of it.

Cam turned on her. 'I'm fine Hannah,' unusually using

her full name, 'you know, working my nuts off leading this team, and let me tell you it's not easy coordinating everything, meanwhile you're wining and dining in London with some ex-boyfriend.'

Hannah could not believe his response. She was lost for words, and nearly laughed in his face, this was not a feature in their relationship. She had never seen overt possessiveness from Cam.

'Ex-boyfriend!' Are you kidding?' she gave a brief explanation of the couple of dates she had with Graeme and highlighted they had not been romantically linked.

'Yeah right,' Cam sneered and walked out of the room to head upstairs.

At first, she was annoyed as Cam essentially was accusing her of something she hadn't done. A whisper of empathy arose, would the green-eyed monster erupt in her, should Cam have met an old girlfriend for lunch? There was an iciness between them when he returned downstairs after a shower, he put the TV on and ignored her.

'Would you switch that off please.' Which he did and she said clearly, 'I did not know Graeme worked for this team and I am under no obligation to inform you of every man I'm going to have a business lunch with. Sadly, senior roles are still held by men, so you're going to have to suck it up, or make huge strides to change the patriarchy!' she couldn't resist the comment, despite Cam's slapped-arse face.

'You didn't have to accept the invitation to go for a drink,' he said quietly.

'Why shouldn't I?' Hannah was growing increasingly

frustrated. 'So I'm not allowed business lunches eh, you're being ridiculous!' She sat beside him, put her hand on his knee and he did respond with his arm loosely around her shoulder. 'Cam, do you feel threatened because I went for lunch with a man I'd known in the past and hadn't even had a relationship with?'

'It's because … I was badly let down by someone years ago who I lived with, and, I thought that was it, for life. It was really awful.' His face said it all.

'What about me?' She said softly, 'two kids and I didn't know an affair was going on right under my nose, how useless am I? I must have been the laughing stock. But you're right, it is so bloody awful to be let down badly by someone you trusted.'

Cam nodded and squeezed his elbow which gently nudged her closer to him, 'I'll tell you all about it someday,' his head dropped, eyes closed, looking really tired, 'but not now, not today.' He wilted into her, and Hannah didn't question him as she held him. She knew she was the reassurance he needed, and he would tell her in his own time.

'I don't want to be intimate with another man. Truly Cam, please believe me. I have never been this happy in my whole life. Why would I do anything to jeopardise what we have?'

'I know H, I don't want anyone else either. This is it for me.' He pulled her closer towards him and she rested her legs over his, in a warm tangled embrace.

'Let's make a deal. I can't bear living in a relationship full of lies and deceit again,' she looked into his eyes … 'honesty always.'

'Honesty always, I'll drink to that.' Cam kissed her and amorous feelings erupted between them.

As Hannah and Cam were responding physically to each other's touch, they were interrupted by loud male voices and a jumble of gangly arms and legs bursting into the room. Evan and Ross were vying for first place, bundled into the doorway, shattering the sensual, serene moment. They were arguing, yet again. It was the same old rant about who had overrun their time on the console, commonly known in the household as, The PS4 Wars! Ross was accusing Evan of going over his time. Cam got up and walked out of the room, Hannah understood, this was something he had to tolerate, and it can't be easy for him at times returning home, weary from work, to this boisterous sibling rivalry.

In her head she wanted to open dialogue, and suggest the boys negotiate a fair plan that would work. It would be a good idea and sensible, if not utterly draining being the parental arbitrator. However, what she chose to say, when there was a break in the yelling was; 'Look boys, listen … me and Cam have been doing quite well recently, so we'll buy another console and you can have one each.' It wasn't particularly the right way, of going about it. However, with the constant everchanging lockdown restrictions and lack of social interaction for her sons, she knew, it was justified. Ultimately it would stop The PS4 Wars escalating to use of weapons! Both boys were initially stunned, then with fist bumps and broad smiles were thrilled. It was fifteen-seconds before another argument erupted about who would get the new console with the added features. Hannah put both her hands up, more or less in the boys faces and said,

'This is a one-time offer! You don't get another chance. Now go and make peace with each other or it's not going to happen!'

The boys looked at each other sheepishly, and left the room. She could hear them muttering and as Ross walked through the door first, she noticed Evan gave him a slight shove. She simply said, 'Evan,' in a low menacing tone. He didn't turn around, but scarpered upstairs. She strolled to the conservatory, feeling accomplished, 'yep, definitely got this parenting business all sorted.'

Cam returned to the conservatory with a bottle of lager in one hand and a refreshing ice-cold vodka and cloudy lemonade in the other which he presented to her. He'd heard everything, and with a huge grin on his face he congratulated her on her faultless parenting and negotiating skills, which Hannah graciously accepted.

'We need to consider Sara, she is part of this family and anytime the boys' benefit, she should have something too,' suggested Hannah.

'That's such a nice consideration H, I'll check it out,' said Cam.

'We are in this together.'

'I do love you … and sorry,' Cam was genuine.

'Forgiven, this time. Been thinking we're going to need a bigger family home so Sara can come to stay, once restrictions are lifted.'

Hannah and Cam often made plans during soft, slumberous weekend nights when he was home from Scotland. Hannah noticed Cam's fatigue and suggested a deputy manager could be appointed at Laurel Trees to offer him respite from constant demands. They continued discussing plans for a new home, leaving the house that had contained pain in the past for Hannah could be a positive move. Another positive move would be to make love to her partner again, but as she turned towards him, in the dark night in their warm bed, she heard his gentle breaths and watched the synchronising rise and fall of his broad shoulders. Softly she slid closer to him, caressing the back of his neck with her mouth, she loved him a lot, but for now he needed to sleep.

26

A three-tier system was introduced in England on 14 October as County Councils were reporting different reproduction rates of the virus. There was resistance to impose a full lockdown to prevent further school closures and more damage to the economy. More restrictions were in place across Ayrshire, with advice not to travel, and hospitality was closed, so work was suspended on Laurel Trees.

Hannah stared at the TV screen's flickering light illuminating her despondent expression. 'More tears, in tiers, it's happening again.' Turning to Cam, with cupped hands around her mug and blowing on hot coffee, said, 'frontline workers are at risk again, clapping every Thursday, and painting rainbows won't help either.'

Cam added, 'can't believe the death rates are rising like this again. NHS staff must be stressed to hell from the first wave, and now going into another depressing, never-ending cycle of tough, grinding shifts.' Cam placed a reassuring hand on Hannah's back, as tears trickled down her face.

'Bloody awful.' Hannah needed distraction, sniffed and

straightened up, 'did Sara like her Glam Camper Playset?' She forced a faint smile.

'She did, Julia will set it all up next time we're online to see her playing with it. She loves putting her dolls to sleep in the camp-beds and apparently it has a little hot-tub, and disco lights, all the bells and whistles; everything a seven-year-old needs in life.' The pain on Cam's face was evident at further separation from his daughter. 'Hope it's not too long 'til we see her again.' He tried hard to be positive.

Hannah agreed, 'we're back to not mixing households again, bloody depressing, isn't it?'

By November, Hannah and her siblings resumed their parental support plan, but she was concerned the last time she saw her mother. Martha wasn't her usual buoyant self, she looked pale and weary. Hannah, standing half way along the path from the front door, where she'd placed the week's shopping, asked how they were.

'Oh well, you know, it's fine sweetheart, but some days … we get a bit bored. It would be lovely for the grandkids to come and visit, or for us all to meet for our monthly Sunday lunches again. You watch the news and it's all so terrible.'

Hannah couldn't bear her mother's crestfallen demeanour. Her childhood home was the place of laughter and raucous activity. Usually, only a few days would pass before family members visited to spend time with them. She felt so desperately sad and wanted to give her mother the biggest hug. All she could do was empathise with cold raindrops dripping down her face and the back of her neck, in hopeful tones, 'there may be some light at Christmastime?'

Though it was looking extremely doubtful. She put on a brave face, talked encouragingly about the boys and Cam, and her work, but she was freezing. Hannah had to leave; she was soaked. Her parents stood at the door and waved until her car was no longer in view. Hannah's rain-stained face mixed with tears, echoing the droplets running down the windscreen. Hannah broke her heart on the drive home, when strange random memories entered her mind.

It was 1990, Lena spun around, blue eyes blazing, knuckle-white fists on her hips, screaming like a petulant child. *"I do everything, absolutely everything for you and this is how you repay me! Look at this mess and no florentines left!"* Astonished at this parental behaviour, a young Hannah couldn't see any mess, but for a few tiny crumbs, and wondered what the hell florentines were? Verna's face was scarlet as her mother, Lena, berated her. On the rare occasion there was anything edible in Verna's house, the girls had eaten two fancy chocolate biscuits each; Hannah realised they were the florentines. They'd arrived home from school, famished, slung their school bags down, fed Stella, the border collie and tucked into the biscuits. Stella lived in the rear part of the house; she was rarely allowed in the pristine front lounge.

Thirty years later, as Hannah drove away from her parents' home on this stormy November evening, she reflected on her childhood when Verna's mother, Lena, had invaded her thoughts. She was in maudlin mood, and clicked-on the car indicator, as headlights and splashing tyres whizzed by, until she spotted a break in the stream of cars, then turned onto the dual carriageway. Recounting long distant memories of the strange contents of Verna's kitchen cupboards and fridge. It was not what children desired; cheeses Hannah hadn't heard of, smoked salmon, cold meats, olives and saltines, which Hannah discovered were a bit like small cream crackers. Hannah had contemplated whether Verna had a mild eating disorder from the lack of hearty meals, and the necessity to look perfect for Lena; the surreptitious calorie counting if they grabbed sustenance when out shopping or meeting during Hannah's lunch breaks. Verna favouring a light salad and fat-free yoghurt, in comparison to Hannah's choice of a plump, ploughman's pickle, bursting baguette, with accompanying crisps and a brownie.

Hannah distinctly recalled holding her breath each time she went upstairs in Verna's huge childhood home, to prevent knocking the slender, delicate ladies-holding-flowers ornaments off the sills or spindly side tables; they were everywhere. It was like an obstacle course to go for a pee. She never touched the walls in case her hands were grubby, she was careful where she walked and how she sat in case she left a mark on the cream sofa or carpet. Thinking about it now, Hannah was still traumatised at the memory of spilling blackcurrant juice, horrified as the spreading blotch turned cream into deepest scarlet, like a bloodied murder scene. Lena suppressed her resentment well, but took it out on Verna who was made to scrub the carpet until her fingers were bright pink, and Lena was satisfied every drop was removed. Hannah never accepted another drink, ever.

These childhood thoughts filled Hannah's mind as she continued the journey home. Few would know of the perpetual emotional abuse that permeated Verna's childhood.

Her successful elder brother Simon, was absent from the house at university, so the perfect, pretty younger offspring gave Lena an opportunity to parade her around. Verna learnt how to perform her role beautifully, for which she was adorned with exclusive imported clothing and footwear no one else had. The price Verna paid was to have the house scrupulously clean from top to bottom. Hannah helped when she stayed for tea. From being eleven years old; they dusted, hoovered, mopped floors, cleaned the kitchen, the bathrooms and the windows; ensured the beds were made, and ornaments and sofa cushions were in exactly the right place. In summer, tending to the garden plants and mowing the lawn was added to the chores. But the girls had fun together, they never really minded. Lena meticulously inspected the work each evening when she returned from work.

Years later, Verna said to Hannah, *"I'm sure my mother has OCD, or depression or something else. She's tired and lethargic for days, then other times full of mad energy."* Hannah recalled Verna missed school occasionally when Lena couldn't get out of bed. They'd discuss Lena's spending sprees, returning home with tons of shopping bags, skipping around like a child at Christmas, trying on outfits. The girls would, *"ooh"* and, *"aah"* as she elegantly paraded around in glamorous dresses and stilettos. When Lena was out, the two girls dabbled with her make-up and tried on her sparkly clothes and high heels. Hannah missed that dazzling Verna grin, complete with dimples.

'We must've looked like two little girl-clowns,' she said aloud smiling, as her car trundled along in the heavy, miserable line of traffic. Hannah had a distinct memory of trepidation, trying to smooth over a brand-new powder-blue eye shadow compact, so Lena wouldn't know their little fingers had been poking around in her cosmetics. She loved the shimmering maroon boxes, tracing, *Charles of the Ritz,* in silver script with her finger. Smiling now, at her own naivety thinking it must have been expensive and worn by princesses because it said, Ritz, yet it probably was. Hannah expressed her worries to Verna that she'd be in trouble after they'd been getting up to mischief. With genuine affection, she remembered Verna's impish reply, *"It's worth it."*

Hannah's smile reflected in the rear-view mirror with fond memories of her own mother, in stark contrast, telling her to buy Astral moisturiser, *"it won't break the bank, and it's the same as the pricey stuff."* Hannah repeated Martha's comment, 'if it's good enough for Joanna Lumley, it's good enough for me.' Hannah was overwhelmed with respect and fondness for her parents, and wished she could give her mam a hug ... a massive hug ... that's all.

Sniffing and wiping her eyes, Hannah needed to concentrate on driving. The weather was atrocious, it was 3 p.m. and darkness was already descending, as early November hail battered the windscreen. As if that wasn't bad enough, she was caught up in an extended tailback. Orange rotating lights ahead indicated roadworks, and as blue lights flashed across her face, she realised there had also been a traffic incident. She called Cam, 'it's going to take ages to get home, there's been an accident, would you crack on with tonight's meal please, sorry I'm going to be late.'

'Of course, hope it's not too much grief. How's Martha and Tommy?'

'Not great. Anyway hon, see you as soon as … who knows, love you.' She ended the call quickly after Cam responded, for fear of him hearing desolation in her voice. Sitting in motionless traffic, irritatingly needing the toilet, Hannah recalled a heinous event at Verna's house, which sometimes drifted forth from her memory store. They were fourteen years old; Verna, Hannah and two brothers who lived on the upmarket estate, were sitting in the lounge watching television. Lena drifted downstairs in a magenta lace-edged silk robe, she crossed the lounge, and entered the dining room through the dividing glass doors. Hannah recalled that robe in every detail. What Verna and Hannah couldn't see, because their view was obscured, was Lena draped over a dining chair in full view of the two boys. Her magenta robe had slid open to reveal a black, lace bra and knickers, stockings and suspenders, exposing most of her breasts and the pale rounded flesh of her belly, hips and thighs.

Verna became curious regarding the brothers' giggles and deft looks through the glass doors. She leaned forward, as did Hannah to see what had attracted their attention. Verna cried out, *"Mother, for god's sake!"* Lena nonchalantly drew the robe together, half smiling, faking surprise saying she hadn't realised her robe was open. The vision, however was indelibly imprinted upon each of their puberty-developing brains. Verna was so embarrassed and had cried openly with shame to Hannah later that night after the boys, pink-faced and sniggering, left the house.

As the seesaw of age raised Verna's natural beauty, Lena's began to descend and fade, and her mother became competitive. Verna wrung her hands recounting episodes of Lena flirting with her friends' fathers. *"She'd turn up to collect me in skimpy miniskirts and tight-fitting vest tops with no bra."* Hannah pictured a stunning Lena in full cosmetic glory, shoulder length bleached blonde hair immaculately done. Verna and Hannah would often chat and reflect upon these shared memories.

Hannah arrived home, relieved the boys had eaten, fish fingers, chips and peas it seemed, from the debris scattered around the worktops. Cam appeared and hugged her, enthusiastically saying, 'I started making the boys' tea and told them to put a timer on their phones to sort it out themselves, and left them to it. They'll soon get fed up of burnt food if they forget,' looking around he added, 'but, they still require cleaning-up coaching apparently,' as he began clearing the debris.

'Great idea,' Hannah commented with a weak smile, knowing Cam recognised the same anguish in her every time she returned from the visit to her parents.

'It's awful seeing them like this I know. But on a positive note, the boys have been fine by the way, no arguing at least.' Cam was getting used to managing the spats with calm reason and humour.

Hannah sank into his embrace, 'thank you for everything you do.'

He held her securely. 'No problem.'

Hannah popped upstairs to greet the boys, returned and slumped onto the sofa in the conservatory feeling weary. The twinkling solar lights strewn along the fence caught her eye as they were ignited by darkness. The maudlin-filled journey home left Hannah in low mood. This spot in the conservatory had been her crying place, secluded from the boys when her marriage failed. Verna had been so kind to her; lending, no, gifting her money when she was desperate and taking her out for drinks or afternoon tea to cheer her up. She arranged for a block booking of massages at a spa and looked after the boys, so Hannah could have some much-needed relaxation and peace. But most of all she offered her time and support, loving friendship and companionship in those dark times. She missed Verna, today was a sad day. Hannah had cut off all contact as a way of dealing with the loss, and was still ashamed it may have been borne of her past resentment toward Leo.

A darker thought crossed her mind, did she harbour a deep envy of Verna; not only her looks, personality and her fantastic petite figure despite having three children, but her affluent home, business success, and seemingly perfect marriage and lifestyle. Hannah scrolled her phone for images of them together, she needed to see Verna's face, and questioned whether their friendship had been real. Images of their joint fortieth birthday celebrations showed genuine joy in them beaming from the screen. Hannah looked at Verna's natural dark blonde hair, highlighted perfectly from sunlight in summer, and mused that, women spent decades at the gym, paid a fortune in beauty products and visiting salons to replicate what Verna had naturally inherited. Despite the rare twinges of jealousy she may have, and who wouldn't, she loved Verna dearly.

Cam sat, handed Hannah a glass of red, 'fifteen minutes for food.' He caught sight of the picture. 'You look gorgeous, who's the woman you're with?'

'It's Verna, she's … she was my best friend.'

'Was? What happened to her?'

Hannah told Cam about Verna and the argument whilst having their evening meal. He was naturally protective and couldn't see she had done or said anything wrong. Observing her sorrow, Cam suggested she re-connects with Verna, whenever she was ready. He also commented, from a male perspective, she may be correct in her suspicions about Leo.

27

Verna. July 2020

Steve entered Leo's room on the mental health unit, and found him crouched in the corner of his bed shouting, 'andate via bastardi!' Steve recognised this now, *get away bastards.*

He spoke clearly and calmly to Leo, 'hey Leo, it's Steve, it's okay.'

Leo recognised the reassuring face of his key worker and asked, 'se ne sono andati?'

It was a challenge for Steve, not only to manage Leo's psychosis, but his switch into Italian often mid-sentence, though he recognised this repeated question, *have they gone?*

Verna was in contact with the unit for regular updates over the three weeks Leo was in hospital. Visits weren't advisable for fear of viral transmission; however a plan was in place to manage video calls upon Leo's request, or if the team assessed it was beneficial to his progress. The latest report was the medication seemed to be stabilising him. He was eating well and engaging with the team, remaining calm most of the time and had a good rapport with his key worker.

Leo was still suffering from night terrors and on a few occasions had further psychotic episodes trying to escape from the shadows, and had inadvertently lashed out at workers who were trying to calm him. Although Leo was showing insight regarding why he was on the ward, the team would continue to reassess his progress and monitor his medication, so he could possibly be discharged with a care plan in place once the night time reactions had calmed.

Verna gave the children regular updates that dad was resting and hopefully he would be given medication, which would mean he could come home soon. She was more honest with Marco, but still tempered the level of truths. Joyce was a regular visitor, bringing baked goodies. She sat with the girls doing various art and craft projects and taught them how to knit, well Amara did learn, but Izzy couldn't concentrate for long and ended up flinging the balls of wool around playing with Rocco. Joyce and Verna on some days would sit with a glass of wine having a comforting chat.

Verna had tackled the financial data from the business accounts, which took days to put everything in order. She had spoken with their accountant and advised to contact her directly, not Leo, in future. She needed to make plans to reduce their living costs. They had four cars, his and hers Maseratis, a Porsche Cayenne SUV to transport family, and their beloved red vintage MGB Roadster, for which they'd had many offers from enthusiasts over the years. It was locked up in one of the garages most of the time as they held onto it for sentimental reasons.

Verna ceased trawling through the many documents on the desk, and looked up as beams of sunlight illuminated her face. She let out a lengthy, audible sigh recalling the day she met Leo as they discussed the sporty red car, also driving away in it from their wedding celebrations at the exclusive, Villa Ortensia in Bergamo. The mountainous scenery speeding by was stunning on their joyful honeymoon touring around Italy. They took it for a run annually on their wedding anniversary, but the beloved car would have to go.

That evening, Verna had one glass of wine too many, and on hands and knees, she dug around the bottom of her wardrobe and found the canvas case which held mementos from special occasions. She partially unzipped it and pulled out the shimmering pale gold silk shawl, embroidered with sparkling bronze jewels and pearls she'd worn as they drove away on their honeymoon. She draped it around her shoulders. The children were fast asleep as she stumbled quietly along the hallway, and momentarily had to cling to the banister as she teetered downstairs. She took some car keys from the back of a kitchen drawer and tip-toed by a sleeping Rocco.

Swaying through the utility room, she enjoyed the slightly dreamy sensation of being off-balance and giggled as she entered the garage. She opened the MGB car door with the familiar satisfying, and gentle clunk of old metal as the key turned in the lock. She sat in the driver's seat. Exciting memories flooded her brain from the scent of the car's interior, she imagined her and Leo zipping along with the roof down. With her head on the headrest, she could feel the sensation of a warm Italian breeze on a blazing hot day caressing her face, and the scent of magnolia and Jasmine. Verna did not know how long she sat there. Exhilaration turned to sadness and tears flowed; she knew her life could never again be so carefree.

Verna woke the next morning, in bed, with the shawl draped around her. Heaving herself up, the overspilled contents of the canvas case, and the MGB keys on the bedside table caught her eye. She rallied, sentimentality would get her nowhere. She forced herself to believe a different future as a successful business woman could be hers; and the Ravassio's would have a positive future; yes, it will be different, but positive! After a large fresh orange juice, strong painkillers for her thumping head and antacids for her churning stomach, she sorted out the children for school, fed the dog, and set to the task of casting more financial wizardry spells tucked away in the study.

Surrounded by printed PDFs of accounts, Verna noted a significant number of payments on hospitality and leisure in Italy; boat trips, lakeside cabins and restaurant bills, not unusual, as Leo had to ingratiate himself with clients and he did enjoy the high life. There were outgoings from exclusive shops in Milan, which accounted for the designer gifts he sent home for her and the children. The euro to sterling exchange had fluctuated with Brexit which meant it was difficult to establish the true cost of expenditure. She massaged her temples in an attempt to quell the crunching headache and gulped more iced water down with another dose of painkillers.

Verna decided to call Leo's former CEO, Fabrizio, his English was pretty good and she was sure they could have a fruitful call. All she needed to establish was, if payments had been made or would be paid to Leo for his consultancy for the period March to May. His number from Leo's mobile was dead and the email she sent was returned as an invalid address. She found the company contact details and left a brief message from VLR Software requesting a return call. Within an hour, her phone rang, it was Fabrizio's son, Toni whose spoken English was excellent.

'Ciao Verna, how are you and the family, how is Leo? I hope you are well in these terrible times.'

'We're doing okay, but Leo is taking some time out from work while business is calmer, he's quite fatigued right now.'

'It is good to have a break. How can we help you?'

Verna explained about the accounts, and asked if Toni could shed light on any forthcoming payments.

After a pause, Toni said, 'but all the contracts were put on hold. I don't understand why Leo would be paid for this period,' softly he said, 'and … it's terrible but my father passed away from Covid in May, so business stopped, and we are still devastated.'

Verna apologised profusely. 'Oh, I'm so sorry I didn't know, Leo must have got dates confused. To be honest Toni, Leo hasn't been well mentally, so this will likely account for his mistakes, and forgetting to tell me about Fabrizio.' Verna was mortified!

Toni was empathetic, 'sorry to hear this about Leo, please pass on my good wishes, I hope he is well soon. I like Leo a lot, we got along well, he was an asset to the company.' Verna offered further condolences, wished Toni well, and ended the call staring at her own bemused reflection in the darkened computer screen. Despite her fuzzy head, she forensically went through the data. She created a spreadsheet, grateful that she hadn't lost all of her administrative business skills, then input the transactions she could find for the time of the Italian contract and it built up a picture of fairly frenetic activity. Why would Leo tell her he had to work at their Quayside apartment? She was mystified. Maybe he had been suffering from delusional thoughts and actions for longer than she knew. He wouldn't be in a position to explain anything coherently for some while yet.

Of all the anomalies, one stood out. There was a deduction from an airline for what seemed to be a single journey flight from Milan to Newcastle in late April on the business account, when Leo was at home. Verna thought long and hard. She was sure it was the day when Leo went into a frenzy of activity explaining there had been a total crash of the system and he had to stay overnight at the apartment to sort it out. Then he arrived home saying he had to return to Italy in the early hours to sort out the mess. There was another deduction which accounted for two return flights to Milan. Her phone screen lit up with an alarm notification. 'Bloody hell, the kids!' She was going to be late picking them up from school.

After a routine mealtime, she ushered the children to their various activities, and once the girls were settled in bed that evening, she returned to examining the accounts. She was stunned and confused and her splitting headache returned, she washed down more painkillers. She jumped as the study door opened.

'You okay?' Marco popped his head around the door. 'I saw the light on, and it's getting really late.'

'Oh ... er yes, so it is son, I lost track.' Verna gave her boy a massive reassuring hug. 'I'm preparing everything for dad coming home, including the finances as he won't be able to work at first. All seems fine,' she smiled, and lied simultaneously.

'Anything I can do to help?'

Verna held back the tears, repeating everything was fine. Marco seemed satisfied with her response and she fell into bed once he closed the door. Despite her numbing exhaustion, she hardly slept a wink.

Leo returned from the mental health unit as he'd made good progress over the last few weeks. It was good to have him home, but he wasn't the same Leo. The advice from his team was to keep everything low key, keep routines and reduce as much stress as possible to help with healing. He was forgetful and often confused, which the children found amusing, however the girls fawned over him at every opportunity, and Marco was pleased he still had the capacity to play on games with him. The family took walks in the fresh air and Verna did everything she could to assist his rehabilitation along with advice from the community mental health team.

By mid-September, Leo had been home several weeks, and life became routine. Verna knew she had to tackle the anomalies and asked Leo directly why he hadn't told her about Fabrizio? His response was neutral, 'oh ... let me see, em, oh yes, I thought I must have told you,' came his cool, detached reply. Verna couldn't decide whether it was truthful or not; the medication masked a lot of his emotions and his memory seemed dull too. She was nervous about confronting him in case it sent him into a tailspin, which would worry the children.

Leo formed a bond with Nigel, having had similar issues in the past, it was a good support for him. Nigel made a suggestion when they were out walking Rocco, 'how about a few days away walking in the Dales? I wouldn't be surprised if lockdown rules change soon the way things are.'

'Sounds good,' agreed Leo.

'Of course, we'll have to, okay it with the wives. I'd rather run it by Verna and as long as she's happy for you to go … if you're feeling strong enough?'

'Great idea, it'll be good for me Nigel, thank you.'

Both Verna and Joyce agreed it was a great idea. Their eyes met and there was an intrinsic acknowledgment of their intention to have a shopping trip incorporating an afternoon tea including a glass or two of bubbly. They could take advantage of the children being in school to become the ladies who lunch, whilst restrictions still allowed.

28

Leo called Verna. 'We arrived safely and the accommodation is great, it's small and friendly. Dent Village is lovely and the Dales are magnificent. I feel weary, but can't wait to get out and about, and take in the scenery.'

Verna was pleased to hear Leo sounding so positive. 'So you should. You need to get some use out of all the new gear you bought for the occasion.'

Leo laughed, he sounded bright. 'This trip is good rehab for me, we've booked for a few days, but they've said we can extend the booking if we wish. I guess I'll see how much it takes out of me.'

'Enjoy it, hopefully it could become a new hobby. Need to go and get the children sorted for lazy Saturday morning breakfast, will catch up soon.' Verna ended the call and the snap of the letterbox told her the post arrived. She lifted Rocco up to inspect his scar on her way to the door. His fur had grown in, and he was no longer jumpy or wincing. He nuzzled her as she put him down.

In stark contrast to the dark brown doormat, a cream envelope had dropped face down. She picked it up, and turned it over. The envelope was quite thick and the stamps were foreign. It was a letter from Italy addressed to Leo, but Verna was mystified who would have sent it. The address was written, as if it had been carefully copied. Her first thought was it was from Toni, who she had spoken with weeks ago. He thought highly of Leo, and had maybe sent well-wishes after she said Leo had been unwell. She would leave the thoughtful message from Italy for Leo's return. Verna placed it on the slim shelf by the door, where all the post rested until it was dealt with or binned. She went about her day; the school run, shopping, a daily coffee with Joyce, then walking Rocco, washing and preparing dinner. A reminder pinged on her phone for daily yoga and meditation practice, to boost her physical and mental strength to devote time and energy into her husband's recovery. Some hopeful feelings abound within her.

On her way upstairs to bed, she spied the letter resting on the ledge. She looked at it and wondered why Leo seemed to have forgotten about Fabrizio's death? Though his thought processes had been erratic, once Leo was discharged from the unit their lives had slotted back into a routine and she was taking everything day by day, and they rarely discussed Italy. Curiosity got the better of her, she took the letter and the remnants of her glass of red upstairs. She hesitated, guilty of opening someone else's personal post, but under current circumstances, Leo wouldn't mind as it was she who'd spoken with Toni.

There was a rarely used letter opener in the study drawer, which she retrieved and climbed into bed, it wouldn't spoil the lovely envelope. She gently slid the sharp pointed tip under the join between front and back, then carefully angled the handle to slice it open. Verna stretched over to take a gulp of the wine sitting on the bedside table, it had become a comforting good friend to her in dark times and it smoothly slid down. She lifted out a letter, but had expected a card or notelet wishing Leo well. Yet it was a letter with some photographs. The paper was thick and the blue ink had absorbed crisply into the paper. It began, *Ciao Leo*.

Before Verna could begin to translate the Italian handwriting, a photograph of a baby fell onto her lap. It was a picture of a new-born wearing a little blue cap in a neo-natal crib. First thought was maybe Toni recently had a child. There was another close-up shot of the baby with its eyes closed, being held by someone. Another, of the beautiful baby with its dark brown eyes open. Another, of a stunning young Italian woman holding the baby with a big smile on her face. Then another photo of the same woman, and Leo standing together with a lake in the background. She was leaning towards him, kissing him on the cheek, his arm was draped casually around her, with a relaxed warm smile into the camera. He was wearing a yellow shirt. The last photo was a selfie of Leo with the same woman on the balcony in his apartment, kissing.

Verna spread the six photographs on her thighs, picked up the photo of the baby with its eyes open and stared into the image, it could be Amara. She glared at the two of Leo with the woman, it was the same woman holding the baby. With shaking hands, she picked up the letter, she couldn't read it fluently but could gather, *tuo figlio Gabriele*, meant, your son Gabriel. Her breathing accelerated, she gasped for air, pressed her hand upon her throat as it constricted; she was shaking uncontrollably as she heaved breaths into her nostrils, thinking, oh god, breathe. The panic subsided a little as her breathing regulated, but the shaking did not. She was frozen in time and space. An overwhelming feeling of nausea rose as her gullet lurched. She didn't have time to get out of bed and reach the en-suite, she rolled to one side and dark pink wine-smelling vomit shot out of her mouth, down the side of the bed and onto the floor.

A stunned Verna robotically got out of bed, found some anti-bac bathroom spray in the en-suite and tried to clean up the watery wine vomit with toilet roll as best she could. She was at a complete loss. Sitting propped up beside the chemical smelling bedding, 'what the fuck do I do now?' she whispered. She shoved the photos and letter into the envelope and slammed it into the back of the bedside cabinet drawer, afraid one of the children may burst into the bedroom if they heard her being unwell, she grabbed the letter opener and stabbed Leo's pillow. Her instincts told her to call Leo and tell him not to come home as she never wanted to see his face ever again. Her mind raced. Maybe he had a fling with a young woman and she was trying to name him as the father of the baby to extort money. It could be anyone's baby, she would support him, that being the case.

Verna was overwhelmed with utter hatred for her husband in the next moment. She knew he had been a stupid, selfish prick who had no insight into the consequences of having an affair with a young woman, resulting in pregnancy. Seething under her breath, 'you utter fucking bastard Leo. A fucking Italian baby. What the hell am I supposed to do now? How could you do this to me and the children … oh god.' Verna cried all night. She hugged her pillow and suppressed her bawling cries into it so the children wouldn't hear her pain.

In the early hours, Verna was alerted to the fact Leo may be home from his trip soon. She couldn't bear to see his face, and she needed a plan. At 6 a.m. she got up, way before the children on a Sunday morning and sent Leo a message saying they'd be out all day and she'd call tomorrow for an update. Verna was great at putting on a brave face which she had done with practiced ease since she was a child, but this … this was different.

The children were occupied once they were up and about, Marco was visiting a friend for the day and the girls wanted to go to Joyce's to bake, and she wouldn't see them until tea-time. Good, it gave her time and space. If Gabriel was Leo's bastard son, she needed a route out of this marriage and it had to be a financially secure route for her and the children. Verna compartmentalised her emotions and clicked into assertive mode, she had maybe a week to formulate a plan. She would survive this; her fierce maternal instincts kicked in, and so would her children! Using a translation website, she input each sentence to ascertain as accurate a meaning of the letter as she could.

Leo. Here is your son Gabriel born September 15 at 6.53 a.m. at Mangiagalli Hospital in Milan. He is healthy and beautiful. You will not see him. You will not know him. He will not know about you. He has love and a wonderful family here in Italy, we will give him everything he needs. I am blessed to have this child. But I am not blessed with the father.

We had happiness, you will remember from the photos. I do not believe now you were divorced. I do not believe now you ever wanted a life with me. For this I hate you. You are a liar! I will need money to bring up my son to have the best life and education. The Avvocato lawyer will send the papers soon. I do not care if you have a good life. Graziella.

29

Verna faked a situation to Marco. 'I'm probably going to be the breadwinner for some time, and need a quiet place to work. I've set up a workstation in our bedroom, and I'll convert the study into a bedroom dad can use if he gets tired. I could be working late in the evenings or up early in the mornings, it'll give him some space to rest.' It was bullshit of course! Verna wanted Leo out of her sight as much as possible until she could expedite her plan. Marco accepted her explanation without question, and enthusiastically helped her rearrange the room.

'What a tip,' Verna commented to Marco through the loft hatch. She was surrounded by old toys, books, Christmas trees and decorations, suitcases, defunct electrical equipment, skis, outdoor gear; and now the rarely used gym equipment from the study Verna and Marco had dismantled to store away.

'Think that's the last of it.' Marco shouted up to her through the hatch.

'Thanks son, I'll tidy up here, would you mind sorting lunch for the girls please, sweetheart.'

'Okay Mum, no probs.'

Verna didn't know what she would have done without Marco helping her rearrange the study. She'd been up since 6 a.m. on this late September morning, trawled the job pages online, and applied for some independent accountancy contracts, hoping her qualifications and business experience would be attractive enough to gain a contract.

Verna was in the loft checking the sturdy cardboard box, full of folders containing the financial information from the study. The folders were in date order, and separated into various categories, clearly marked should she need to access information quickly. One folder marked, Business Affairs, she'd named with heavy irony, contained details relating to Leo's extra-marital activity; purchases, travel bookings and hospitality during the period he was working in Lodi. As she closed the lid and sat in silence, she wondered if the evidence may be required, not only for tax purposes, but in divorce proceedings. The ominous box was placed in the farthest corner of the loft, Verna climbed down the ladders and raised them into the hatch.

At the new workstation in the main bedroom she opened the password protected files on her Mac. She'd meticulously scanned and uploaded financial information from original hard copies. Leo's old phone contract had lapsed, however the phone was secure within the, Business Affairs folder, sim card intact, if ever needed.

It took a week to convert the study into a spare bedroom for Leo. She was pleased with the result. The three-quarter bed was delivered speedily and would be adequate for him on his own with a bedside table and lamp. She transferred all of his clothes into the spare wardrobe, and bought a tall boy for his other clothing and put Marco's' old TV on top. There was a small shower en-suite, so Leo would never need to come into the main bedroom. All this to create an atmosphere for the children, things were normal, between her and Leo.

Verna was alerted to the post each morning to intercept any correspondence from Italy, particularly relating to financial demands for child support. She thought about returning them, *not known*, as Leo may well be, not known at the address in the near future.

On the mental health unit, Steve, Leo's key worker made a follow up call to see how his former patient was doing. He couldn't get an answer from Leo's phone, so he called his wife.

'Hi Verna, thought I'd ring to see how things are going?'

'Oh hi, Leo is away on a walking trip with a neighbour.'

'That's brilliant, it'll be excellent for his recovery. Fresh air, company, exercise and wide-open natural spaces.'

'Uh huh.'

After a pause, Steve said, 'hope it's all going to plan with his medication and the community contact is working out, he's being discharged from all services soon. So … yeah, thought I'd catch up before then.'

'All fine here.'

'Okay, so … I'm glad everything's good at your end. I bet the children love having their dad home in one piece.'

'Yes, they do.'

'Right … well, em, tell Leo I've been in touch, and … er,

hope all goes well in the future. If you need anything, keep my number handy.'

'I will, thanks, bye.'

Steve heard the phone click and got the distinct impression, that was one wife not too enamoured with having her husband home. A colleague drifted by and asked if everything was all right, as he seemed deep in thought. 'Em … yeah, maybe … not sure.'

In her current state of mind, Verna desperately held onto a slim chance the Italian baby may not be his and they could repair their relationship; she was coming to terms he'd had affairs, but felt wretched thinking about her children if they separated. She had only ever truly loved Leo, and though devastating, she must focus on future plans. She couldn't deny the visceral hurt and betrayal that tore her apart deep inside her being. 'He won't take issue with the new regime, once he's aware I know about Gabriel,' she said as she looked around the set up in, what was now, Leo's bedroom.

The day Leo returned from the Dales after an extended eight-day break, which Verna had gratefully agreed, the children were at the window as Nigel's car pulled up. Amara darted out of the front door, flung herself at Leo, yelling, 'daddy's back, daddy's home, I love you!' full of joy, and tears of relief. He held her so close, it brought tears to Verna's eyes, she worried about Amara's separation anxiety. He got into the house and Izzy trundled along the hallway and squeezed under his arms too, as he crouched to hold them both. Once they'd kissed him all over, they dragged him into the kitchen.

Marco held out a hand to shake his and they fell into a warm embrace. 'You're nearly as tall as me now son!'

Rocco jumped and sniffed at his master, who held him up to his face; Leo was covered in dog saliva in seconds. Joyce smiled, proudly presenting an array of baked goodies. Leo hugged her and said, 'I haven't really thanked you enough for everything you've done to support my family.'

'It's been an absolute pleasure Leo,' said Joyce. 'We'll leave you to have family time to yourselves and—'

'Oh no, you're not going anywhere,' interjected Verna, 'you're both honorary Ravassio family members now,' and handed a glass of wine to Joyce, suggesting Nigel gets changed and pops back for supper. They were like surrogate grandparents to the children; she was blessed to have them next door. Plus, she didn't want to be alone with Leo and reiterated they were never intruding and were welcome any time. She hoped Nigel and Leo would go out for more regular, long walks.

Verna had to admit it was a wonderful evening, the children didn't want to go to bed, however Joyce took the girls up and Leo, Nigel and Marco had a man-to-man chat in the conservatory. They shared issues, and talked freely about the stresses and strains which led Nigel and Leo to poor mental health. The chat was naturally tempered for Marco's sake. As she looked at her husband and son, how she wished Leo was back in the comfort of his family without complications, and they could look forward to a life together. They could, if Verna chose to deny the existence of her husband's bastard son. Once the party was over, and tales of the wilderness were done, their guests left and the children were in bed, Leo and Verna went upstairs. Verna, opened the study door and Leo was mystified at the vision inside. Fortunately, Marco would have his headphones on, so she could explain.

'I've made a few changes, and set up an office in the main bedroom which I'll use for starting up my business. I've sorted out the finances and were okay for a good six months, but the cars will have to go. I've set this up as a bedroom for you to rest, and have peace and quiet. Marco's donated his old TV too, and there's a shower, so it's got every convenience you need.'

Leo's exhilaration, became despair in a second. He turned his healthy, tanned face to his wife. 'What's all this about Verna? Please ... what's going on?'

Verna didn't want an argument disturbing the children tonight. She'd keep the illegitimate information to herself until she decided to divulge what she knew. For now, there was one thing she was certain of, 'I know you had an affair, Leo.' She walked out of the spare bedroom and closed the door on his bewildered face.

30

Leo responded to the sound of a baby crying in a cradle at the end of the bed. He held the tiny infant, who was soothed by his touch and gentle voice. He walked through the apartment to the flower-strewn balcony, gently rocking the warm fragile body in his arms.

'Leo! Leo!' He heard Graziella's voice. He lifted the baby to his face and kissed the downy soft cheek.

'Leo, Leo!' He roused at Verna's, not Graziella's, voice. She was peering around the bedroom door. He looked at her, confused at first.

'You're going to be late taking the kids to school. C'mon get up!'

He realised, it was the same, unnerving, recurring dream.

'Daddy look!' Izzy was spinning around in circles, became dizzy, fell over, bumped her head on the bedroom door frame and bawled. Leo dragged himself towards the high-pitched noise emanating from Izzy's delicate mouth and lifted her, rubbing her head and kissed her pink soft cheek. The similarity to the recurring dream was stark. Leo was unsure how long he could tolerate being a househusband. Days of endless tedious domestic tasks and trying to manage meeting every individual demand of his children. He looked towards the closed bedroom door hoping Verna would emerge and take over, knowing she could hear the commotion, and if she appeared, Izzy would default to her care. He soothed Izzy making a fuss and tried to distract her with the help of Amara. It must be tough for Verna listening to a distressed daughter, but she remained steadfast it seemed, he had to cope. Izzy calmed, Leo took her downstairs and made breakfast, made sure they had school requirements for homework, gym kits and lunchboxes.

Marco was already in the car when Leo lifted Izzy into her seat. 'Dad we're going to be late! I can't be late again!'

'It's okay son, we'll be there on time.'

Once the children were ensconced in school, Leo drove to the nearby lakeside beauty spot, parked up and wept. Verna hadn't said anything after she revealed she knew of the affair. She wouldn't discuss it, saying when the time was right, they would. She was ice cold. It was like purgatory living with her these past few weeks, so he did his duty and cared for the children as required. His distress subsided, his blurred gaze welcomed the early winter sun's weak rays through the windscreen. A flock of birds lifted into the air. Leo watched the flickering highlighted reflections underneath their wings as they flapped across his field of vision. He wished he could fly away too. Closing his eyes, he sensed light behind his eyelids, but no warmth as that of a summer day. Leo was used to Italian mornings, full of brightness and colour, not the drab, dark taupe of a British winter day.

Leo wished he was there, away from the pressure, to a life where he pretty much pleased himself. He could maybe return and face everyone. He could try to make peace with Graziella and achieve a reconciliation, if she'd have him. He could say Verna gave him an ultimatum over the children, and he hadn't really wanted to return. Leo wondered why he desired the alternative lifestyle to the one he was living. He recognised the constricted feeling of being trapped with Graziella and longed for his English family life, and now he wanted the opposite. He thumped the steering wheel with both palms.

'Why can't I simply live my life! A life I've made, and be happy with it? What the hell is wrong with me?'

Verna had no idea how many times he lay in bed alone, confused, disconnected and terrified of his secret being revealed, yes, she knew about the affair, but surely, she would've mentioned the baby. He wept tears for his child in Italy, Graziella must have given birth a few months ago. He hoped the baby was well and wondered if it was a boy or girl. He may never know or ever have a relationship with the human being he was intrinsically connected with. The beating he took from Graziella's family was her parting shot, and there would be no more contact, apart from financial requests. Even if Graziella changed her mind and tried to make contact, Verna had changed his mobile contract, so he'd never know. Graziella would assume he'd cut off all contact.

On returning from the lakeside, he took a coffee up for Verna, he had stopped knocking before entering, it was his bloody house after all. He geared up his inner strength and normality to walk through the door.

'Kids all fine, they're doing great but Izzy has no concentration whatsoever. Trying to do simple homework with her is a nightmare.'

'I know, been thinking of getting an education assessment as she's falling behind her group. It could be the impact of the pandemic as they've missed so much education.'

'Verna,' Leo sighed, 'would you please look at me when we're talking. I know you're busy doing the best for our family; but it's difficult constantly having conversations with the back of your head.'

Verna tapped the keyboard a few times, then slowly turned the swivel chair to look directly at him. Leo noticed she avoided eye contact most of the time, unless they were discussing or interacting with the children. He knew she was emotionally remote from him by choice.

'I think, look I … I'm struggling more than you know. Can we please talk about what's happened and let me explain. I know I've made a terrible mistake,' then he said meekly, 'maybe we could set up couples therapy or whatever, I'll do anything, please.'

'I guess so. I really can't bring myself to talk about it yet. I must focus on work. I'll look into family therapy or something,' but Verna's manner was detached.

'No, I'll do it. There needs to be more commitment and responsibility from me.'

'Okay, whatever you think.'

'I know the last few months have been all about me, but we need to reconnect and I never ask you how you're doing? I was thinking, you haven't mention Hannah, you two were as thick as thieves. Are you in touch by text and stuff, I know it's not been possible to meet up of course?'

'Occasional messages, as there's not much to say with the pandemic. Boring lives you know.'

Something about Verna's sharp reply and fleeting insincere smile seemed odd to Leo. It seemed she was somewhat startled at the sound of Hannah's name.

'She was always a good friend to you. A lovely person, and she was a brilliant support when we had the babies and I was working away. I do feel guilty I didn't award her that contract years ago. I mean, both designs were good, but Hannah was more professional, her research and application to the task was far superior.'

'You could never resist a pretty face though could you Leo?' Verna glared into his eyes. He returned a remorseful stare. She turned away and simmering with resentment.

Talking again to the back of her head, 'I'll contact Steve from the mental health unit, and see if he can recommend a couples therapist, it'll be good to chat with him.' Verna shrugged, Leo approached the door, turned and was going to suggest she should buck her ideas up and communicate, but he wasn't confident enough to challenge her. He deserved everything she threw at him. He sat in the conservatory and sipped his coffee, looking at piles of laundry when the letterbox snapped. He retrieved the post and his worst nightmare lay in his hand. An official legal document from an Italian law firm.

He grabbed the car keys and shouted upstairs. 'Just going for a drive! Here Rocco, here boy.' Rocco scampered along the hallway eager to get outside. Leo parked at the same spot he had been earlier and read the information. The full implications of the financial request hit him; they were astronomical! He wept again as he discovered he had a son, Gabriel, who was over two months old. He hadn't seen him, and may never see him. Leo was clueless how to manage this financial shock. Would his life mess ever end? There were times, Leo thought about choosing his own way out of it all, but when he looked at his son Marco, he knew he would never walk down that path. He was empty inside.

Rocco wasn't impressed with the non-existent walk. His master was being strange, no barking, no sticks to catch, no scratches, nothing.

Leo started the car and decided to return and tell Verna everything. It may mean losing his life as it is now, but he hoped with all his heart, above all else, she wouldn't deny him access to his children. The loss of one child was enough.

Verna had shouted downstairs at the sound of the door closing, 'Leo! Leo!' She concluded he'd gone out, and returned to her desk. Verna had a plan which she had discussed with various business support agencies who may help her with the current minefield of available grants and new-business bursaries. 'Maybe I don't need you any longer Leonardo Ravassio,' she said, 'though you're useful as free childcare for now.' Verna was looking forward to becoming a successful businesswoman again and she would be ruthless to get what she wanted, starting with Leo.

31

'I'm popping next door Nigel,' Joyce announced from her hallway, as she went for a Saturday afternoon coffee with Verna.

'Door's open!' came a shout from her neighbour's kitchen.

Verna made two frothy lattes, but seemed distracted.

'How are you Verna, you seem a little low?' Joyce was tentative, but glad of the warm drink.

'I am actually Joyce, not sure why?'

'It's been difficult for everyone during this pandemic it's not surprising a lot of people are feeling quite depressed.' Joyce got the sense Verna wasn't being open. During their frequent chats, Joyce opened up and expressed to Verna that Nigel had been a bit of a philanderer in his day. She observed recently something was quite off between Verna and Leo.

'I'm not sure that's exactly what it is.' Verna hesitated and chewed her lip. 'When you mentioned Nigel may have been, a philanderer, as you put it, I have had my suspicions about Leo. How did you find out?'

'Oh no Verna, so sorry to hear that.' Joyce's heart sank. 'Well … on the occasions when I believed he had girlfriends, I think it happened twice, at least; his behaviour changed, you know, distracted, secretive, and … elated,' she looked at her hands resting in her lap. 'We had counselling as part of his PTSD recovery and though he seemed to want to confess, he said little about the detail; but he was young and temptation got in his way. He was thoroughly ashamed and wanted to move on. Easier said than done,' her eyes flashed with resentment and continued, 'we worked through the situation, but I had to make a decision whether to stick with the marriage or not. Our boy was only three at this time so it would've been devastating for him, and for me. Are you sure about Leo, or do you have a sense there is something going on?'

'I'm convinced something's gone on in Italy, which triggered his psychosis. I've told him of my suspicions, and I'm waiting for the time to discuss it with him fully, but the children are always around.' Joyce noticed Verna turn and look behind her, checking the conservatory door was closed so Leo wouldn't hear their discussion. Verna said, 'it's okay he's playing on games with Marco upstairs and the girls are Harry Pottering in the bedroom. Leo's been too ill to rationalise anything, and I don't want him going into flight mode and worrying the children. It's not fair on them. They're so excited with Christmas looming too, so I wouldn't do anything to break up the family yet.'

Joyce recalled her painful years of distrust, a similar look was etched on Verna's lovely face, she was holding back. 'My best advice is to think long and hard about what you want for you and your family. I do think couples can make it after an affair, but the emotional trauma and building trust again takes years to achieve. I had no-one to talk to, stationed in army barracks. It wasn't the sort of thing people discussed openly, although everyone knew it was going on. I'm always here for you sweetheart.'

Verna said, 'that must've been so difficult for you. To be honest I have been giving a lot of thought to how badly let down I have been by men. My father worked away my whole life and had little influence or interest in me. He was more focused on my brother Simon. He's seven years older and moved out to university when he was eighteen. He's relocated to Bournemouth with his husband Jeremy and their three adopted children. They wanted a fresh start, so in a way he's abandoned me too.'

'The only memory I have of dad is his absence and keenness to get me married off, so another male could take financial responsibility. He has a brother, but I've not seen my uncle for many years. My wonderful father is currently living in Spain and onto his third marriage.' Verna sneered.

'That's sad, for him because he's missing out on his wonderful daughter, and three absolutely beautiful grandchildren. I don't understand why people act this way. I've often meant to ask about your family because you don't mention them much, especially your mother, but I shan't intrude, family business is personal, I know that.' Joyce gave a knowing nod, reliving the strain of years of faking everything was running smoothly in her troubled marriage.

Verna laughed. 'That conversation is for a night on the gins. I have so many tales I could tell you about my wonderful mother Lena. To be fair, I do think she a had long-standing undiagnosed mental health issue, resulting in early onset dementia in her late fifties, and she had to be hospitalised when she couldn't cope. She was on her own because my father left her about five years previously after an affair. She had plenty of male attention, but never settled and some of her choices were dubious. In the end she couldn't manage at home. She came to live with us for a while, but she could be overbearing and demanding and I had three children to care for, so it didn't work out. She's now in her seventies and is quite ill. I visit each month, not during the pandemic of course, but it's quite sad to see her, she was so beautiful.'

'Is that her picture?' The image of Lena amongst the family photos along the sill could've been a Vogue front cover. 'Yes, beautiful, like mother like daughter.' Joyce smiled. 'I'll come and visit her with you if you like, when it's allowed of course. I used to volunteer in an elderly care home, so I understand how difficult it is for relatives.'

Verna adored her saviour. 'Honestly Joyce I don't know how I would've coped without you these last six months.' The women looked into each other's eyes, sitting close together, they fell into a gentle understanding embrace.

Verna became upset, Joyce stroked her back. 'It's been an absolute pleasure, and given me purpose in life, gets me out of the house too.' Looking down again, Joyce recognised she needed the companionship as much as Verna. 'If I can do anything at all to help you and the children, I will … and, take your time with Leo. You will know the right decision when it comes to you, believe me you will.'

'I need some space to talk with him.'

Joyce straightened in her seat. 'How would you feel if the girls had a sleepover at my house?'

'Really? Yes, that would be great, they'd love it. Are you sure? Izzy can be a handful.'

Joyce nodded and swept her hand aside brushing away Verna's concerns.

'Marco will be fine, he rarely comes out of his room, and it would give me a chance to clear the air with Leo.'

Joyce's eyes lit up, 'I'll bake with them, we can watch movies, it would be lovely.' Joyce finished her coffee. 'How about tonight?' she got up, 'I'll go and tell Nigel, he'll be pleased, he's really getting into the Disney movies. I think he enjoys them and I've noticed tears in his eyes at the sad parts, the big old softy. It's quite funny,' she laughed and left.

'We're having a bubble sleepover at Joyce's tonight!' an animated Amara said to her dad. She was hanging around Leo's neck beside him on the sofa as they snacked on lunch together. Verna sensed Amara knew there was something not quite right and had become clingy with both parents, but especially Leo. Izzy didn't seem to notice anything going on around her in her own little world, and Marco spent most of his time online in his room. But Amara … Verna needed to tune in to her daughter's emotions, especially in the light of her confronting Leo about his affair.

32

Leo decided tonight would be the night he would divulge everything to Verna. He could no longer live with the pressure of keeping secrets. He thought for hours wondering how he was going to broach the subject. What should he say? What could he say? Whatever he said it would be devastating for Verna, his children and potentially for him if it meant his marriage was over. It was a risk he had to take. He had been experiencing night terrors recently. Verna did not know anything of it because he was in the spare bedroom, however, on occasion he had sat in bed reading all night when it was really bad, trying to distract from the anxiety of shadows. Whilst Leo could rationalise they were not real, he feared the prospect of mentally losing control again. It was unnerving and when his thoughts strayed to the beating, he physically winced and held a fetal position under the bedclothes.

Amara was so excited, she'd packed a bag bursting with clothing. 'Don't know if I want to wear my, Hedwig, or Gryffindor pyjamas?' Because she couldn't decide, she put both in her bag. Amara continued her obsession with everything Harry Potter. Laughter rang out from Amara's room, 'come here, look! Izzy wants to take Rocco on holiday too!' Verna, Leo and Marco arrived and joined in the hilarity as Izzy had put Rocco inside Leo's large backpack and zipped it up so far that only his head was poking out. Rocco sat patiently looking around, eyebrows raised, wondering what the fuss was all about, he was quite comfy, thank you very much.

Amara helped Izzy pack, Leo and Verna heard her reading from the list she made; 'toothbrush, clean knickers, vest, pyjamas, and don't forget Peppa Pig blankie.' For children used to travelling abroad to exclusive family resorts, their children had adjusted well to new experiences, no matter how small. It was 1.30 p.m. but as the girls were so eager to go to Joyce and Nigel's, they left with her after she popped in to check they were still coming for a sleepover.

'It's fine,' Joyce had insisted to the girls' parents with Izzy on her knee and Amara snuggled into her, 'we've got plenty to keep them occupied.' So off they went.

Verna knocked for Marco, no answer. She slid into his bedroom, 'you okay if me and dad pop out for a drive? The girls are already at Joyce's. If you need anything, call me or pop next door.'

'Okay.' Marco acknowledged, not turning from his screen. Before Verna closed the door he spun around with a pleading look. 'Can we have takeaway if they're out of the way?' She smiled and nodded, then heard, 'Yass!' as she closed the door.

'Let's go for a walk.' Leo was a little startled to see Verna holding Rocco's dog lead in her hand. It would be less than two hours until twilight. He assumed Verna would be locked away working upstairs, and he had settled down to an afternoon watching television.

'Sure, yes great!' he was thrilled with the minuscule attention she was offering, though with trepidation. Verna drove to one of their favourite walks around the lake. There were few people around, mostly returning from a wintery walk. The bare trees, the frosted water and icy breeze reflected Leo's desolate mood.

'We need to talk, or at least you do,' Verna stated.

Leo held his gaze focusing on Rocco's tottering, bouncing behind on the path ahead. 'I know.'

'I'm not stupid Leo. I know something happened in Italy you haven't told me about. Did you have an affair?' Verna stopped in her tracks.

Leo's momentum took him a few steps further. He turned and looked into Verna's deep blue eyes, reflected in the sharp cold air all around.

'Leo, I'm going to try and stay calm, but you have to tell me. Do not mess me about.' She looked resolute. He couldn't hide now, not now, not here in the bleak expanse surrounding them. She walked ahead, shivering against the diminishing temperature. He instinctively moved to put his arm around her, but her mood was like the weather, icy and unrelenting, so he resisted.

'Okay,' he took a deep breath unsure where to start, and decided to start at the end. 'I was badly beaten up. I didn't fall in the bathroom.' The silence told him to continue. 'I was beaten by two men who are relatives of, a woman … a woman I was having an affair with.' He turned to her, waiting for a response. There was nothing. 'I told her, it was over and she got her brother and cousin to come to the apartment and beat me up. I thought I was going to die, it was horrific.' He looked at her again. Still no reaction. 'Verna, I'm lost here. No idea what you want me to tell you?'

'Everything.'

They walked, boots crunching along the path with each step as dusk descended. Leo told Verna about Graziella, missing the vital information he was terrified of saying aloud. Confession was a relief, but the consequences were frightening. 'She turned up at Newcastle Airport the night I said I had to work at the apartment. I am so ashamed of what I've done, and I don't deserve you or the children. I had to return to Italy with her, to tell her it was over, so I could come home, for good.' Leo's tears came thick and fast. He observed Verna's blank expression, once his emotions had subsided. What was she thinking?

'Who was Juliette or was it, Julianne?'

Leo stopped in his tracks. 'What?' He could not believe what she said.

'You heard.'

Gob-smacked, he realised there was no point lying, but found it difficult to speak. How on earth did she know?

Verna remained silent.

'Oh god Verna, I won't lie anymore.' He looked skyward; his insides were churning like a washing machine on spin. 'I had an affair with her a few years ago.'

'How many women Leo?' Verna's eyes remained downcast.

There was no point fabricating an answer in an attempt at damage limitation. Barely audible, he said, 'a few.'

'Anything else you need to tell me?'

Leo's mind whirled. Bloody hell does she know about the baby! How could she? He had only now received the legal information himself. The familiar firework went off inside his head. There was someone or something along the track in the black gnarled branches of the trees ahead. Spindly hands were reaching out toward him. His deepest familiar fears encompassed him, as terror filled his eyes, he couldn't move or speak.

Verna recognised from Leo's vacant stare he was on overload and lost inside his mind. It reminded her of the night sitting in the garden prior to his psychotic episode. There was no point forcing him down the anxiety path, it would get her nowhere and she needed him to function for the children's sake. 'Hey, it's okay, let's head back.' She handed Rocco's lead to him, encouraging him to call for the dog. Verna had learnt how to distract Leo and give him a physical task when he drifted into scary virtual headspace.

Verna was in control, striding to the car, she thought, he hasn't even got the balls to tell me the truth. She was thinking clearly. He had omitted the fact he'd lied to Graziella about being divorced and hadn't mentioned Gabriel. There was no empathy for Leo at all. Her ability to close down emotionally, and deal with the disappointment she'd been on the receiving end her whole life, had served her well. Through gritted teeth from anger and frozen air, but trying to stay calm, Verna said, 'I'll explain what's going to happen. You will remain in the spare bedroom and continue to care for our children while I build up my business. For now, it must appear things are fine between us for the children until after Christmas. If you choose to leave any time after then, you are free to do so.'

Leo seemed to have returned to the present. She heard his words imploring her he'd do anything to try and work it out; saying how much he loved her and how much he hated himself; he wanted the chance to change and save their marriage. It was likely from her neutral-expression, Leo knew exactly where he stood.

Verna had stopped listening as her mind was racing. She was internally incandescent! It took all of her restraint not to shove the lying bastard down the embankment to plummet into the glacial water. However, she must stick to her plan in securing hers and the children's financial future by keeping dialogue open. She needed him to continue caring for the children, to keep the family stable until she could execute her plan for freedom, ultimately, she didn't care what happened to him. The icy air followed them into the car, Verna did not speak to him on the journey home. She decided to keep the knowledge of Gabriel to herself for now and wondered if Leo knew he had a son in Italy, and whether he cared.

33

Lockdown was reintroduced and the weekly bubble sleepovers at Joyce and Nigel's ended. The girls were bored; being home-schooled again wasn't helping. Amara and Izzy wanted to go Christmas shopping with Verna, she wasn't too thrilled about the shopping trip as it wasn't straightforward negotiating two lively, excited children within Covid restrictions. However, Verna realised she'd been absent with Leo providing the childcare while she was busy building up her business portfolio.

'You two must be on you best behaviour,' she said to the eager little faces looking up at her and nodding. It had taken half an hour for them to decide what outfits they wanted to wear. 'Poor little things, getting excited about going shopping,' she said to Leo, who's gaming day with Marco was planned. She always engaged in child-related conversations with him. 'I'll take them for a browse around the clothing section; they can buy a few small treats, a bag and hair trinkets. Gone are the days when I could give them anything their little hearts desired.' She aimed verbal punishment at Leo, she couldn't help it, this time it was to the back of his head. He did not acknowledge her statement, but she knew he would be feeling hurt inside, however it paled in comparison to her own pain.

As she arrived in the superstore car park, Verna spotted a great-looking guy walking towards a new dark-blue sporty Ford Puma several bays along. He wore a maroon crew neck fitted sweater with a dark grey body warmer, black jeans and expensive-looking sports boots. His tousled dark hair reached his jawline, and as he tucked one side behind his ear and turned his face, he briefly caught sight of her looking at him from her driver's seat. She looked away, a little embarrassed. Two teenage boys and a woman followed. The woman had shoulder length, thick straightened dark hair, swept to one side. She wore a colourful top in a distinctive ethnic print, under a fitted longline jacket, indigo slim jeans and the most amazing strappy biker boots. She looked casual and classy, she resembled Hannah.

Verna's eyes flicked to the boys. My god that's Evan and Ross, and … Hannah! Verna had a million thoughts at the vision in front of her and wanted to call out her name. Hannah looked fantastic; her subtly highlighted longer hair looked great. She must be wearing contacts, not those awful jam-jar bottom glasses, Verna thought with a broad smile on her face. So, that's her new man, handsome in a rustic way, definitely Hannah's type. Verna smiled warmly, her heart was skipping beats, as she became aware she looked, and felt, like a downtrodden bag-lady, her gaze lowered to her dog-hair covered jeggings and dried-in muddy walking boots, she was so distracted she hadn't changed them. 'You look great Hannah Kay, and happy,' she whispered towards the content family getting into their car. The wallowing despair hit again as Izzy and Amara began whinging and arguing. Fiddling around to find her mask, she let them out of the car. She stood in front of them admonishing the girls saying they wouldn't get any treats unless they behaved. Verna was on a short fuse these days, she didn't see the Ford Puma pass by her.

'Look over there H, she looks a bit like your friend in the photo, is it her?'

Hannah looked in the direction Cam indicated. A fleeting view of Verna guiding her girls out of the car appeared, she was admonishing them, and did not look happy. Hair scraped back, no make-up, how unusual, she looked tired and sort of hunched with an absence of her usual elegant poise. 'Not sure, it may have been.' Hannah did not want Cam to stop the car and insist they reconciled in the car park. As they drove away, she looked in the wing mirror, Verna was striding towards the store, with the girls tottering behind.

Verna and the girls arrived home, with excitement they showed Leo their purchases. He let them drape their new bags around him and put bejewelled slides in his hair. He was a lovely father, Verna acknowledged this, but her positive thoughts inevitably strayed to distaste. Could they ever come back from this, she remembered Joyce's advice; *"think long and hard about what you want for you and your family. You will know the right decision when it comes to you."*

Her curiosity about Hannah got the better of her. 'You ok to see to supper Leo? I need to do a little more research for the business.'

'Only if they behave.' He wagged a finger to them and they snuggled down into him. They loved their dad so much.

Verna accessed and scrolled Hannah's social media pages, a little voyeuristic for her. There were a few recent posts of her, Cam and the boys. My they were growing up, she thought, and Evan's light grey-blue eyes were exactly like Hannah's, she and Cam made a handsome couple. There was a post from some months ago announcing Hannah was leaving BlueSea Graphics to go solo, with a link to her website, *HK Creative*. Verna read her web pages. It was creative indeed, with a funky, contemporary user-friendly website, which Verna guessed her brother Grant would've set up. Her winning bid for Riverside Quays was featured with pictures of her looking radiant, professional and streamlined in a charcoal grey suit and wearing heels, Hannah never wore heels! Verna scrutinised a close-up shot showing her subtly made-up face, manicured nails and sleek hair. The top she wore brought out the colour in her eyes. Verna looked into those eyes, she missed her so much.

Verna wondered if Hannah would design her own business theme, then thought she may not be interested given the high-profile organisations she was now working with. 'You really missed out on a true talent Leo, to impress some young totty, you stupid, stupid man.' Verna often spoke to her husband, in his absence, the words floated away in thin air. Verna wished she had taken the opportunity to approach Hannah at the supermarket. A simple acknowledgement would have been enough. She determined at that moment, she would make contact with Hannah, but she did not know how, or when.

34

Cam, November 2020

A big snowball of white fluff flew into Cam's arms. Sara squealed at the sight of him. She wore her furry winter-white coat, red sparkly woollen hat and mittens and multi-coloured unicorn wellingtons. Cam surreptitiously handed his car keys to Niall, to transfer Sara's Christmas gifts out of his car boot to theirs while Sara was distracted. Julia and Niall brought Sara to the park at the halfway point rendezvous between Newcastle and Leeds for a Christmas cuddle with her dad. They found a picnic bench by the riverside to sit, and the smell of soaked wood, the dark grey clouds above, and sodden grass underfoot indicated they wouldn't be out for long in the cold drizzle.

'Really appreciate you doing this Julia. I would drive all the way down, it's no problem,' said Cam.

'It's fine, Niall likes a drive out and it's handy for getting Melody to sleep, she's horrendous!' She beamed lovingly at the bundled-up nine-month-old baby in the buggy who was starting to wail, 'always hungry, with … an assertive personality let's say.'

Cam laughed and peeped over the covers to see her. 'She's a cutie, even when she's screaming. Seems like yesterday when Sara was so small, she was as good as gold wasn't she?'

'She was … and still is.'

'I'll walk her, she may drop off? Could do with moving around, it's a bit nippy,' said Niall as he walked away pushing the screaming infant in the buggy.

'What's up poppet?' Julia asked Sara as she leant into her.

Sara turned to Cam. 'Daddy, the lady, erm …' putting a delicate finger on her lips and looked upwards scanning her memory.

'Hannah.'

'Yes! She's nice.'

'She is.'

With a coy look. 'Are you going to get married?'

'If she'll have me, maybe.'

'Will you have a big wedding?'

Sara climbed up on Cam's knee. Julia and Cam glanced at each other knowing exactly where this was going. Cam tucked her into his coat and shielded her from the weather. He never tired of soaking in her perfect, flawless skin, looking into her big brown eyes and today, stroking her rosy plump cheeks.

'Maybe, why do you want to know that little miss?'

Sara whispered in his ear, 'you'll need a bridesmaid.' She turned his face directly to hers and held it firmly within centimetres, nodding with a serious expression. He caught the scent of chocolate on her warm breaths from the novelty reindeer treat he'd brought for her, which she devoured in an instant.

He whispered back, 'if we do get married, you will definitely be a bridesmaid.'

Sara jumped off his knee and spun around, clapping and bouncing like a dandelion clock in her fluffed-up coat.

'She's desperate to be a bridesmaid, goodness knows where it's come from. As you know I don't do marriage, happy in a partnership, weddings are never mentioned,' Julia suggested, 'it's all the princess stuff they're fed on TV.' After a pause, 'do you think you and Hannah will marry? She seems really cool, I like her.'

'I may pluck up the courage to ask her soon. She's lovely, so thoughtful, gone right over the top with choosing Christmas gifts for Sara and got a little something for Melody too.'

Julia looked crestfallen, 'oh no, I haven't got anything for her boys.'

'Hey, no worries.'

Julia fiddled for her backpack to give Cam some money to get Evan and Ross a gift, which he refused. Julia didn't work and Niall was furloughed, and not sure if his job would be reinstated.

'Listen why don't I get them something from Sara? A massive selection box or whatever would be sweet. I don't want to set a precedent Julia, honestly if Sara wants to, she can make birthday cards for them, and we'll sort a small Christmas gift every year for her big step-brothers. Actually, that sounds quite cute, doesn't it?'

'Yeah, it does,' her smile waned, 'here's the Tasmanian

Devil.' Melody had finally gone to sleep, and Julia wanted to transfer her to the car so she'd have a good sleep on the way home.

Cam grabbed Sara, had a never-ending cuddle, told her he missed her and would ring on Christmas Day to check Father Christmas had been, then grinned as she put her hands on her hips. 'Of course he'll come to my house Daddy!' They parted and he returned home, considering if he would propose to Hannah.

Hannah was Christmas shopping while Cam was seeing Sara. The supermarket shelf held a vast array of bright festive boxes of chocolate truffles. Hannah glared at them. After her pathetic attempt to appease Verna, she was finally getting the hang of shopping with a discerning eye, selecting items to please, but not max-out on spending. Ironically, Hannah could now afford to be more generous, realising her gift-giving psyche was over-compensation for her perceived inadequacies. It was difficult to buy anything for Cam; he would say he had everything in life he needs, 'me, of course,' she said to herself and believed it. Masks and two metres distancing were handy for making surreptitious comments in public.

Crossing between the end of the aisles, there was Verna! There was no mistaking her luxuriant blonde hair scraped into a pony tail, with Amara and Izzy trailing behind. Hannah instinctively looked away before she was spotted, and wondered if she should hide, or stalk her at a safe distance. What would she say if they met? Verna wouldn't be rude, but if she blanked her, it would be hurtful. Hannah stood calmly waiting for the right words to appear. She rehearsed if their eyes meet and a flicker of recognition was held, then maybe she'd speak. Even in a mask you could tell if eyes were smiling. Hannah realised she missed the girls and Marco too. Amara was growing and looked the image of Leo, whilst Izzy was Verna's double.

Hannah became aware of other shoppers glaring at her standing in the middle of the aisle as they tutted, skirting around her to maintain two metres distance. She decided to continue shopping and would acknowledge Verna if they met. She had the advantage knowing Verna was in the store, unless, Verna had seen her first and was avoiding her. As Hannah approached the checkout, she spotted Verna leaving. She was bending over Izzy, holding her hand, and looking frustrated. Amara seemed, quiet, it wasn't a harmonious scene. Hannah was disappointed in herself, an impromptu meeting could have been an easy way for them to reconnect.

Later Hannah regretted not taking the opportunity to approach Verna at the supermarket. A simple acknowledgement would have been enough. She determined in that moment, she would make contact with Verna, but she did not know how or when.

On 24 November the government announced, three households could socialise over a five-day period between 23 and 27 December, but they could not mix with anyone outside of their social bubble. There were many television broadcasts and radio phone-ins from thousands of people asking a variety of questions whether their particular circumstances met the guidelines, which were vague and confusing. One caller suggested, *"this is a load of crap, written on the back of a fag packet, they haven't a clue what the f–"* the call was cut off.

The Kay family were struggling with the Christmas conundrum, so Hannah and Ellie agreed to make things simple, they would not visit their parents over Christmas. Heart-breaking though it was, it was the right thing to do. They arranged, weather permitting, a wave-at-the-window gift exchange. Their elder brother Jake and wife Megan would go on Christmas Day with their four children and partners, whilst younger brother Grant and his partner Shona would stay away and hopefully comply.

'The fewer people who mix the better,' said Ellie, 'I hope Grant doesn't turn up with their laissez-faire approach to lockdown as mam will let him in the house. I don't understand how they don't get it. They could easily pass on the virus to mam and dad who could become quite ill.'

Hannah agreed, 'hate seeing their desperate faces waving at the front door when their house would usually be bursting at the seams. I'm okay with keeping a distance, but some people's attitude infuriates me.' Hannah sighed. 'At least when it's all over we'll know we were part of the solution, rather than part of the problem.'

By the 19 December, an announcement was made scaling activity back to 25 December only, for temporary Christmas social bubbles. It was incredibly complicated and disappointing. Many people had booked travel and families were preparing their homes, having bought gifts and shopped for planned menus to welcome guests for the festive period. In the Kay-Wallace household, Christmas Day went well, Evan and Ross were on top form, they were getting along famously, and Ross was learning how to banter back to Evan to fend off, big brother bullying, tactics. He had a keen mentor in Cam who would feed Ross lines of retort, he was a good student in the art of sarcasm. The family had dropped off gifts days earlier to Cam's comment, 'it must cost you Kays a fortune for Christmas and birthdays.'

Hannah explained. 'We worked out a long time ago setting a strict modest limit on gifts was how we would do family celebrations and only give gifts up to age twenty-one for all the children, then a cash donation towards a night out is usually most welcome.' She smiled, 'it mystifies me how our parents manage to buy each child and grandchild a gift, they must save out of their pensions all year round.'

Hannah was enjoying a mulled cider, whilst Cam was a little melancholy, 'it was so lovely seeing Sara open her gifts today, shame it has to be online, can't wait for all this to be over so she can be here. Things aren't getting any better are they?'

Hannah added, 'I can't bear watching the news. God knows how health and essential workers are coping. There's going to be some real mental health issues in the future from the trauma people have experienced.'

'I'm glad everyone has stayed healthy,' said Cam. 'I worry like hell about my dad and the heart thing. I think it's in the family, the men die young.'

'Better get you checked out then, don't want you dropping down dead on me. We've only been together a year!

D'you remember, The Bridges Bar, Saturday 19 December last year?'

'I won't drop dead, promise, and of course I remember. We'll go there next year for our anniversary.' Cam kissed Hannah as they lounged on the sofa. 'Speaking of the wonderful Sara, she asked me a question ... if we got married, could she be our bridesmaid, apparently she's desperate to be one.'

'Well, in that case, we better had.' Hannah looked at Cam's satisfied smile.

'I will if you will H.'

'Why not?' she grinned, they hugged and nearly tumbled off the sofa.

'I've got the distinct impression I'm a bit drunk, are you?' asked Hannah.

'Yes, I've got the distinct impression you are drunk. But me?' shaking his head, 'no ... no, not a jot.' Cam got up to get more drinks, tripped walking into the kitchen, and knocked the oven dish of left-over stuffing onto the floor. 'Good job your stuffing is rock hard, otherwise it would've been all over the place,' he laughed.

'Cam!' Hannah yelled.

He popped his head around the door, 'yea?'

'Get stuffed!'

On Boxing Day, Hannah woke with a hangover. Mixed tones of man and boy voices drifted upstairs, as Hannah snuggled into cosy Christmas bedding, hugging Cam's pillow. His masculine scent alerted her pulsating hormones, and she hoped he'd come back into bed. Then, as she lifted her head, realised it wouldn't be a good idea as she was incredibly shabby indeed. Hannah flopped in smug contentment, she had a lot to be grateful for; everyone had remained healthy this year, she and Cam had broached the subject of marriage, and buying a bigger house together, she was excited to have Sara for sleepovers, her boys got along great with Cam and they were doing okay, despite these strange times. Hannah ran her fingers through her hair, then swept her arms and legs wide in a starfish pandiculation, thinking about her amazing future work prospects too. It was one of the most chilled Christmases she'd ever had. Despite the pandemic horrors and her pounding headache, Hannah's life was good.

35

Hannah, January 2021
Evan caught Alisha looking at him on the last few occasions they had passed in the school corridor months ago, they held each other's gaze. Alisha had the most amazing dark brown eyes, cute dimples and full lips. He imagined kissing her. Evan had never kissed a girl, he hadn't had the opportunity, and wondered how it felt, and how to do it properly. He hadn't noticed girls' hairstyles either, but Alisha's shone like a curtain of glossy black silk threads. She reminded him of the exotic characters he used to watch in Disney movies when he was young. In his eyes, she was perfectly beautiful. He always glanced around to see if she was anywhere in sight when leaving classrooms or entering communal areas.

It was 8 January 2021 and Evan's long-awaited return to school was finally here. He looked at his reflection and loosened his school tie, he needed to look relaxed and nonchalant. It was only a few days ago when Ross yelled his daily, *"Cyclops!"* insult at him regarding the, thankfully disappearing, huge zit in the middle of his forehead. Evan went to slap his kid brother, who ran downstairs to his mother's sanctuary. Hannah admonished Ross for the insults, as he flashed another, got-away-with-it, smirk to his furious older brother following behind.

Evan was about to add a little more wax to his thick brown hair, but didn't want it looking too polished. He needed to keep the nonchalance theme going. He tousled it up, smiled at his reflection, said, 'Harry Styles,' and happily left to meet his friends to walk to school. He was disappointed he didn't see Alisha all day when he returned home.

'Evan,' Hannah said the instant he was home. He poked his head into the kitchen where she broke the confirmatory news, 'sweetheart, I think schools are closing again, so sorry.'

'What! When? Why?'

'Immediately, because of the spread—'

'For fucks sake!' Evan darted upstairs. 'What the hell are they playing at?' Hannah gently rebuffed him for swearing, but totally appreciated his frustration. Ross grinned at his brother being told off. Evan was raging as he clashed around his room, mixed with sounds of a young man crying, Hannah was upset, and shed a few tears in anger herself. Her boy, ripe for teenage angst, was starting to struggle with the uncertainty and life disruption.

'What's up?' asked Cam nodding towards the ceiling resonating with bumps and bangs as he sat catching up on social media. He didn't expect the ensuing rant from Hannah, and with an expression of mild shock, placed his phone down on the coffee table, moving the hot coffees out of the way from Hannah's swiping reach.

'Young people in this pandemic have been hit so hard with constant changes. That bloody algorithm exam fiasco was disgraceful, now this, opening schools because they're safe, apparently one day, then closing them the next for fucks sake!'

'What about the online guitar lessons?' suggested Cam using any words he could conjure up to calm Hannah, then quickly, 'not the same as seeing your mates of course, but it may distract him.'

Hannah nodded, 'I'll check out the list of tutors again, but best to wait until he's more receptive. He'll dismiss anything I suggest while he's in this bloody awful mood.'

Ross sniggered at his mam swearing, and sat back with hands behind his head, elbows raised, in smug satisfaction, he was delighted school had closed again. Cam realised Ross was itching to have a pop at Evan being in a foul mood, he explained to Ross firmly, it was definitely not the right time to poke the bear.

The next day Hannah called Ellie, when her face appeared she asked, 'are you having mood swings? I worry so much about the demise of bees, then within minutes I am astounded astronauts on the space station are growing plants. I'm following, Earthwatch and NASA online because it gives me hope for humanity.'

An unusually subdued Ellie agreed. 'I can't take much more of it. Over 120,000 people have died and that's, ironically, a conservative estimate. So many people, no longer here, it sometimes feels like the world is coming to an end. I can't bear watching the news, but feel guilty as if I'm ignoring the devastation.'

'I know,' Hannah was downbeat, 'takes so much energy to manage your feelings, January is so dark and dreary, it's a crap month at the best of times. I haven't crossed the doors for days, don't feel like going anywhere. Poor Evan is devastated about school closing again, he's gone into a real funk and won't come out of his room. Cam does his best to engage him and I've offered to get guitar lessons online, but we can't seem to encourage him with anything. I do worry about young men and their mental health. His fifteenth birthday must've been such a let-down at home, no friends, just us and takeaway.'

'Poor Evan,' said Ellie, 'not surprising Geoff is busier than ever the way mental health cases are skyrocketing. At least there's this,' Ellie splayed her hands, 'we're lucky to live in an age of online communication. Can you imagine if this pandemic occurred when we were teenagers? All four kids stuck in the tiny house with our parents with no Internet, no online games, no decent telly or streaming sites, it would be dreadful, we would've killed each other!'

'But think of the hours of fun playing Kerplunk and Buckaroo,' added Hannah.

Ellie laughed. 'Seriously though, I hope this latest, roadmap out of lockdown or whatever it is, doesn't have politicians debating whether scotch eggs are a substantial meal on national TV, or confusing tiers no-one can get their head around. Christ on a bike, piss up and brewery comes to mind. It's a real worry about our parents, they aren't doing well after the dreadful let-down of the Christmas gatherings fiasco.'

It would be over two months until Evan returned to school. He happily braced himself against the blustery March wind and joined several of his school-mates for, yet another, first day back at school. Hannah watched him leave the house, he was growing up too quickly, at fifteen turning into a young man. Surely it had only been five minutes since she was hurrying her sons to get ready for school, now delighting in the memory that little children never walk in a straight line, and her boys loved to wear their superhero outfits wherever they went.

Evan was messing around joking with some mates in the expansive computer room during the afternoon break. All gathered around a few spaced-apart consoles, when Alisha and two girls walked in. She sat in Evan's eye-line and flicked a glance at him before looking away. Evan did not want his friends to notice as he couldn't bear the thought of them showing him up in front of her. Days went by and Evan lost sight of Alisha, he panicked in case she had left or something. He couldn't get her out of his head, day or night, then miraculously she entered the computer room ahead of him. He craned to see if her friends were walking ahead … no, she was alone.

What does he do, what does his say? Everything he rehearsed in his wildest imaginations of such a scenario sounded creepy, not brilliant as he hoped, in his head. As Alisha placed her bag on a desk, he wondered, should he sit beside her … or opposite … now that would be creepy. There were few people around and Alisha, like him was clearly doing some extra work during the break. He would sit at an angle a few desks away, that would be okay. Evan could feel his neck and face flushing, his hair was a bit greasy today, but no spots had erupted recently ... good!

Nonchalantly he swung his bag onto a desk diagonally a few rows away, well within Alisha's peripheral vision. She was intent on the screen. Evan stared at her, she was gorgeous, in fact, perfect. Shit, if she looked up and caught him ogling, she'd think he was a weirdo. What if she thought he had followed her? He was panicking a little, hoping no one else would bundle into the room and disrupt the atmosphere. He knew his voice would sound stupid, especially if it cracked half way through a sentence, but he had to take a chance. Alisha always smiled at him, though maybe she was simply being polite.

Evan cautiously kept darting his eyes across to her location, enough to catch her eye if she looked up. Deep in thought, Alisha's gaze lifted, Evan took a chance and lifted up his bag, faking looking for something, to distract her stare. It worked; she looked directly over to him as he turned his face toward her.

They both smiled. 'Hi,' said Evan.

'Hi,' replied Alisha, 'quiet in here for a change.'

'Yeh,' what the hell does he say next, 'just catching up on homework and stuff.' Inwardly thinking, stupid, stupid, stupid! Why can't I think of anything more interesting?

'Me too, I—'

A loud rumble interrupted Alisha's flow. It was Evan's mates. Harvey was yelling, 'c'mon Evo, you not coming to footy practice? Been waiting ages?'

His response of ... 'err, yeah, just, you know, working hard here,' was met with jeers and taunts. He gathered his belongings and could see Alisha was smiling at the interaction. As he lifted his bag onto his shoulder, his mates were leaving the room, a couple of the less responsible ones pushed and shoved, trying to trip each other up, with little regard for distancing. Evan deliberately walked in front of her desk, with a smile and a low, 'see you around.'

'Yes, sure,' she replied, looking up at him with those heavenly dark brown eyes. Close up, Alisha was even more beautiful, she looked great with her black braided hair, swept over on one side. Evan felt a connection deep inside his chest, a lovely secret between them. He couldn't wait to see her again.

36

Verna, December 2020

Restrictions were having a detrimental effect upon many families, the Kent variant of the virus, meant no-one was travelling in or out of South east England, which remained in the highest band, Tier Four, total lockdown. Joyce and Nigel were bereft. They were to have their son's family travel from London. Between sobs, Joyce explained to Verna she wouldn't now see her grandchildren, hadn't seen them for months, and they were so looking forward to time with their family. They were utterly devastated.

'They haven't a clue what they're doing, the bloody imbeciles.' Joyce never swore! 'Why the hell did he say families could visit, then do a U-turn and pull the plug. We've bought all the food, I took an age decorating the tree, we've prepared the whole house. They knew about the variant before now. I'm so ... f, fu ... flipping angry!' her face flushed and tears spilled.

Verna had never seen the usually gentle, calm Joyce so upset, and genuinely thought she was going to blurt out crude expletives. She calmed when a large gin and tonic was handed to her.

'It's small consolation, but of course you're welcome here for Christmas Day.' Verna had a moment of inspiration. 'We have a large screen monitor, and Marco will set it up so you can connect to your family online if you like.'

'Oh, that would be lovely Verna, thank you. We do computer-call the children, but only on a small screen, and we're always cutting them off.' She smiled meekly, 'they do laugh at our attempts with technology. We had such lovely gatherings with them over the summer.' Joyce became visibly upset again.

'I only wish I'd thought about it beforehand Joyce you could've done calls from here anytime. From now on, we'll set up regular sessions as we don't know how long this lockdown is going to be. Verna had slight misgivings about promising Marco would give up his screen-time too frequently, however she'd work something out. Verna hugged Joyce. The women had developed a deep, mutual understanding and although there was an age-gap, their friendship was solid.

Verna's relationship with Leo was necessary, if distant and platonic, she could bear to be close to him briefly, and let him take her hand, only when the children were around for show, releasing the hold to his resistance at the earliest opportunity. She avoided physical contact with him, and the children hadn't seemed to pick up on anything, though Verna was highly attuned if Marco showed signs of curiosity. The children were simply pleased to be together as a family, and she wasn't going to allow the illusion to snap away in an instant.

Christmas was simplicity itself, for the Ravassio family, as they weren't going anywhere, their annual family jaunt to Lapland was never going to happen. An online gathering on Christmas Eve with Verna's brother, Simon's family had gone well, as the children excitedly chatted about their expectations of Christmas morning, which seemed to take an age to arrive. The girls opened their gifts with enthusiasm, and Marco maturely understood money wasn't as abundant, and had stated, *"a few new games would be good."* Rocco in his Christmas collar was diving into discarded wrapping and yelping with delight. Verna made a pact with Leo, they wouldn't buy each other anything, and was amused as he was totally taken aback, she usually loved expensive gifts. She impressed upon him they had to be more economical. A token gift was exchanged to make it seem normal to the children.

Joyce was hilarious, she was a little tipsy and the girls hooted with laughter at her attempts to copy their flossing dance. Marco set Nigel and Joyce up online and the Ravassios introduced themselves to the extended family, then left the pair to enjoy some private time. They were online for ages; Marco had to intervene and re-connect when Joyce, or Nigel inadvertently cut them off three times. Verna enjoyed their laughter and considered how Joyce and Nigel had made their marriage work, after troublesome years. Maybe there had been hope for her and Leo over his affair, and life could've been perfect again, if it wasn't for his bastard child.

Verna had a few drinks, and dwelled with sorrowful grief for her previous life. Anything now would be second best. Her marriage was over and the strain of living under the same roof with Leo was tough. She was upstairs in the ensuite, looking into her face in the mirror and quietly fumed, 'you lying, fucking stupid arsehole Leo. You had everything and you've wrecked it all.' Nigel and Joyce emerged from Marco's room after their family call and headed downstairs. Verna rallied, she refreshed her make up, held her shoulders back, put on her practiced smile and went downstairs.

37

Weeks flew by following Christmas, until two months had passed. The Ravassios were busy as the children prepared for another return to school. Leo continued his main parental role, whilst Verna diligently pursued more accountancy contracts, she rarely left her office-bedroom. Leo was accepting of their situation, a loveless marriage, expediting daily domestic routines, and Verna's distinct detachment from him. Knowing the break had to come soon, Verna endeavoured to be as prepared as possible.

In early March, she called her brother Simon, his face, illuminated by warm light, appeared on Verna's screen. A picture of health and happiness, he said, 'Hi Verna, early start?'

'Always is,' she smiled into the screen, 'but I needed a chat with my big brother with no interruptions, how's life treating you?'

'All fine here thank goodness, and you're as beautiful as ever. You should pay us a visit, the south coast is the warmer end of the country, bet it's still freezing up North. Don't know how many times I've suggested it, but you were always jetting off somewhere exotic. The kids would love it here, and the new place is big enough to accommodate you all.'

'Don't tempt me.'

They spoke about the children, about their lives in general, it was so lovely for Verna to welcome his joy into her life.

'How's our mother, no better I guess? Bet you've not heard from dad, I get the occasional message, but that's it.' Simon paused. 'You ok sis, you seem … a little down?'

'I'll be honest Simon there's stuff going on here with Leo and his business. Things are a mess.' She glanced at the door to ensure it was firmly closed.

'Hey, I've got time now, tell me all about it, I don't like seeing you like this.'

Verna was grateful for the opportunity to offload to Simon. She offered up an overview of Leo's illness and referred to his affair, she kept it singular, minimising the fact he probably had several and no mention of a baby.

'Though I want to come up there and punch his lights out, it's not helpful for you. Come and visit us,' he urged, 'seems you need a break and we can talk things through. It's about time the six cousins had some fun together too, and I think restrictions will have eased by the spring break maybe.'

Verna chewed on her lip, obviously considering his suggestion, 'know what Si … think I'll take you up on your offer. You're right, I need some time out and the kids could do with some fun. But it's, well … the money.'

'No worries, I'll sort it, and we won't discuss it after this convo, ever, okay?'

'You're a star.'

'Well, I know that sis, pfft! Let me know whenever you're ready and it'll be done.'

After the call, Verna gave out a huge satisfying sigh and smiled. She thought about the image of her brother looking healthy and relaxed sitting in the glow of light around him in the brighter south coast weather. She wanted to be there with him, the only close family she could connect with. Verna looked forward to bathing in a wonderful warm atmosphere with happy people. It would be an experience full of love and laughter, and she could leave thoughts of Leo far behind her, only a few weeks to go, first she had to persevere with Leo.

After weeks of perseverance Verna suggested she and Leo took a walk whilst the children were in school, she was ready for the crushing conversations. Leo recognised the prompt really meant; we need to talk. He obediently grabbed Rocco's lead, who bounded joyfully in anticipation at the sound, and the pair patiently waited for Verna at the door to embark on a bright spring walk around the lake.

'I'm taking the children away,' announced Verna, shaking Leo from his pensive state. 'We're staying with Si for a couple of weeks.' They took their routine walk around the lake, where they often discussed their uncertain future, more precarious than Leo thought.

Leo said, 'I've been in touch with a company I worked with years ago, to see if there are any contracts I could pick up,' he waited for Verna's response. Although communication had eased into respectful dialogue, Leo bit his lip, anxious every time he made any suggestions. 'I'll take it, you're okay with me making enquiries.'

Verna shrugged. 'Anything that brings money into this family is fine by me.' With a derisory stare, dark blue eyes sparkling, 'anything to get out of the mess we're in. I'll be in Bournemouth with Si's family for a couple of weeks, do what you want. I'll clear the extended absence at spring week with school. They can fine me if they like, I need this trip.' Leo's expression indicated he was astonished she was straying outside the rules, due to her former attitude towards parents who remove their children during term time. She smirked, she had changed, so had he. Everything had. They discussed the practicalities of timing and conjured up a reason to tell the children why Leo would not travel with them.

'Tell them you have some new work lined up, or … we need someone to look after Rocco, whatever, make it plausible.' There was a flat disinterested tone whenever Verna spoke to him, unless the children were around.

'You're good at putting on an act, aren't you?' Leo questioned.

'What's that supposed to mean?'

'The pretence, everything is okay when the children or Joyce and Nigel, are around.'

'If I said what I really think, or expressed how I felt inside, I'd end up on a mental ward too.' Verna spent each day suppressing hurt and anger. 'You have no idea Leo. None.' She walked ahead of him, quickening her pace. Turning back, she quipped, 'oh, and Si has offered to pay for our flights and other travel expenses; board and lodgings at his place is free obviously, and I'm sure he'll subsidise other outrageous costs for taking three children on holiday for two weeks.' She knew her words would pierce and deflate Leo's pride, but she meant it. The remainder of the walk was in uncomfortable silence, and they remained in stalemate.

During dinner, Verna announced the exciting news to the children, they were going to see Uncle Simon's family for a holiday. Amara leapt onto Leo's knee with a big hug, Izzy clapped and Marco said, 'wicked!' Verna looked intently at Leo.

'Okay, calm down, but I can't go I'm afraid guys. I've got some new work contracts coming up, so I have to stay here, and besides, who would look after Rocco?' he appealed.

Amara burst into tears, 'Joyce will take care of him, can't you work from Uncle Si's place Daddy, please!' Her anxiety separation from Leo was evident each time there was a hint they would be parted. Leo held her reassuringly, promising to chat online every day. Marco looked at Verna, there were questions in his eyes, were they staying together as a family? Both children sensed the disconnect between their parents, she was sure, maybe they observed the charades and lack of meaningful reassuring touches. The playful banter had left this family, and it was noticeable.

A few days passed, and the excitement of travelling to see their cousins softened the blow for Marco and Amara. Izzy was oblivious of any emotion and lived purely in the moment of each day. They had online calls between the families, which were exciting. Leo briefly engaged at the beginning of the first call, then Verna revealed she had told Simon about his affair, adding, 'but only the one, any more discretions would have been too humiliating. Si was keen to have a word with you, but I asked him not to ... yet.'

Marco was impressed with the eldest cousin, Connor, from their online contact. 'Hey Mum, Connor is into music and plays guitar, he's joined a band, says I can practice with them, it'll be so amazing.'

'I know son, he does look like a surfer dude with his long hair, rock band tees, and trendy shorts.'

'Surfer dude, trendy shorts? Don't you dare come out with anything like that when we visit.'

'Afraid I'm going to show you up or something?' Verna grabbed his shoulders and said to his face, 'that's what mothers do, it's allowed.'

Marco was taller than Verna by a few inches now, he screwed up his face, 'sssoo embarrassing.'

Verna noticed Leo's smile at the tenderness between them. It was Amara who worried them both. She had lost some of her sparkle. Approaching eleven-years-old, Verna questioned, was she simply emerging from playful childhood, and transitioning into the many changes preadolescence brings; or was she reacting to the underlying tension between her parents?

The holiday arrangements were made. Verna in no uncertain terms, advised school the children would be absent for an extra week at May spring bank holiday, and offered to pay whatever fines were necessary. She received mixed reactions from various teachers, some thinking it was a wonderful idea, to those who met her plans with disdain for her children to miss out on more education than the pandemic had inflicted. Either way, she was going, she was an exemplary parent with exemplary children, she'd supported their education, and deserved this one piece of freedom. Simon had booked their flights to Bournemouth. He was true to his word and never referred to cost.

The family bundled through Covid protocols at the airport after the one hour fifteen-minute flight. Izzy sat cross-legged on top of their suitcases on the luggage trolley. She insisted upon taking, and wearing Joyce's straw hat with bright red cherries around the headband. The hat was miles too big drooping over her eyes, but she refused to remove it. Amara was looking cute in her sports leggings, trainers, navy Harry Potter hoodie, emblazoned with sparkly silver stars and golden snitches. Marco had chosen the coolest jeans and T-shirt he owned. He kept pulling at the ends of his hair to stretch it as long as possible to be like Connor, and he'd missed a recent trip to the barbers. Once outside the airport building, the children leapt upon Uncle Si with exciting tales about the flight. Verna and Simon shared an extended hug, her relief was palpable in his reassuring arms. He soothed, 'hey sis, you're okay now, you're here.' She could have wept. She was relieved, tired and excited all rolled into one shell of a human being.

They settled quickly into Simon, and his husband Jeremy's extensive home. Teenagers Marco and Connor would sleep in the basement bedrooms, usually used as extra living space for guests, which also conveniently had an extra bathroom. There were four bedrooms and two bathrooms upstairs; Simon and Jeremy's room, Connor's large bedroom was adapted for the three girls; their middle child twelve-year-old Rose with Amara and Izzy, though Rose could use her own bedroom if she needed space. Nicky their seven-year-old son, remained in his own smaller Lego-filled bedroom.

The living space on the middle floor, was a huge open plan minimalist area with chunky L-shaped sofas, thick rugs, marshmallow-soft cushions and luxurious throws. It was a sensory and tactile area. A beautiful large studio photograph of the couple with their children adorned a side wall, along with beautiful wall art on the other walls. The dining area and kitchen covered the other half of the space leading out onto a large patio area and neat lawn, surrounded by mature trees.

An alcove leading into a little-used study off the main living area was converted to another bedroom for Verna. Jeremy had exquisite taste and had redecorated it in pastel shades, with beautiful bedding and accessories, including a tranquil carved Buddha in one corner. He said, 'it's the quietest place in the house. I thought you may appreciate a peaceful calming space.'

Verna replied, 'you know what you've done don't you?' to Jeremy's consternation, 'I'm not going to want to leave.' With a broad smile she hugged him.

The two families took a walk along the beautiful sea front after unpacking. They had ice-creams and ate al fresco at a family friendly pizzeria in the early evening. They were all exhausted after breathing in sea-air and a huge meal. Once the children had calmed, and settled for the night, the adults enjoyed gin cocktails, courtesy of Jeremy, or Uncle Jem, to his nephew and nieces. They enjoyed catching up, though it wasn't a late night, Verna was exhausted.

She woke in the morning to the different sounds and smells all around her. Her body was gently encased in the mattress which had a floaty quality as she stroked the smooth bedding. Rolling her head in super-soft pillows, she looked intently at Buddha in the fractured rays of sunlight streaming through the blinds, it gave her a feeling of serenity. She hadn't slept so well in months. Reluctantly rising and pulling on a zip hoodie over her pyjamas, she padded into the kitchen where Si was ready with a pot of fresh coffee. The children were all in the basement den, and the sound of their pleasing laughter and chatter rang out as they watched cartoons on the huge cinema-size television.

'They've all been fed and watered and promised a picnic on the beach today, it's going to be a warm one. We'll get there early to grab a spot, as it'll be busy.'

Verna sighed after a gulp of soothing coffee and swept her hand wide, 'what a wonderful life you have. I'm so happy for you, and as for Jeremy … he's simply delicious.'

'This has been a new lease of life for the children and us. You remember a bit about their background?'

'Yes, you explained the overview when they were adopted, so I would understand their responses. What gorgeous little humans they are … honestly Si, so beautiful inside and out.'

Si filled with pride said, 'they have their moments, when fear and insecurity creeps in. We have post adoption services here and they can access counselling if and when, but on the whole, doing great.'

At that moment, little Nicky came into the room with

slumped shoulders, and glistening sad eyes, as the big guys didn't want him in their space while playing guitar. Simon cradled him and said he would speak with the boys if they were mean to him. He also reminded Nicky how everyone should have time-out if they needed. Nicky cheered up when he was told he could choose something from the treat box, which he did, then sat on the patio clattering his big box of Lego out onto the play mat.

'I'll have a word with Marco, I'm not having him being rotten to the little one.' Verna reassured. 'He loves this lifestyle, it's going to be hard to get him home.'

'Won't he miss Leo?'

'They've lived with extended periods separated from Leo, so I don't think they really notice after a while, it's mostly been me and them.'

At this point, Connor and Marco appeared in a shock of luminous coloured swim shorts, revealing gangly legs ready for the beach. Verna caught Marco's eyes, made facial gestures to him and nodded towards little Nicky. Marco understood. 'You need your swim shorts on Nicky, c'mon hurry up!' Nicky instantly looked up with glee to run and put his swim shorts on, being gratefully accepted back into the big-guys club.

Minutes later, the girls emerged in swimsuits. Verna noticed Izzy's was on inside out. 'Our little dizzy Izzy is a one-off.' Verna said. Uncle Si read them the so-called riot act about safe beach behaviour, with the caveat of them immediately returning home if they didn't abide. The coastline was a fifteen-minute walk, he'd prepared every convenience required for a family day out, bundled into two large backpacks he and Verna carried; whilst the older boys carried the bodyboards and beach toys.

They found a spot close to the water's edge and placed themselves where they could supervise each child's movements. Izzy was the only one who disobeyed the rules, hurtling towards the sea. Marco was superb, he was used to his youngest sister's renegade responses and flew after her, carrying her back from the water's edge. Simon reiterated the beach safety riot act, explaining the parameters exactly. Verna asked Izzy to repeat what Uncle Si said, reminding her she'd have to go home. Izzy took Marco's hand, repeated the rules and promised she would be *very* good. The reassuring presence of her older brother helped Verna feel completely relaxed. With ever-present eyes on the children, she gazed at gentle, glittering ocean reflections resting on the beach chair, shovelling her toes into the warm finegrained sparkling sand. The soothing warmth of the sun, the distinctive sea-salty smell, and sounds of gentle waves, gull's cries, and children's shrieks of laughter was the tonic Verna needed.

On their return from a wonderful day on the beach, the children were enjoying snacks down in the den. 'Any idea what you're going to do Verna?' asked Simon. A cool lager was handed to her as they walked to the loungers and settled on the patio area.

It was a bright, warm, late afternoon, as she watched tiny beads of water rolling down the cool bottle. She swept them away with her fingers, took a drink, looked at her brother and said, 'not a clue.'

Jeremy arrived home saying he'd secured his days off,

joining them on the patio. 'The kids will sleep well tonight and we have a chilled-out day planned tomorrow,' said Simon. Jeremy gave his hand a grateful squeeze, as they smiled lovingly.

In the morning Verna was startled by Uncle Jem's voice. 'Bing bong! Morning yoga in five.' He was attempting to rouse the children, but after their energetic beach day and movie night treat of staying up late, none of them wanted to get up. Verna emerged from her sanctuary, 'looks like it's you and me Verna.' They went out onto the lawn as the sun glimmered through tree branches, spreading its golden warmth and bright joy. Jeremy practised yoga for many years to counter the stresses of his work as a renowned criminal barrister.

Verna recognised he was supremely fit; his petite fifty something body, had clearly defined muscle-tone and his healthy skin glowed with a perfectly even, light tan extending to his receding silver hairline. Verna imagined his piercing blue eyes would be intimidating when being cross-examined in court, but today they were a soft cornflower blue. Verna and Jeremy had a wonderful yoga session, she felt peaceful, balanced and grounded afterwards. Over a healthy fruit smoothie, Jeremy spoke tenderly about the time he met Simon at the exclusive leisure club Simon owned and how they fell in love and married within a short period of time.

'Simon hasn't returned to employment as yet, maybe when the children are older. He's completed a post graduate teaching qualification, I don't know how he's managed it,' his blue eyes flashing, 'eventually he hopes to work in education, as it would tie-in with the children's school holidays. We always wanted to be parents, and time was running out, for me at least. Simon has given up his career to be a stay-at-home dad and I'm so grateful to him for taking on three ready-made children full time. My work is demanding, but at least it gives us a lifestyle which is healthy for them.'

'I remember when Connor and Rose first arrived,' said Verna, 'they were five and three, Connor seemed like a toddler, and Rose was like a baby. She's still petite now, and seems younger than her age. Must have been hard work when a third came along.'

'It was a no-brainer, when the agency advised information their birth mother had another baby, we immediately made enquires to be assessed to adopt Nicky too. He was a gorgeous seven-month-old when he joined the family, and he's doing really well. Can't believe they are fourteen, twelve and seven now, it's flown by. Rose lacks confidence, however she's bright as a button, bordering on gifted, but we don't want to pressure her. Connor required a lot of support, initially, however the move here was the making of him. The free outdoor lifestyle is ideal for him to express his frustration and to run off his energies. He still doesn't concentrate on any one thing for long, and has aggressive outbursts, which are reducing, but he has stuck with his interest in music.'

'Marco is besotted with him. It's lovely for me to get to know my nephews and niece more. Although it was hard when you and Si left the area,' Verna was downcast, 'but, I do understand why you made the move.' Simon and Jeremy did everything to support their growing, demanding family. Verna looked with admiration at Jeremy, and Si who now joined them, coffee in hand.

After morning greetings, Simon said quietly, 'I've … well, we've noticed Izzy has some delightful idiosyncrasies—'

'Tell me about it,' Verna said, 'I'm going to arrange an educational developmental check when we get home. She's beautifully eccentric, nothing like the other two. Some of the things she does and says are odd, and make me love her more, but she's falling behind in sequencing and language. You haven't seen this yet, but whenever we're on escalators, she stands perfectly still, silent, looking at the top or the bottom. She shows no curiosity, doesn't look around or anything, then when she steps off at the end, returns to normal. Same when aeroplanes pass overhead, she stops and stares until they've gone, sometimes even lies down watching them no matter what she's doing, she shows no fear, so it's not that. The way she uses cutlery is quite the feat too, it's weird but wonderful. I've looked into dyspraxia as she has no coordination or concentration whatsoever, and writing frustrates her to bits, which may explain some of her delightful idiosyncrasies.'

'We've read extensively about developmental issues as you can imagine,' said Simon, 'I guess it could be a spectrum disorder perhaps. We're all on it in some way.' Jeremy and Simon shot glances at each other and laughed. 'Jeremy has major OCD issues.'

'I'll have you know, my issues really help to fully understand children, who have a variety of emotional responses to life.' Jeremy concluded with an authoritative, yet playful nod.

Verna enjoyed witnessing the two men's secure emotional relationship, humour and easy manner. She was somewhat jealous she didn't have that now with Leo, and wondered if she ever had. A twinge of longing often spread across her face as overwhelming sadness pressed a heavy weight upon her. After a moment, Jeremy said, 'forgive me if I'm talking out of line Verna, but if you need any legal advice about anything at all, please, ask.'

Verna finished her smoothie, slid her sunglasses down to shield the 10 a.m. unbearable brightening sun, and to cover her glistening eyes said, 'thanks Jeremy, I do need to be making decisions soon.'

The younger children roused and gradually emerged zombie-like from their rooms, starving for breakfast. Nicky and Izzy plonked themselves on the play mat tipping all the Lego out and soon became absorbed. Rose crept onto Jeremy's lap, their non-genetic physical likeness was stark. He engulfed her with a hug and kissed her forehead after drawing back her wispy white blonde hair, she was a quirky, stunning child with exactly the same cornflower blue eyes as his.

Amara sat next to Verna, had a jaw-breaking yawn and rested her head on her mother's shoulder. Verna slid her arms around her. 'You ok darling?'

Amara's response was divided by another huge yawn. 'Per … fect!'

Marco plodded into the kitchen, his large bare feet slapped on the tiled floor. He heaved his weary body onto a breakfast bar stool, resting his chin on his hands. Simon placed a large plate of warm crescent croissants and plump pain-au-chocolat in front of him. The sweet aroma jogged him into alertness, 'mint! thanks uncle Si'

'No sign of Connor?' asked Jeremy.

Marco laughed, 'he's flat-out uncle Jem, still snoring his head off.'

Verna looked at her three children with loving adoration, it certainly was time to be making decisions for their future, and hers.

Leo had transported Verna and the children to the airport before their trip. It seemed odd, the wrong way around, usually he'd be the one leaving, and he wondered about the many separations they'd had. As he watched Amara skipping her way through the huge revolving doors to departures, and Marco taking responsibility firmly holding Izzy's hand, with Verna looking great, he was excluded from this family adventure, and it hurt.

On returning home he took Rocco for a walk and said, 'just us two boys now buddy, it'll be quiet around here for a while.' He was sure the dog nodded. He tidied up the wreckage his family left behind and when he was done, scanning the huge neat kitchen, the central hub of family activity, the silence unnerved him. Soon music emanated throughout the house, and he left all the doors open upstairs so he could look into the children's rooms when he passed. He'd been separated from his children many times and for longer than a fortnight, but this was different, it was definitive.

Leo was exhausted by late afternoon and after a brief chat with Joyce and Nigel to say the family had arrived at their destination without any hitches, he decided to have a lie-down. He sighed with contentment, no demands or routine tasks, he would make the most of this fortnight of pleasing himself. He folded the duvet back, about to clamber into bed, and was stunned at the vision of a cream envelope on the pillow, clearly addressed to him in blue ink.

38

Hannah, March 2021

As Hannah left her meeting in Leeds City Centre, her hatred for multi-story car parks loomed large. She entered the concrete monstrosity via a littered, urine-smelling lift to her floor. She scanned the rows of cars and wondered where the hell hers was, grumbling internally, even though there weren't many cars, it was the same at the supermarket, she could never remember where she'd parked. She turned at the sound of footsteps echoing behind her, no-one in sight. Hannah pulled her watercolour-print silk scarf close around her neck on this chilly March evening. Continuing her inner musings, she thought it would probably take an hour-and-a-half to get home. Thank goodness this meeting was in Leeds, no traipsing to London again, she loved the work's but commuting was a pain.

Hannah fumbled for her keys in her bag with internal commentary; hang on, did I put them in my pocket? No, not in there, if I hadn't been delayed by that bloody truck, and rushing to get to the meeting I'd have parked elsewhere. 'Got them!' She held the cold steel bundle and clicked the fob, the car pipped and the flashing lights indicated her direction. She sensed a presence and turned her head.

A slim man with a shock of wild hair and filthy clothes was walking directly behind her, he stopped, looking right at her. He was about ten metres away, then started walking in her direction again. Hannah thankfully reached the car and pulled the handle, but turning her back on the man felt perilous. She braced herself for a solid whack on her head! A sharp stab! Hands around her throat! Panting, she yanked the door open, inwardly repeating, stay calm, stay calm.

She dived into the seat relaxing momentarily, when her head jerked sideways, as she was sliding backwards out of the car. Her scarf was tightening around her throat, she tugged at it, frantically unwrapping the end from around her neck. The momentum of release rendered the attacker tipping backwards as the scarf whipped into the air. She heaved herself upright, and sharp pains on her scalp told her, he'd grabbed handfuls of her hair, as she slid out of the car again.

Her brain in fight mode screamed, No! This will not happen! No! Self-preservation and instantaneous images of her son's faces imbued her inner spiritual force. With both hands she punched as hard as she could into his stomach and groin, emitting a primeval, survival screech which echoed all around the bleakness. He bent double releasing his grip. She banged the door shut, a voice in her head screamed, lock the fucking door! She couldn't think, the scream wasn't in her head, she was yelling aloud, 'turn the fucking key, turn the fucking key!' Her rock playlist exploded into life, as his face appeared at the passenger window, yelling, he banged on the roof. The image of the heavily lined old face, rotten teeth and matted hair was now indelibly imprinted. He exposed his genitals at the window as she zoomed forward.

'Come on Hannah think for fucks sake! Which way did you come in? It's ok, you're safe inside the car. He can't get inside the car.' Her breath came in gasps. On auto pilot, she drove around until she spotted the exit, he was walking towards it, sauntering, with not a care. She revved the engine, put her foot on the accelerator and drove, headlights beaming towards him. He turned as the headlamps illuminated his sickly grinning face. Fury filled her being as she raged towards him. He was not going to take anything from her; her dignity, her respect, her security, her life! In a split second before impact, she swerved and he disappeared at the side of her car. Driving slowly, she couldn't see him. Had she killed him? In the rear-view mirror, a dark mound on the ground, moved, and rolled over onto its knees and staggered up to standing. The fucking bastard was still alive, she reversed to turn the car and headed towards him.

Hannah was driving without one conscious thought about how she was going to get home. After fifteen minutes, she somehow ended up on the motorway heading north, and her breathing calmed. Hannah realised Cam would be home, it was Friday, she sighed with relief and called him, 'I'm okay don't worry, but I was attacked in a car park after the meeting.'

His shocked voice asked if she was hurt and if she was okay driving, offering to come and get her. Hannah's voice was calm, 'I'm okay, I'm thinking clearly and focusing on driving safely. Please don't ask me to explain now Cam, I need to concentrate on getting back, I'll tell you everything when I'm home.' Hannah couldn't get over the fact she was incredibly calm, but knew she had to distance herself from what had happened for now. She continued to play her car rock playlist, at the loudest, bearable pitch and enthusiastically joined in with Foo Fighters, *My Hero*. As long as she kept singing loudly, and concentrating, she'd be home soon; she'd be safe soon.

Cam grabbed her and held her tight the second she entered the house. She was acting normally not wanting the boys to get wind of any distress. She met his eyes with an unspoken message as Ross came to the top of the stairs with, 'Hi Mam, were getting takeaway again, yay!' He dashed back to his bedroom. No sight of Evan, but his familiar, 'hiya Mam!' rang out.

Now it hit her, she may never have seen their faces again if things had turned out differently in the car park. Keeping tears back with a rasping throat to stem the flow, she flung off her coat and stumbled into the conservatory. A large glass of wine was already poured. She took a long drink. Cam was glued to her side. 'You okay honey?'

'No.' She fell into his arms, trembling and crying. 'Close the door and watch for the boys' … she sobbed … 'don't want them to see.'

He rescued the wine glass before it fell out of her hand as she went limp. All doors were closed, so there was an early warning if either of them appeared. 'Hey Hannah, hey it's okay, it's okay. You're safe now. I'm here, no one can hurt you,' he soothed. Cam held her tight and stroked her hair. 'What happened H? I'm so fucking livid this has happened to you. The bastard will be dead if I get my hands on him, you ought to tell the police.' He was right, but didn't want to push.

Hannah took two large gulps of the smooth red wine, 'he may already be,' and started to explain. With clarity she recounted the event. Once the trembling eased, Cam gently traced the red mark on her neck with his finger. 'This may sound strange, but it would be good to get a picture for evidence.'

'Evidence?' Hannah hadn't thought anything like that, but agreed. Cam took a few quick shots of the injury on his phone. 'My scarf is probably still lying on the ground in the car park,' there was a smooth area of skin she caressed with her fingertips, she didn't need to see a mark.

'It'll help us catch the scumbag, wonder if there's any CCTV. I hope I get ten minutes with him.' He cradled her in his arms all evening and during her call to the police. She was exhausted, but desperately needed a shower before bed. She needed to wash and rinse away the sight of her assailant, the feel of him, the smell, the look on his face. She scrubbed her hands with a nailbrush, and scraped her nails into her hair and scalp three times as that's where her skin had touched his. It felt contaminated.

After a disturbed night's sleep, the couple sat in the calm of the conservatory, when Cam suddenly yelled, 'the dashcam, the dashcam!'

'Pardon?' Cam leapt off the sofa, leaving coffee swill on the table, and half eaten toast on his plate as he shot outside. He returned with a small black device.

'This could provide the evidence we need.'

Hannah was queasy, still vulnerable, recovering from the assault, the assailant's face imprinted in her mind. She needed to erase the memory, not have Cam banging on about evidence, she wanted everything to return to normal in her safe, ordinary world.

'Good job you took my car otherwise we wouldn't have the evidence.'

'Okay … okay, Poirot, calm down. What on Earth are you on about?'

'The dashcam will have recorded everything, so we can identify the bastard to the police.' Cam was highly animated asking if she knew when the cops would be coming to take her statement. Hannah had no idea, as the officer she spoke with mentioned she'd get a call from her local force. Cam was fiddling with the unit to find the footage, which should have captured the last two hours of Hannah's evening journey from the car park to home.

The replay began. 'I really don't know if I want to see it,' she said fearfully, as if something different may have happened. The attack had shaken her to her core.

'I'll watch it through first,' Cam said. She nodded to him, at the sound of tinny rock music which overwhelmed Hannah's indistinct words.

Cam watched the footage. In the half light of dark evening, the windscreen view showed headlights spanning the expansive car park with half empty bays. The car moved forward and the rectangular windscreen image swung right then left. Hannah's voice drowned out the music. *Come on Hannah think for fucks sake! Which way did you come in? It's ok, you're safe inside the car. He can't get inside the car!* Cam was shocked at the panic in her voice, he paused the image and looked at her. She nodded, he needed to see it, but she found the sound of her own loud, terrified voice unnerving.

Cam watched more footage. The view of the car park exit centred in the windscreen. A figure was walking towards it, the figure grew bigger as the car headed towards him. The painted white T shapes of the parking bays, and roof strip-lights speedily flashed by. The face of an old scruffy man with raven black beady eyes was now leering into the windscreen, then a look of pure terror replaced it. The rectangular image abruptly slowed and took a severe swerve right as the figure disappeared from view.

Cam placed his hand over his mouth to hide a shocked expression, with a muffled, 'Jesus Christ Hannah.'

Hannah was calm. 'Shouldn't mess with a perimenopausal mother, should he?' She sipped her coffee. 'Still think the cops should see that?'

'What the fu—'

'I didn't hit him! You would've seen the car bump or heard a satisfying crunch if I had.' Hannah stretched and yawned. Cam rewound the recording. They watched it together, she knew the more times she went over it, the less scary it would seem, she had survived. Hannah shrugged. 'He wasn't dead. I looked in the rearview mirror, he got up, but … really slowly,' she said with a satisfied smirk, 'I was going to go back to finish him off, but didn't want to be done for manslaughter.' The gratified look remained on her pale, tired face. 'You going to make your speciality bacon butties for us all hon?'

Cam nodded with a hint of a smile, he took a long admiring look at her and crushed her in his arms. Still smiling, he stood, shook his head and padded to the kitchen to make the butties. Evan and Ross were told about the incident and knew the police were calling to take a statement. They were told a man was trying to steal cars, and their mother had reported him. They watched a brief snippet of the footage of her driving away, Cam had disabled the sound of their mother's abject fear. They were astonished when the car sped up towards the man as the image stopped. Hannah explained, she'd frightened him because he was really abusive towards her, and reassured he'd ran off before she reached him. Evan wanted to post the footage of his, *Grand Theft Auto,* mother on social media, but Cam quickly suggested the police would need it as evidence so it shouldn't be viewed in public, in case it prejudiced any police investigation. Also, they couldn't be in the room when Hannah was interviewed because of confidentiality. Hannah looked adoringly at her serious faced, fast-thinking man.

A tall, slim fair-haired male officer and petite, young dark-haired female officer arrived to take Hannah's statement. Cam played the footage, and Hannah noticed a glimmer of a smile on the female officer's face at the point the assailant thought he was going to die. Hannah explained he was definitely not hurt as he did walk away, pointing out the footage would have shown a collision, which they agreed. Hannah's recorded panicky voice and the assailant's banging on the roof, exposing himself, plus the marks from the scarf on her neck, corroborated her account of the assault. Evan and Ross spoke with the police officers before they left, who understood the boys knew nothing of the nature of the attack. They said their mother had been brave and chatted warmly with the boys.

Two police officers arrived at the run-down terraced house, in a deprived area of Leeds, and knocked on the door. It was the last known address on the system for Patrick Dean.

Known locally as, Pervy Paddy, he had been charged with indecent exposure in the past. He was often seen hanging around parks and reports of him following and intimidating women were made, but no offence was committed on these occasions. The ancient wooden door and window frames were rotten and crumbling. One floral faded yellow curtain hung loosely across the filthy window. PC Nate Smith was bending to observe the window frame, 'those windows are going to fall out soon—' the door opened a fraction and a scrawny woman's face peered around it. 'Is Pat in? We'd like to speak with him.'

There was no resistance. The woman opened the door, shuffled along the hall back into the kitchen. Not turning around, she said feebly, 'he's upstairs,' then closed the kitchen door. The two officers entered the premises.

'Bloody Hell Nate,' said PC Theresa Walker as they walked upstairs, 'where do they buy these sticky carpets from?' She turned to wince at him as the increasingly powerful smell of fish, human waste and cannabis filled her nostrils.

A broad grin spread across Nate's face, 'same place they get the air fresheners from I guess.' He sniffed dramatically, 'this one's, Hint of Arse Gravy, I believe.'

'Pat, Pat, are you here?' Theresa pushed a bedroom door open, avoiding the bathroom door, where the deep-flavoured aroma was emanating. A man was spread out, fully dressed in filthy clothes on a single, stained mattress on a threadbare carpeted floor. The range of detritus surrounding him included, cigarette papers, matches, filthy clothes, an old radio cassette player, which looked as though it had been modified non-expertly with wires springing out of it. Lots of mugs with engrained tea stains were gathered on one side of the mattress, with a few empty large plastic bottles of cheap cider on the other. Lying across Pat's stomach was a pretty silk scarf in a watercolour-print.

'Don't think that's his,' said Nate.

'No, not Pat's colour that. You never know he may have bought it as a gift for his lovely lady downstairs.' Theresa suggested, 'an arrest for robbery here?'

'Definitely got a serious category crime.' Nate replied.

'Don't know about you Nate,' said Theresa, 'but I'll be happy to seize the scarf, and call that a complete search, haven't the stomach to rake through Pat's worldly belongings.'

'Agreed,' said Nate, 'even though he's gone to all the bother of tidying up for us.'

Theresa toed the mattress to rouse Pat, which did the trick. He was truly shocked to see two police officers leaning over him and tried to scramble up. Theresa cautioned him and said he was being arrested for robbery in a city car park three days previously, and they were going to search his bedroom. Pat, resignedly, nodded his head. Nate explained he was required to attend the police station where he would be interviewed. Pat's dull eyes showed little acknowledgement and he simply nodded again, slowly stood and limped towards the stairs.

Hannah received a call from Detective Constable Katrina Easton from Leeds Police. She introduced herself as the Officer-in-Charge of the investigation into Patrick Dean's assault in the car park. Hannah was pleasantly surprised, not believing there'd be a conclusion to the sorry story, but always hoped they did get the bastard. Kat explained the progress of the investigation so far, and asked if Hannah would be willing to take part in an identification procedure if needed. She would not need to return to Leeds as it could be carried out via video locally. From the dashcam footage, and the fact he was in possession of her scarf, it was unlikely she would need to. Kat confirmed Patrick Dean would be interviewed, and she'd keep Hannah updated as the investigation progressed. Hannah confirmed she was willing to attend, and did not want the scarf back. Katrina thanked her, relieved she did not want the item returned, as it was evidence. She also deemed it unnecessary to describe, for what purpose, Pervy Paddy had been using her scarf.

39

Hannah was working on her new projects, and no surprise she won the contract to design the branding and logo for The Hexagon Retail and Leisure complex in Leeds, from her submission ideas. She hoped there'd be no further need for face-to-face meetings in London or Leeds for a while. Hannah suffered moments when she shuddered thinking what may have been if the car park incident had gone a different way. She utilised the breathing techniques she had found online for calmness when her anxieties arose, which was becoming less frequent and the waking up crying in the night had at least stopped. Cam sensed the moments she went into panic mode and held her close. Her hyper-sensitivity raged as she looked at each potential male as an assailant she passed, even in broad daylight. She never took runs alone any longer through the wooded area close by, preferring that route only if Cam was with her. She stuck to residential, highly populated areas with other runners, dog-walkers and cyclists. She was seriously thinking of taking self-defense classes and buying an alarm or spray, though she had read the latter was illegal in the UK.

Hannah accepted her work would involve travelling to different venues, so she'd research the areas and look out for well-lit routes, always taking taxis to her destination. She planned to wear flat shoes, and would remember to have knuckle keys handy, which may provide some defence. Cam said he would be her bodyguard, he truly meant it. If she had to travel away, he would drop everything and accompany her. Hannah appreciated his support but it angered her to think, in the twenty-first century, women continued to live in fear of attacks. During a recent conversation with Cam about work, Hannah candidly mentioned her ex-colleague, Graeme, as she was sure he had put in a good word for her. It did not elicit any negative reaction from Cam, she was pleased to note.

'We've got a few viewing appointments today, H, remember?' Cam interrupted her thoughts.

'I hadn't forgotten, but what time?'

'First one is at eleven.'

'You're kidding! I haven't even showered yet.'

'We're only going to view houses, you don't need to get dolled-up.'

'Hah, dolled-up? That's one of your dad's, isn't it?' she smiled. 'I know but they're really posh places, I can't go looking like a burst sofa.'

'They won't be arsed how you look if we buy a house, and they won't get close enough to smell you, it's all Covid-safe, socially distanced.'

'Not funny Cam, not funny, you should have told me the time.'

Hannah shot upstairs leaving a bemused Cam, who

didn't realise he was her personal human alarm clock. She emerged ten minutes later, he leaned towards her, sniffed, and said, 'nope, no Sweaty Betty smells.' She thumped him, then they jumped in the car and sped away. 'We've got our Covid jabs tomorrow afternoon H, just giving you twenty-four hours-notice.' Hannah pursed her lips at his sarcastic eye roll.

Three pairs of blue plastic overshoes rustled with static along the wide light-grey carpeted hallway. The face-masked figures, Hannah, Cam and the estate agent, Carol, were simultaneously lathering their hands in sanitiser. Coiffured Carol, the broadly-built, pushy sales agent led the two around the vast, beautiful five-bedroom house on a new estate, which seemed to have sprung up within weeks in the exclusive neighbourhood.

'I wished she'd stop stating the bleedin' obvious, we know it's the sodding kitchen,' Cam said in mask-muffle close to Hannah's ear.

'Sorry,' asked Carol, turning towards the mutterings, 'did you have a question?' Cam innocently shook his head.

Hannah was trying not to laugh at the sycophantic sales pitch from Carol, who probably wasn't used to such types wandering around the exclusive show house. God, she's irritating, she thought. Carol was clearly not going to let them have a wander themselves. She opened every door and cupboard herself, presenting empty interiors with glowing descriptions in a fake posh voice. At one point Cam was going to reach for a cupboard door handle and she exclaimed, 'ah-ah!' putting her finger up as if reprimanding a child, 'there's a pandemic on you know!'

Hannah met Cam's crinkly eyes as he whispered, 'is there really, Carol the Cupboard-Nazi is stating the bleedin' obvious again.' Carol spun around, with a quizzical look in her heavily mascaraed, wide-eyed, but irritated stare. Hannah knew Cam was pulling a face right at her. Hannah was bursting inside trying to stifle any sound, glad of the mask coverage as she coughed to cover a leaked-out laugh.

'Hyacinth Bouquet or what?' Hannah squeezed out the words between giggling gasps, as they clambered into the car. They were creased up with laughter at scowling Carol, glaring from the doorstep as they drove away. This was the third similar house they had seen, on a similar estate and they were blurring into each other.

They had an in-car conversation about which property best met their requirements for school location, separate bedrooms for three children and a room that would convert to a work studio for Hannah. They envisaged a downstairs room as a music and gaming room for the boys, with huge telly and sound system. Hannah didn't imagine a year ago she would be walking around show-houses she never dreamed she would own.

The couple had taken a punt visiting an old infant school. It was partially renovated into a five-bedroom home with attic conversion, before the former owners ran out of money and had to sell, Cam was keen to see it. The house was located along a lane from a vibrant village, close enough to the boys' school. The instant Hannah and Cam walked through the door of the spacious, quirky dwelling, they knew it was going to be their next home. The former tiny village infants' school had served a sparse population, it was closed when a huge academy style education complex swallowed up nearby fields to accommodate the growing number of families moving to the area.

'There's so much to consider,' another in-car conversation ensued, 'you having the time and energy to complete the renovations may be a bit much, with Laurel Trees too.'

'You've got your heart set on the attic studio space for work though, haven't you?'

Hannah grinned. 'It would be a stunning home for the children, in a perfect location.'

'Well … my house has sold, it'll be a bit tight, but we could stretch to the schoolhouse while living in your house for a period of time until renovations are complete.'

Uncharacteristically, Hannah clapped her hands with unbridled joy.

40

From May 2021, most Covid restrictions had eased in England, for businesses, education, retail, and leisure. Life was beginning to return to some normality when Cam began renovations on, The Willows, an obvious name for their new home, having a mature weeping willow in the large garden. Hannah had designs on a shady seated area during the summer months, beneath its draping gold-green fronds. She wrote out their new address; The Willows, Starbeck Lane, Dayton Village, it sounded idyllic. It was. It would take several weeks until they could move in as Cam's priority was to complete Laurel Trees in Scotland. He showed Hannah images of the imposing stone building, the portico front entrance, the two huge bay windows at either side and several of the internal rooms.

Hannah said, 'it'll be stunning when it's finished. Can't wait to go and see it.'

'Got all the original features too, enamel sinks and a pantry to keep fresh produce cool, no fridge for Aunt Marie. Bathroom fittings will be fun, but I've got an excellent skilled team and I've promoted Iain to deal with matters in my absence. I'd trust him with my life and he's happy to stay in Scotland for the duration of the renovations.' Cam was full of pride.

'Ellie's looking forward to restoring the paintings, artefacts, and the vintage jewelry,' added Hannah, 'she's renamed her studio, Lorna's Emporium, and Jayne wants me to have an overview of decor.' Hannah looked at photos of the interior stonework, fireplaces and the wooden balustrade which adorned the sweeping entrance and stairs, she smiled. 'It's a real family affair.'

Life for Hannah and Cam was running smoothly until Hannah received a frantic call from Iain one morning at 9.20 a.m. telling her Cam had collapsed when he and another worker were removing some old heavy units from the cellar. It seemed he had fallen backwards onto the stone floor and was unconscious.

'What? … oh no, God no! Is he all right?'

Iain tried to calm her, and explained he was breathing and had a pulse when he checked him over and called emergency services. He gave her details of the hospital, and he was on his way following the ambulance. He wouldn't be allowed in, but would report any updates. Hannah immediately called Ellie, no answer, she called Megan who arrived as Hannah was on the phone to the hospital. Megan took one look at the sickening pallor of her sister-in-law's face, gave her a hug, and went to make a hot drink. Hannah was distraught as she ended the call, her hands shook as she tried to lift the mug of strong, sweet hot tea. Megan, sitting close by, held her hand as she explained what was happening.

'They're doing various tests, have taken bloods and are monitoring his heart,' Hannah burst into floods of tears.

Megan affirmed, 'they'll be doing everything possible to determine what happened. He's a strong man, he'll come through this. When can you speak to him?'

Sobbing and wiping her dripping nose and red swollen eyes, 'he … he's still in the treatment room … drowsy, they're monitoring him because it's a head injury. Oh Megan, it's all my fault. He works so hard … both houses, travelling to Scotland. He helps with the boys … and, everything, he must be exhausted.' Megan put a reassuring arm around Hannah to soothe her as she continued, 'there's heart stuff in the family … oh god what if it's his heart? What if he's injured his spine or something and … it's all my fault, just because I wanted an attic studio!' Waterfall tears streamed down her face. Megan held her tightly trying to calm the spiralling anxieties. Hannah's mobile rang, it was Ellie. Megan answered explaining what the missed call was about, Ellie was on her way.

By the time she arrived, Hannah was on another call to the hospital. She ended the call and explained Cam had regained consciousness, but was nauseous and disorientated, so she couldn't speak with him. 'They want him to rest and make observations overnight as he was out cold for half an hour. I've asked if I can talk to him on the phone, so they'll let me know later.' Hannah cried again, 'I can't bear anything happening to him. I've waited this long to meet the man I love, and I'm not going to let anything take him away from me,' she said fiercely.

Iain called Cam's sister Jayne, who in turn called

Hannah. 'Mam and dad are naturally distraught, and we made a family decision not to tell Julia yet, until we have more information. Don't want to worry her or our little Sara,' Jayne couldn't get the words out without her voice breaking down. 'Let's travel up in the morning, they won't allow us to visit, but at least we can be nearby if he needs us.'

The call ended with arrangements to travel to Scotland the next day. Ellie offered to stay over and look after Evan and Ross, and Megan agreed to help organise the boys for school. Over an hour later Hannah's phoned pinged with a message from Cam. *Hi H. How u doing? Don't worry I'm fine, bit of a bump, medics said nothing serious. Will ring soon, having some grub. Love you xxx* 'It's from Cam!' She kept re-reading the message, examining each word, to ensure she got the message right and read it aloud twice. Within the hour Hannah's phone rang. It was Cam making a video call. She pointed to the ceiling, indicating she'd take the call in the bedroom, she told herself, don't cry, don't cry, don't cry as she answered.

His ashen face appeared, propped up on crisp white hospital pillows smiling, 'hi gorgeous.'

Hannah burst into tears.

'Hey, I'm fine, don't cry.'

'I … I was scared, it's so lovely to see your face.'

'Great to see you too. So sorry I worried everyone, poor Iain must've got the shock of his life, told him to get some rest, he's a good lad.'

'How are you feeling now?'

'Okay, a bit shaky. Don't remember much once I fell, apart from lying there a bit dizzy, then the next thing, people were talking, and I was in an ambulance. I was disorientated for a while, like in a dream, but they've obviously sorted me out.'

'Do you know how it happened?'

'Sort of, Iain and the other lad explained the heavy chest slipped and knocked me down the stairs, I've got a few bruises to show for it, and I was out cold. The paramedics couldn't revive me, so they brought me in.' He shrugged. 'It was an accident Hannah, it happens, no one to blame. They've done a few tests, shining lights in my eyes, heart monitoring and so on, they're keeping me in overnight to keep an eye on me.' His voice sounded weary, he looked into the screen and she savoured his crinkly weak smile, but her eyes watered again.

'Don't start H, or you'll have me blubbing.'

'I know, sorry ... I can't bear the thought of anything happening to you.' She wiped her eyes.

Cam looked upset, 'nothing's going to happen to me H, or to you. We're all good.'

'You've been working too hard, so we're going to scale everything back.'

He rolled his eyes at her, 'I'm fine, everything's in working order and if you were here now, you'd know about it,' he grinned.

'Exactly,' she brightened, 'I want you all in one piece and fully functioning.'

'Not a problem H. It'll be good to have some time out at home. Can't wait to be back.'

'Well ... we have got some planning to do.' Cam looked puzzled.

'You know … we can't disappoint little Sara, can we?'

'Oh right, I see, the bridesmaid thing.'

'This has made me realise what I want in life Cam, and what's really important, you and me and our children, that's all, nothing else matters.'

He moved the phone closer to his face, 'love you H.'

She looked deeply into his tired eyes. 'Love you too. Can't wait to see you tomorrow, I'm coming with Jayne in the morning, so … try not to die in the night or I'll be bloody furious.'

'I'll do my best not to.'

'You'd better not or I'll kill you. Get some rest, sleep well and I'll see you tomorrow.'

'I do feel sleepy now.' Cam said mid-yawn. 'Night H, love you.' He blew a kiss into the phone, Hannah returned the gesture and ended the call. She held the phone against her heart, feeling reassured. He looked okay … normal, but he mustn't have realised it was only 4.30 p.m. A few tears fell, as she breathed deeply, then popped into the bathroom to splash cool water on her face. She dried her eyes and gathered her emotions, then headed downstairs as the boys were home from school.

Whilst Hannah was talking with Cam, Megan and Ellie explained to the boys what had happened. Ross was silent with tears in his eyes, and Evan sat dumbfounded on the sofa. Hannah sat between the boys. 'He'll be fine Mam, I know he will,' reassured Evan with his arm around her.

Hannah was trying to ring Cam, but couldn't remember the number, then she remembered, and kept repeating it to herself. But, each time she tried to tap the numbers on her phone, the wrong digits appeared on the screen and she had to start again and again, time after time. She was panicking, she must talk to him! She was shouting and pleading with people passing by to help her, but they walked by ignoring her. She woke crying, her throat was dry, she'd been sobbing in her sleep.

The deeply disturbing dream, resulted in a mini panic as she lay in bed. What if something had happened to him during the night! But, surely the hospital or someone would've been in touch, she checked her phone. Hannah looked over to Cam's side of the bed, to his book reader on the side table, his phone charger and the T-shirt and jeans draped over the laundry basket. Her whole being was swollen with grown-up love for him. It was 5 a.m. when Hannah decided to get up after the disrupted night. She rallied, sat bolt upright, she would see him and everything would be fine. She convinced herself it was a blip, brought on by fatigue, she would nurture him back to health when he was safely at home. A surge of energy prompted her to get on with the day. Jayne was picking her up at 8 a.m. glad she was driving as Hannah hardly slept all night. Megan would be arriving to get the boys sorted for school soon; she was so grateful her family were there to cushion the impact and share the emotional trauma.

Hannah sipped a potent aromatic coffee in a silent conservatory as dawn light filled the room. She looked at the dated multi-photo frame with disdain, she hadn't got around to changing it for something more contemporary when she had her home re-vamp. The pictures of her boys growing up were centrally placed, though bleached from years of sunlight, she'd replace them for some without Adrian. She savoured those of her family, and a brilliant shot of her colleagues from BlueSea Graphics on a night out.

There was also an image of Verna and Hannah celebrating their fortieths, looking glam, cocktails in hand in a classy wine bar. Hannah pondered how Verna looked when Cam pointed her out in the store car park. The look on her face, what was it? Sad … the fleeting glimpse revealed, sorrow. Hannah would always regret the hurtful accusations she made about Leo. The old adage, life is too short, to lose what they had; thirty years of friendship, was true. Hannah determined in that moment, she would contact Verna.

41

Jayne pulled up at the house, Hannah was waiting at the door. Jayne got out of the car looking fresh in a turquoise t-shirt, lightweight joggers and pumps. 'Two women going on a road trip?' Jayne's question and arms-out gesture brought to mind Hannah's reply.

'Thelma and Louise,' suggested Hannah after placing her overnight bag on the back seat. Her outfit mirrored Jayne's, but for a pink t-shirt.

'Precisely!' nodded Jayne.

As they set off, Hannah said, 'just spoke with Cam. It's good news, he's been stable overnight and if he remains in good health for the next day or two, they're sure he's going to be fine.'

'Great,' the relief was apparent in Jayne's voice. 'I feel more confident knowing he's had a good night and there doesn't seem to be any residual issues from the fall.'

'I was so worried about him. We've made a pact, he's putting a hold on the renovations to The Willows for now.'

'I can't wait to visit your new home, it sounds fantastic.'

'It was strange ... you know, soon as we stepped through the door, it was instantaneous, we looked at each other and knew it was going to be our home. Kismet, I never understood what it meant until that moment. The Willows will make a lovely family home, and it'll be great to have Sara to stay now restrictions are eased. We've got a separate bedroom for her, which I can't wait to kit out and decorate with her choice of décor, hope it's rainbows, unicorns, and sparkles.'

'It will be, don't worry! She's quite the gorgeous thing. I wasn't surprised it didn't last between Cam and Julia to be honest. They were good together at first, but it was more like a close friendship than an enduring long-term relationship. They met when she was on a night out with friends in Newcastle, and after a long-distance relationship, she moved up and they rented a flat until Sara was born. Cam worked hard to buy the house, but it became clear it wasn't working out between them, then Julia wanted to return to Leeds. She came across as a little immature, although she's only a few years younger than Cam, but it's good they get along well. I'm glad he's met you now though,' she turned and smiled, 'you seem happy together.'

'We are, it's working out for us both, and I've got nothing but praise for the way he's taken to my boys, it's not easy. They get on my nerves at times and I gave birth to them!'

'Yea, he is patient. Okay ... looks like we've got a good day for this run-up to bonny Scotland.' Jayne pulled onto the dual carriageway, 'shouldn't take more than a couple of hours till we get there.' Both women, donning sunglasses in the bright May sunshine, settled in for the trip.

'Really appreciate you driving Jayne. I had a terrible night last night worrying about Cam, but now you can dish the dirt, you can reveal all his secrets, we've got hours to get the lowdown on Cameron Wallace.'

'You'll be happy to know, there isn't any scandal in his background. He's been a good lad most of his life. He's had a few run-ins when he was younger, out with his mates. Ask him what they got up to in Ibiza,' Jayne said with a smirk, 'but he's never been into anything nefarious ... that I know of.'

'I'll definitely ask him about that.'

'Has he mentioned past relationships?'

Hannah shook her head, 'not in any depth, and I haven't pushed him.'

'He's wanted to forget all about the worst time ever when he broke up with Delphine,' explained Jayne, 'hmm that name?' Jayne spotted Hannah's quizzical look. 'Her father is Mauritian and her mother is French. I'm sure Cam was attracted to everything that was exotic about her. Stunning girl.' Jayne's comments were less than inspiring, and Hannah's insecurity demons roared with glee.

'Cam proposed and everything seemed to be going well. Delphine was planning the wedding and they were looking at a huge property together. The bombshell came out of the blue, Delphine arranged to meet him and announced it was all off, it seems she didn't want to make the commitment. It's not as though they were really young, Cam was twenty-eight, they weren't teenagers, and they'd been together four years. He was devastated. Truth is, Cam hasn't fully explained what Delphine said, all we knew was he came home in absolute shreds. He went to his bedroom; he'd left a flat-share to move back into the family home to save up, and became depressed. Our parents were concerned at his drinking and missing work. I tried to get through to him, but he refused to see me, it was awful, I hadn't seen him like that, he was like a different person. He was unshaven, gained weight and honestly looked quite unkempt at times, so unlike him.

'He lost touch with his mates, even though they tried to maintain contact. A couple of them called round to the house, but he refused to see them too. Then, I don't know what happened, something clicked, and he called me to ask if we could meet for a coffee; it seemed he had turned a corner. So … we met, had a long talk; he didn't reveal the detail, you know what guys are like, but did hint there was someone else, I don't know the full story yet. I was relieved he was back to being the Cam we know and love, back to himself … my little brother,' Jayne added softly. 'From then he got in touch with a couple of his close friends and went out for drinks. It was a quick turnaround; Cam was out, enjoying life, playing cricket, keeping fit, trips away, and it wasn't too long before he met Julia.'

'Poor Cam. What a bitch … er sorry, don't even know her, but she is. He didn't deserve that.' Hanna's protective instincts had kicked in.

Jayne laughed. 'Well, it's freed him up for you.'

'True.' Hannah held out an opened packet of chocolate coated peanuts, which fortunately hadn't melted with the benefit of decent air-con. Jayne grabbed a few, washed them down with gulps from a bottle of sports drink Hannah passed to her. The journey was easy, the roads were clear and it was a crisp, bright day.

Once the mini sustenance snacks were done, Hannah commented, 'the Delphine saga explains a lot. Cam became upset when I met with an ex-work colleague who I'd briefly dated. But we worked through it. There's no one else for me and I'm sure he feels the same.'

Jayne became quite animated, 'ooh wedding bells?' briefly turning to Hannah, she was thrilled at the prospect. Hannah simply smiled in response.

Time went by quickly during the journey as they chatted. Hannah received a message from Cam, he was discharged from hospital, Iain picked him up and he was at Laurel Trees resting. All works had been suspended for the time being. When Hannah arrived, she was astonished at the imposing size of Laurel Tree House, even though she had seen pictures of it. The exterior of the house was more beautiful than in photos, looking stately in the surrounding grounds.

Cam was waiting at the door, 'Ah, my two favourite women.' Holding out his arms, Hannah threw herself into them, she couldn't let go of him. He released an arm to hug Jayne and gave her a peck on the cheek, 'great to see you and thanks sis for bringing Hannah.' They had the update on the hospital treatment and how he was feeling, all glowing at the speed and skill of the NHS staff. They spoke with Iain, who was ready to leave as they arrived. Iain had cooked a sumptuous Scottish breakfast for Cam, and had made up the two available bedrooms, he and Cam were using, with fresh bedding for the guests.

'You'll make someone a lovely wife someday,' said Cam

Iain smiled, 'it's the least I can do after you giving me this great job. But now I'm going to leave you in the capable hands of these two wonderful women, and I'm going for a drink. A bloody big drink!' he laughed.

Cam said, 'it's well-deserved mate … well deserved.' Shaking hands, then hugging, 'thanks for everything. Will catch up soon. I'll let you know when the work will restart once I get the go-ahead from these two,' nodding his head towards Hannah and Jayne.

They went inside and Hannah was even more impressed. The high-ceiling rooms oozed elegance, and although they were partly refurbished, she could tell the place would look classy with the contemporary quirky touch Jayne envisaged. In the evening they ordered a huge Indian takeaway they were ravenous, it took an age to arrive. The delicious aromatic spiced food was laid out on the large dining table and as they crammed it into their mouths, Jayne suggested promoting Iain to site manager for a while, Hannah agreed, adding, The Willows could wait

Jayne went to the bathroom, and in her absence, Cam held Hannah's face, looked into her eyes and said, 'it wasn't my heart. The furniture we were moving was too heavy, and it knocked me off balance. It was an overambitious mistake, that's all.'

Hannah grabbed him and squeezed him with all her might, 'No more overambitious mistakes then, okay?' Cam nodded in reply.

They repaired to the expansive main living room, and Hannah rested, full-length on one of the tapestry sofas to aid her digestion. Although she wasn't partial to whisky, Jayne and Cam did enjoy a tipple of the Highland brew as an after dinner digestif. Cam had, 'only a wee dram,' and steered clear of any more alcohol. Hannah decided to join in, and as the evening drew on, the two women became quite inebriated.

Jayne spoke lovingly about Aunt Marie and her interesting life. 'Marie may have been a childhood nick-name from her parents perhaps, as the name Mhàiri is on her birth certificate and is usually translated to Mary.'

Hannah held up a picture of a rather stiff-looking Mhàiri, 'Ellie could paint this, it's quite regal.'

Cam seemed to enjoy observing his sister and his partner running hand-in-hand down the path of enthusiastic nostalgia as they became more animated and dramatic with each tot of whisky.

'You! … have got the best woman right here right now Cameron Wallace,' Jayne pointed a drunken finger at him, 'you're a lucky man.' With her arm around Hannah, they sprawled, heads together on the floor with documents strewn around them. 'I used to do Cottish Suntry Dancing when I was a wee bairn.' A drunken stupor prompted Jayne to give Hannah some basic lessons.

'Is there such a thing as a Highland Fling then?' Hannah swayed somewhat as she got up ready for her tutorial.

They whooped and hooted, leaping about as Hannah tried to follow Jayne's steps, arms aloft, whilst Cam played traditional Scottish country music on his phone. He looked on laughing at their uncoordinated attempts to dance, thoroughly enjoying their antics. 'Neither of you will be capable of doing anything if I become ill, or need to go back into hospital!'

'You'll be fine ... I can still peek on the sone,' said Jayne.

'Sorry?' smiled Cam, tipping his ear towards her.

'She means, peek on the phone, er ... I mean,' Hannah stood still, spoke slowly and pointed her finger to emphasise each word, 'em ... speak on the phone.' then nodded triumphantly as if to validate her achievement at stringing the few words together coherently.

'Not convinced,' said Cam.

Hannah plopped into his lap on the broad sofa where he'd been lounging, as Jayne wobbled to the door. In a broad Scottish accent, she bade them, 'guid nite, am away tae ma bed!' continuing to sing, 'I love a lassie, a bonnie, bonnie lassie—' there was a loud thump. Cam and Hannah were alerted, then relaxed as footsteps continued along the hall.

'She'll be fine. Better get you up the stairs too. Probably no happy sex tonight,' Cam said as he guided Hannah to the stairs.

'Overambitious mistake,' Hannah shook her head as she swayed.

The following morning Cam was up and about making coffee, having poured two ice-cold fresh orange juice drinks. Hannah, wearing Cam's shirt over her shortie pjs, held onto the bannister all the way down the sweeping staircase, for fear of falling and ending up with another trip to hospital. She made it to the kitchen and was part way through the life-saving orange elixir, when head in hands, Jayne appeared.

'Paracetamol?' Cam enquired.

'I'd nod, but my head might fall off.' Jayne slumped at the kitchen table.

He laughed and handed her two tablets with a large glass of water. 'Hannah, you don't seem too bad?'

'I didn't have too much, it's an acquired taste for my palate, so I took it easy.' She winced, 'could do with a couple of those myself.'

Cam supplied the medication. 'I was going to make you both a full Scottish breakfast this morning with tattie-scones and everything, but don't think you'll manage, so it'll have to be Lorne sausage sarnies.'

Jayne held one hand over her mouth, the other out-stretched to stop him even mentioning food. Hannah frowned and mouthed to him, what are they?

'Traditional Scottish sliced square sausage meat, fried and—'

Jayne held up her hand again and rushed out of the room to the bathroom, to the sound of Cam's laughter.

42

Leo, May 2021

Leo couldn't believe his eyes as he stared at the six photographs he'd spread upon the bed. They'd slipped out of the envelope as he picked up the letter from Italy. His shallow breaths were amplified in the silence. The world had stopped turning. He became aware of the pounding pulse in his temples, drumming in tune with heartbeats in his chest. In a low whisper he said, 'get a grip, stop panicking, stay calm, and breathe.' Drawing a deep in-breath through his nostrils, he tried to harness every single technique he'd learnt from his mental health worker, Steve, to maintain regulation. He was too stunned to move. He inhaled deeply, had he taken his daily medication, Steve said it was imperative he did. Leo couldn't remember.

He picked up the photo of Gabriel, his soft brown, baby eyes looked up into his father's face. It was heart-warming looking at his fourth child, his Italian son, his baby Gabriel. The letter said he was healthy and he looked it. Leo picked up the photo of him and Graziella in the apartment. It seemed like a hundred years ago, yet now he could smell the distinct scent of citrus and woody vanilla from the bougainvillea strewn balcony.

A sudden jolt of shock hit him as he realised Verna had known about his secret for … how long? The post mark on the envelope looked like September 2020. Gabriel would be eight months old now. Verna knew about him and never said one word, not even when they discussed his affair with Graziella months ago. Leo was stunned at Verna's ability to retain such control. Why had she left it until now to reveal this information? He wondered how she must've felt when the letter from Italy arrived when he was in the Dales with Nigel.

Leo was incredulous and full of mixed emotions. His fixed gaze rested on the envelope and Graziella's immature-looking handwriting, angry that Verna hadn't told him about the letter, or his son. Though Leo was the cause of all the pain, her actions were somehow cruel. Leo checked his phone, there was no message from Verna … yet. He was unsure whether to send a text acknowledging the revelation. He drudged downstairs, his world was crumbling around him. Leo was a social drinker, yet now he craved alcohol, something to soothe his inner anxieties, so poured a large rum and coke.

In the living room he was compelled to look at the huge family portrait above the fireplace, taken two years ago. All five, in white clothing grouped together smiling, no, they were laughing. The photo caught a spontaneous, natural family moment; the children were joyful and Verna looked stunning. He looked into Verna's beautiful face and said, 'so that's why you re-arranged the house and separated the bedrooms, making me believe it was about an affair, but you knew about Gabriel. All this time you've been planning your future.' He was certain her smile broadened.

He sipped the strong alcoholic drink in a daze, sitting for how long, he couldn't tell. The house was silent, but for the faint shuffling of Rocco at the door. Leo was too ashamed to let the dog see his face. He finished the drink and allowed Rocco into the room, 'you have no idea what I've done buddy.' The letter rested on the arm of the sofa. It made him sad to consider Graziella may have been anticipating a reply and would assume by now, Leo did not want anything to do with Gabriel. Should he reply? There were feelings of elation and connection that his child was born in the same hospital as him, and was living not far from where he spent his childhood. He envisaged Graziella having the same relationship he had with his own mother, Claudia, the parallels made him feel strangely content.

One thing Leo did realise was his marriage to Verna was well and truly over. He looked at Rocco, the content recipient of having his ears and chin scratched by his master, 'I've been so stupid, thinking I could keep this big secret forever.' He told Rocco about Gabriel, and showed him the photos, he was the only living being he could talk to about his baby son.

43

Lost hours passed, it was late evening, and still no message from Verna. The children would surely be in bed now. Leo glanced through Graziella's letter and stared at the photos. He retrieved the solicitor's child maintenance letter, which was secreted away in a cabinet in the spare bedroom. He let Rocco out into the garden, and fed him, the evening walk wouldn't happen. Like and automaton, Leo set to coffee making, the alcohol had made him sleepy, but he needed to think. The pervading coffee aroma roused his senses, he had time to plan his next move. Verna would leave him penniless, she had been planning the finances for months and controlled everything.

Gulping strong coffee, Leo scrutinised the, Enforcement of Maintenance Order, for Gabriel. The spare money in his secret personal account, which Verna knew nothing about, was decreasing rapidly, and there was no access to any further funds. His only option was to approach his father, but his stomach churned at the thought. Many times, Leo cursed his father who had stopped contact with him after his mother, Claudia, died. It was mutual, however he then received legal communication of his removal from his father's will, denying him any claim on the family estate. His father intended leaving their family property in, Sarnico, and all worldly goods to the church. Leo knew Claudia would be enraged about this.

Leo placed the maintenance letter aside, and thought longingly about his mother. Impulsively he retrieved his favourite photo of her from the array of framed images on the sill in the conservatory. He kissed his fingertip and tapped it on her face. Claudia looked so happy and beautiful, with her arms around her toddler son, by the lake near their home. He became aware of Rocco irritating him, whining for water. He stood abruptly, returned to the kitchen and splashed water into Rocco's bowl, he poured another large coffee and headed back to the conservatory, closing the door.

Leo stared into the perfect image of mother and son. He could sense Claudia around him and closed his eyes. When he was in Italy, the sight of the familiar white and gold pack of her cigarette brand, or the tobacco scent walking past a café evoked powerful memories, he instantly pictured her. Leo could distinguish the aroma of those cigarettes from all others, and it reminded him of her, but ultimately, they had killed her. There were times he thought he'd glimpsed her, and was saddened when he realised it couldn't possibly be so. The beautiful soul was gone before she reached fifty-two.

Claudia died not long after he and Verna married. The wedding had been brought forward so she could see her son settled, and photos showed the ravages of her disease, which stripped her of her beauty and exuberant persona.

She knew she would not see grandchildren. He had loved her deeply, and the loss was cutting and visceral, it hit him like a steam train some days. He despised his father even more, why couldn't it have been him?

Leo closed his eyes, Claudia's voice was in his head, laughing, singing, and calling his name. He recalled childhood memories of them baking together. They'd take boat trips on the lake. The two would ride on her bicycle around the town, there was a photo somewhere of him sat in the basket on the front when he was tiny. Every image showed her holding and kissing him. He could envisage her black wavy hair, her big brown eyes and cute smile. Many people commented she resembled, Audrey Hepburn, with her delicate facial features. He smiled as he absorbed the memory of her beauty. He traced his finger around her face and spoke her childhood name, 'Mammina, Mammina.' It came to him, Amara was going to look exactly like her, he could see it already.

He took the photo upstairs and gently placed it on the bedside table in the main bedroom. He would see it every night and morning, and if he woke in the night. After a troubling evening wondering how to approach his father, and having many attempts to write an appropriate letter; his only option to make contact, Leo flopped into bed. He curled up, looking at the photo of Claudia, and encouraged his brain to retain precious memories replaying them over in his mind. Just before he slept, he noticed a spider, legs splayed, static on the wall.

44

In the morning, Leo rolled over, enjoying the rebellion of being in the marital bed. He glanced at Claudia's image, and noticed the spider was gone. He'd slept late and soundly, unusually. The familiar surroundings of the furniture, bedding, bedside lamp and the scent of the bedclothes, and of Verna, brought some comfort. He knew she'd be irritated at him being in their bed. He smiled, small victories. Rubbing his eyes, and glancing at his phone … no message. His thoughts turned to the child he had with another woman and his acceptance Verna would never be able to overcome his betrayal. Leo's mood changed, it had frequently over the last twenty-four hours, he hadn't felt such desolation since his mother died. Rocco was whining downstairs, as his phone buzzed, which startled him. A text message from Verna read, *Children fine having a great time. Need to talk, I'm sure you understand now. Please call Amara.*

It was short and to the point. His marriage was over. The overwhelming silence of white noise in the house buzzed in his head, he had to get out. Rocco was let out into the garden, and he sauntered back after a few minutes relishing the much-needed relief. Leo took a carton of citrus juice from the fridge, took several gulps, grimacing as the tart liquid hit the back of his throat, then got dressed. As he lifted Rocco's lead the bouncing bundle scampered to the front door, Leo picked him up, and involuntarily cried into his soft fur. Rocco tipped his head in a curious manner at the strange actions of his master, then seemed to shrug dismissively, he was going walkies at last!

Leo drove for miles along remote Northumberland country roads until he spotted a roadside van and bought a hot drink, he couldn't face food, but the polystyrene encased, excuse for tea, was disgusting. He recalled Steve telling him to maintain regular meals. He called Steve, who wasn't on duty, so he left a message. He desperately wanted to confess everything to him or someone, anyone. He wanted to wash his sins away, to repent for all the wrongs he had committed. 'Confession!' he said to Rocco, who lifted his head towards Leo, with a sideways glance, bemused at the change in his master's demeanour.

A vivid memory of drawing back a curtain and sitting in a small dark, square enclosure with a latticed opening, sprang into Leo's mind. He was seven years old, yet he could now acutely smell incense. A deep-rooted need to see, Father Boselli, washed through him, he'd presided over his mother's funeral and conducted the service when he and Verna married. He did an internet search, fortunately getting a signal in this remote place, and gladly discovered he was alive and serving the local community in Sarnico, Leo's home town.

Father Paolo Boselli was known for his services to poor communities, and had a passion for the flora, fauna and landscape of the area, often taking lone excursions into the mountains. Leo discovered there was a retreat, maybe he could go there. He was empty and bleak, he needed someone, anyone, anything to comfort and fill the dark void inside him. He wanted to be forgiven, but knew he didn't deserve it, atonement was his only course of action. Though he hadn't spoken to his father for many years, a compulsion to make contact with him, and Graziella, was irresistible. Leo splashed the remaining tea out of the car window, and threw the cup in the back of the car. Rocco straightened abruptly, ears up, astonished at this outrageous messy behaviour.

Leo set off towards a local beauty spot where he could take a long walk and gather his thoughts. It came to him like some divine intervention in the forefront of his mind with a mental list; contact Father Boselli for confession and guidance. Make peace with his father. Visit his mother's grave and talk with her. Find a retreat in the beautiful mountains. Reconnect with his home town, and walk the familiar streets. He was lifted by these thoughts. In his mind's eye he pictured himself going to church, buying bread from the bakery, taking a bike ride, going on boat trips and swimming in the lake as he had as a child, when he was supremely happy. Leo in his shifted state of thinking, wondered why he had ever left Italy to live in England, and forsake his homeland, his family, friends and his religion as he derived great comfort from it now. Maybe this is why he had behaved in such a way all these years with the affairs and lies, he had never been fulfilled. It all made sense to him now.

He recounted prayers he learnt in school and church as he walked with Rocco, who glanced up at him, confused, eyebrows raised at the unfamiliar human words. As Leo drove home a peaceful lightness entered his being. Feeling the warm sunshine and breeze on his skin from the open car window, he knew his future path. The house appeared different as he walked through the door. He enjoyed the solitude, he didn't need the noise, the hustle and bustle of family life. There was a voicemail from Steve, which he deleted, then blocked the number, and all the contacts for the mental health unit. He also deleted the recent contacts he had made in his search for work, he no longer needed that in his life.

Leo booked a one-way flight to Milan with his secret account, leaving in a fortnight. He found a number and connected with Father Boselli, his comforting, though faint, quivering voice filled him with a contentment he hadn't experienced since he was a child. Leo asked him to make initial contact with his father, Antonio Ravassio, explaining they had been estranged for years, but Leo now wanted to make peace with him. If possible, he would like a telephone number if he was agreeable; Father Boselli was happy to assist.

The names Graziella and Gabriel on his mental to do list, had a virtual question mark beside them. How fitting his son's name was saintly. He would deal with that and the financial issues when he went home … home, to Italy. The overwhelming desire for Leo to engorge his soul with love, Italian memories, and religious meaning took precedence over his need to fulfil his duties, as a husband and father.

45

Verna and the children had the most wonderful time staying with Simon, Jeremy and the cousins. She was refreshed having the benefit of several meaningful and progressive conversations with her brother discussing her options. She found it exceedingly painful to talk about Leo's affair with Graziella, and whilst she hinted there may have been more women, she wasn't explicit and did not mention Gabriel. The betrayal was too much to bear and state aloud. If she said it ... it was real. Verna had a plan for separation, which kept the children's relationship with their father alive. It was up to Leo if he told them about Gabriel, however, she desperately hoped he wouldn't for a few years yet. Jeremy coached her in practical strategies to help secure financial support, child maintenance and keeping her house. Simon reassured her, they were available any time of day and night and empathised with the strain she must be under, living under the same roof as her duplicitous husband. On the family's return home, Verna experienced a sense of dread climbing into the car at the airport. Fortunately, she didn't have to make conversation with Leo.

'Daddy it was brilliant! Uncle Si and Uncle Jem's place is a … ma … zing!' said Amara. 'I love my cousins, so much, we've had such a lovely time.' She sighed.

Izzy repeatedly sang theme tunes loudly to the cartoons they had watched. Verna noted Leo seemed irritated at the level of noise as he glanced straight-faced into the rear-view mirror.

Marco added, 'I've learnt loads of guitar riffs Dad, I'll play them when we get in.'

The three recounted collective memories of fun-filled times at the beach, days out exploring, lovely cafes and restaurants, and repeated Uncle Si's ridiculous jokes.

Marco fell silent by the time they arrived home and shot straight upstairs, dismissing Joyce's welcoming smile and array of baked goodies. There were gin cocktails for her and Verna and mocktails for the children. Marco eventually emerged and Verna wondered if he had been crying, and whether he was missing Connor, jamming with his band and the beach lifestyle; or it could be he sensed the reality things were not right at all between his parents.

It was a happy homecoming thanks to Joyce and Nigel in the main, who patiently listened to the children's stories and looked at many images of where they had been. Verna noticed Leo seemed different. He had his upright, confident swagger back, bantering with the children and their neighbours like old times. Though she couldn't bear to look him in the eye, he exuded a new-found calmness, which she found odd.

Leo took the luggage upstairs and once the welcoming celebrations died down, Verna's lead-weight in the pit of her stomach forced her to take a much-needed, quiet interlude, 'just popping upstairs to sort a few things,' she said on leaving the room. No one really noticed. She took half an hour in contemplation of her future and half-heartedly sorted through the jumble of clothing flung into the cases. Out of character for her to not have everything packed in a neat, tidy and orderly fashion; she recognised the haphazard jumble reflected her life. She noticed her bed had been slept in and was affronted by it; returning home was proving difficult and she knew she wanted Leo out of her life. The strain of faking that her marriage would survive was exhausting.

As she passed the spare room, where Leo was supposed to be sleeping, she noticed some trinkets on the tallboy unit. She approached, and reached out, first at an ornamental crucifix, the framed photograph of Claudia, and one of Leo as a child with Claudia at a lakeside. Verna hesitated, standing transfixed, hand outstretched toward a strange item, a candle depicting an angel. The black wick in the centre of white molten wax revealed it had been lit. The words, St Gabriel the Archangel, was etched under the image. Verna whispered under her breath, 'what, the, bloody, hell is all this?' The reference to Gabriel, was stark. Considering she had been rational and pragmatic about their separation, a surge of hatred welled-up for Leo. She wanted him out of the house immediately! She needed to talk with Simon soon; the protective, secure barrier she had lived in for two weeks had come crashing down. She was exposed to raw humiliation and the treachery ate into her soul. Wondering how she was going to mask her hatred, she headed downstairs to organise bedtime for the children.

Later, Leo commented, 'sounds like they've had a brilliant time, the kids are full of praise for their cousins.' Verna knew Leo wouldn't mention Simon or Jeremy, he wasn't comfortable around gay men.

'It was great, and I've made a decision, I want you to leave as soon as possible, I have all the support I need from Simon. I've had some sound legal advice too, so I suggest you appoint a solicitor.'

'Okay, fine.' Leo was dismissive.

'Did you hear me ... I want you to leave.'

'Yes, I totally understand. As long as the children are okay with that.'

'The children!' Verna muffled her outcry. 'Yes, *my* children Leo. How many have you got?' It was about to spill over as she was struggling to cope with his dismissive responses. 'And what the fucking fuck is the fucking crucifix and the fucking candle all about?' The dam had broken.

Leo turned and looked toward her and said calmly, 'been thinking I should reacquaint myself with my country, my family and my religion. I hadn't realised they have been missing all these years.'

Not only had Verna been betrayed by other women, and a baby, she was now competing with the lord. In a low menacing voice, she didn't know she had, she repeated, 'your family, do you mean *this* family Leo? You really have lost your sodding mind.'

'What will you say to the children when I'm gone?'

'I'll tell them you've gone insane, and had to go back into hospital, but I *will* tell them the truth about all your lies and deceit when they can get their precious little heads around it. You can get out of our lives forever. Go back to your Italian tart and bastard son!'

'I've got a flight booked to Italy tomorrow actually, it's a one-way trip.' Leo's eyes sparkled, he was smiling and was showing no distress whatsoever. 'So, okay,' he shrugged, 'whatever you want.'

'I'll be seeking a full financial settlement and I'm keeping the house.'

'Fine by me.' Leo was almost joyful.

'Get out, take your stupid altar with you. Go and fucking worship somewhere else, because you have clearly never honoured our children, or me.'

Leo headed upstairs. Verna gulped down the rest of her gin cocktail, then poured a glass of wine. Leo returned with a weekend bag and backpack, he ruffled Rocco's head and said, 'see you around buddy.' Then, as if it was perfectly normal, held his arms out towards Verna inviting her for a hug, as if he was merely going away on a business trip.

Verna spat out a mouthful of wine laughing. 'You've got to be kidding!'

Leo turned and picked up the car keys. She spotted the crucifix and the candle in each of his jacket pockets. 'Oh no, you can get a taxi to wherever you're going. You're not taking the car.'

'Okay.' He took out his mobile.

Verna was astounded at Leo's passive behaviour. 'What will you do for money? You don't have any access to the bank accounts.'

'I've been in touch with my father, and we've talked. He has transferred some money into a bank account for me, and he's decided to reinstate me to the family estate.'

Verna's mouth dropped open. 'Your father! You haven't spoken to him since Claudia died. You've certainly been busy since we've been away,' incredulous at this turn of events.

Sweeping headlights flashed down the hallway. Leo walked to the door, opened it, looked back and said, 'it's never too late to re-connect with those you love.' Rocco had sped along the hallway thinking he was going for a late evening walk, only to be rebuffed by the front door closing in his face. He turned and looked at Verna, baffled, then followed her into the living room and jumped upon her knee.

A few moments passed. The sound of the taxi faded and Verna became aware of Rocco's warmth curled up on her knees, and the regular gentle rise and fall of his soft body. As she stroked him, her shoulders softened; the weight of peaceful silence surrounded her, holding her down securely. A veil of calm draped over her being. Leo was gone. She sent a text to Simon; *You said I could call anytime. Still up? You'll never guess what's happened! xx*

Simon's contact number lit up Verna's screen immediately. 'You okay! What's happened?'

'I'm fine … well, I think so.'

Jeremy's face appeared. 'You're not hurt, are you Verna?' looking concerned.

'No, nothing like that, my pride is maybe.' She couldn't help but giggle to Simon and Jeremy's utter bemusement. Once the involuntary laughter passed sufficiently enough to speak, Verna described the latest saga, deciding to tell them everything, including details about Gabriel.

Simon was horrified, barely able to contain his anger. 'Why couldn't you tell me how bad it was? Oh Verna. Good job he's leaving the country, I'd fucking strangle the bastard if I saw him ... sorry,' Simon never swore. 'I can't believe you're being so calm!'

'I've known about Gabriel for months, but had to wait for the right timing given Leo was in hospital, and I needed him for childcare too during the pandemic restrictions, then Christmas came along and ... I had wondered if we could come back from it. Not only was I competing with other women, but a baby, and now the lord god almighty.' She burst into laughter, this time they joined her.

'So, he's found god. It's hilarious if it wasn't so tragic,' laughed Jeremy. 'Wait! He hasn't taken the letter and photos, has he? That could be proof of his infidelity.'

'If he has, he's taken copies, I scanned and re-printed the letter, and switched the original photos with copies, it looked authentic.'

'Excellent!' said Jeremy, 'have a dig and see if there's anything incriminating anywhere else.'

'Don't worry, I've got boxes full of stuff in the loft,' Verna said triumphantly, 'all the business accounts, records of flights, including the single flight when Graziella came over. To be honest, it's not surprising he's gone loopy with the stress, but the stupid bastard deserves it.'

Simon said proudly, 'now you see why my little sister was a successful business woman, attention to detail.'

'Brava Verna, brava,' said Jeremy.

Verna was contemplative. 'You know, maybe he should've gone into the priesthood as his father wanted, perhaps that could've been his path. He may have been more fulfilled, and not stressed to hell for years running the business. I've got three wonderful children out of the marriage, but I am concerned he shaves his head and buggers off to a monastery. He could bequeath all of his family inheritance and worldly goods to charity, like the welfare of starving cats in Milan or something, and there'd be no funds for the kids, or to keep the house going 'til I set up in business again.' Verna couldn't help but smile, 'honestly I thought I was unlucky having a mother who is barking mad, but to have a husband howling at the moon too, it's way too much!' Verna rolled her eyes and burst out laughing, but now bordering on hysteria as nauseating, nervy feelings rumbled within her.

'Absolutely, they don't spoil a pair,' Simon laughed. 'Loony Lena and Loopy Leo!' He looked into the screen searching for the truth of how Verna was coping and said clearly, 'you're going to be fine. We are here for you one hundred percent. I'll be on the next flight, you only have to say.'

'Thank you Si, love you bro. Thank goodness there's some sanity in my life. I can rely on my neighbours for support too, they've been superb,' then to herself, 'wait 'til I tell Joyce.'

'Leo's father has money it seems, let's keep that in mind. I know some brilliant family lawyers who work internationally with child maintenance and parental contact. We'll be ready,' offered Jeremy in serious tone, then softly, 'don't forget about your yoga meditations sweetheart, we can hook-up online and do it together. We're here for you.' Simon was nodding, Verna ended the call feeling a little more positive, she was part of a loving family, and a good team. Leo was gone, and she didn't need to concern herself with him, but must secure her home and the future for her children. She would arrange a time to explain to Joyce he wasn't returning, so she could help support the children when the time came to tell them. This was the only point when Verna felt utterly broken.

Hannah crossed her mind as she thought, so this is how betrayal truly feels. They had always shared the same sense of the ridiculous in life situations, and there was plenty of material here. She could do with her good friend who she could say anything to and above all, would understand the difficulties. Hannah would laugh and cry with her, but would mostly not pass judgement.

Verna scrolled the contacts in her phone, stroking the soft bundle in her lap, and was going to send Hannah a message. Unsure how to start, she realised it was well after midnight, and put her phone down. She recalled times when their outrage at Adrian's behaviour would turn to raucous laughter, joking at his, and Ginger Gezza's expense. Verna could imagine what Hannah's humorous responses about Leo might be and managed a smile.

46

Italy, June 2021

Leo arrived at his family home, near Lake Iseo in northern Italy, emerging from the hire car with his shirt, sweat-stuck to his back from the stifling journey in summer heat. His elderly father was sitting out front in a floral blaze; he had always kept the garden beautiful for Claudia's memory as she loved flowers. He stood as Leo walked towards him and held out his arms. They embraced, both men in tears, wondering how they had become strangers. Antonio grasped Leo and patted his back in their embrace crying, 'Leonardo, oh Leonardo my son, you have returned to me.' Tears streamed down Leo's face, his father's warm embrace, the memory and loss of his mother tore him apart. The family home hadn't changed much apart from essential maintenance and decoration required over the years. The house was one of a cluster of a dozen, within a ten-minute walk from the lakeside, with the surrounding hills rising majestically behind the town.

The house seemed small, he remembered the mezzanine floor leading to his bedroom, which was unchanged.

The downstairs area was dominated by a huge dining table that could comfortably seat eight people, yet there was his father dining alone most evenings. The outdoor terrace where Leo played was now covered with a wooden frame and trellis entwined with vines to shield the blazing sun. The terracotta pots filled with flowers were in the same position, their scent evoked distinct memories of him helping Claudia to water the plants. Leo had mixed feelings about being here, memories of his time with his mother were bittersweet.

Excursions around the town over the next few days to places he knew well, were fulfilling and he met many families who were living in the same houses. Nothing had changed. He spent hours at his mother's graveside talking with her. It gave him enormous internal peace. He laid a stunning bouquet of hybrid pink-edged yellow roses, Claudia's favourites, at her graveside and said he would return soon.

Conversations with his father, Antonio were strained at times, but as long as he kept it to a religious theme, it worked. Leo knew he couldn't stay for the long term. His head was clear, he didn't have to think about his wife or children or his former lover and their baby, as God would guide him. This was a new life for him, however, he needed to express his remorse to Graziella as part of his atonement. He would do the same with Verna and the children when the time was right, it was all part of his master plan. Leo made contact with the solicitors dealing with Graziella's maintenance claim and asked if they would pass on a personal letter to her.

Dear Graziella,

I hope you, you're family and beautiful Gabriel are healthy and happy. I did not know about Gabriel's birth. Your letter and photos were hidden from me for several months. Please believe I wasn't ignoring you or Gabriel. He is a perfect child and I know you are a wonderful mother to him.

I have given up my business and left England, as things haven't worked out with my marriage. I have returned to my father's home, and have regular counselling with my priest. Each day I gain strength from my faith to be a better person and now understand the wrong I have inflicted in my life that has hurt others.

If you feel it would be good for Gabriel to see me, I would be so happy, but would accept your terms if you don't want contact. Maintenance payments will continue, and if you need anything else, please let your solicitor know. I will do anything to put right the pain and suffering I have caused you and your family. I want you to know how desperately sorry I am that I hurt you. I was wrong and you did not deserve my behaviour.

Please give Gabriel a kiss from me, if you feel it is right to do so, and try to accept my humblest apologies, Leonardo.

Leo was perched on the bench outside the humble cabin he rented in the Bergamasque Alps. The stunning view filled him with grateful thanks. Leo was euphoric with an enlightening feeling. If he stepped off the edge of the pathway in front of him to the valley below, he would float to the ground, knowing his saviour would protect him. He said a prayer thanking his lord for the beauty surrounding him and for his forgiveness, then set off to walk into the mountains. As he walked, he thought about the response he received from Graziella's solicitor. She had agreed to meet him with Gabriel once under supervision from her family. The meeting was a few days away, which made him content, another opportunity for forgiveness. He continued walking with a spring in his step from the lightness within.

Graziella was anxious at the thought of seeing Leo. She had spoken with her family who agreed it wouldn't be acceptable for him to have any role in the child's life. Graziella was aware Leo may have parental rights for contact through official channels, so she hoped this meeting would satisfy any requests he may have. The security of having her brother and cousin observing in the vicinity of the meeting would ensure Leo wouldn't do anything stupid, like try to snatch her son.

The busy open park area for the contact was in the centre of town, avoiding any remote locations. Graziella spotted Leo heading towards the play area. He was still a handsome man, though looked thinner and older than she remembered from over a year ago; his dark hair had a peppering of grey. He caught sight of them and waved. She lifted her hand in response and looked towards the location where her family were stationed, who acknowledged they had seen Leo approaching.

'Ciao!' Leo greeted her warmly and they engaged in a conversation about Gabriel, including his health, his growth and his personality. He gazed at the beautiful nine-month-old infant sitting on his mother's knee. He complimented Graziella and Gabriel saying they both looked beautiful and well. She was absolutely stunning; however, Leo was not interested in adult attraction, he was saving his energies to devote to his faith. He said little about his recent circumstances or the complete separation from his English family and his former life, giving minimal answers to Graziella's questions. She was incredibly curious.

Leo seemed satisfied to have seen his son, and Graziella offered him an opportunity to hold Gabriel as she knew there was no threat from him. Leo was non-committal but did gently stroke the dark brown, soft hair on Gabriel's head, held his tiny hand and kissed it. Leo continued to talk about the Archangel Gabriel, and how their child Gabriel's existence was God-given. He thanked Graziella and reiterated he would support her, and she should maintain contact at his father's address. He promptly stood and walked away without looking back, eager to return to the small cabin-haven he now called home.

Graziella was unnerved by the transformation in Leo; from the charismatic, ebullient and sexy man she had once loved; to the benign, devout man she had just met. She held Gabriel close, stroked his plump, warm legs and kissed his silky-smooth fat cheek. Gabriel's big brown eyes looked into hers and he gave her a cheeky smile, revealing two small square, white lower teeth. She squeezed his tummy and he broke into jubilant giggles.

47

Verna, July 2021

'This is rather complicated.' said Verna to Olivia Mordue, the pinstripe-suited, dynamic solicitor, dealing with her divorce.

'Certainly is,' agreed Olivia. 'You do have options if you want to keep the house, but it would require you earning a specific level of income, which may mean taking employment until your business venture is established.'

'I haven't been able to set anything up with everything that's been going on, but the child maintenance income from Leo's father is enough to cover basic costs. Leo has no income by all accounts, and I'm unsure what to do about the rights of the business.'

'If you can sell the VLR Software name and goodwill, it would boost your funds, but the pandemic has made a dent in multi-nationals absorbing smaller concerns, especially with no active contracts. The options with your Quayside apartment are good however, either selling it to make a profit, or rent it out to provide monthly income. We can look at those figures, then judge what is preferable.'

'It's worth renting it out through an agent for now, I can't deal with anything more than that.' Verna's energy reserves were dwindling. 'If I pool everything from the sale of the company, and the cars I could pay a chunk off the mortgage, but it means a significant level of income will still be needed to pay for utilities and maintenance. School costs alone for three children aren't cheap, never mind the amount of food we need; then there's birthdays, Christmas, holidays, clothing, you name it, and I don't want them to suffer.' Verna tried to raise a weak smile.

'You will need Leo to engage, and sign his agreement to any financial transactions, particularly if you sell your house and the apartment,' suggested Olivia, 'but I don't know how difficult it will be if he's definitely gone A.W.O.L.?'

Verna heaved a deep sigh. 'I need to go and think about everything. Having to work, starting up my own business, caring for three children and having a sick mother isn't conducive to a stress-free lifestyle. I couldn't bear having to scrimp and save for everything, only to keep a massive house on a posh estate.'

'Well, your option to sell and buy a smaller place would free up some collateral, which would extinguish the mortgage, and subsidise living costs, plus any residue could be invested into a business.'

After the meeting Verna drove away and couldn't stop sobbing. She had to stop and pull over, unbeknown to her, into the same passing place as Hannah had after the awful kitchen argument, eighteen months ago. Verna couldn't see that well through puffy, watering eyes. She questioned what on earth she had done to deserve this, her tears came thick and fast. Verna looked at her left hand, the audacious engagement ring and wedding band mocked her. She took them off, said, 'I might get a few quid for those,' and placed them in her pocket. She looked through the windscreen with flashing random snapshot thoughts, and for some reason she couldn't recall the last time she had meaningful physical comfort from a man. It was a strange thing to occur to her, it led to misgivings about whether she would meet someone else, or end up alone once the children were grown up. She started the car, it stalled, she tried again, it fired up, and she set off home.

Feeling thoroughly depressed, she did a fake smile to Joyce, who'd made the children's meals, and after a brief chat about Izzy's recent educational assessment, said she had to go and search for some financial details her solicitor wanted. It was a diversion, as she wasn't in the mood for a chat with Joyce.

Joyce put her cardigan on, 'how's Leo doing? He's been in hospital a good-few days now, any update?'

With a glance around, closing the kitchen door Verna decided she wanted everything out in the open and said, 'he's not coming back Joyce.'

'What?' One look at Verna, and Joyce knew, 'Oh no,' she enveloped Verna in her arms, but she didn't acquiesce. 'What happened, how are you doing? I guess the children don't know?'

Verna shook her head. 'They don't. He's gone for good, back to Italy.' I told him to leave, there's much more I haven't told you. I'd like you to be around when I tell them.

'Really! Didn't he even explain anything or say goodbye to the children?' Joyce was flabbergasted.

Verna shook her head again, 'I believe he's had some sort of break-down, he had a … a crucifix and … angel candles around the place when we came back from Simon's.'

'Dear me … how very strange. Hmm, we need to think carefully what to do next.'

Verna appreciated the, we, in Joyce's response. 'I may have to sell up, not sure I can afford to live in this house,' tears pricked Verna's eyes and Joyce looked devastated, but rallied.

'Well … whatever happens, me and Nigel will support you and the children.'

Verna did acquiesce this time and fell into Joyce's maternal embrace, 'I can't thank you enough Joyce.'

Joyce agreed to have the girls to sleepover on Fridays, and would be around every day to help with cooking, cleaning and washing, whatever Verna needed while she looked for work. Joyce was as mad as hell, 'Bloody men, they have no idea what they put us through.'

'Are you going to give Nigel some grief on behalf of all womanhood when you go home?' Verna smiled. It always amused her when Joyce got on her metaphorical high horse.

'Oh, he's had plenty of that over the years let me tell you,' Joyce, arms folded, said firmly before she left, 'I'll be back later when they're in from school.'

Verna drifted upstairs, and opened Marco's bedroom door, she knew she had to do this. He was on a study day revising for an end of term assessment, so she took advantage of the girls being in school to have a conversation with him. As it was a Friday, Verna hoped she could manage any emotional fallout over the weekend regarding the news about Leo.

'You do know dad hasn't been well son,' said Verna as she sat on Marco's bed. Marco didn't turn around, but she noticed he was nodding. 'Sorry to interrupt your studies, but, dad ... dad's gone, he's gone to Italy and I ... I really don't know if he's coming back Marco. I wanted to let you know. Everything is up in the air, and we haven't been getting along—'

'Was he seeing someone? Was he having an affair?' Marco turned his thunderous face to look at her.

'Wh ... what makes you say that?' Verna was desperate in case Marco had overheard her conversations at Simon's house.

'I knew something was up between you. I just knew it, when dad had the breakdown and all the hospital stuff, losing his work and everything. I knew he wasn't right and something had happened in Italy.'

'This is so hard to say, but yes ... he was having an affair. I tried to shield you all from it, but it's no good, our marriage is over.'

Marco hung his head and looked away. Verna took his hand and encouraged him to sit beside her on the bed. They both cried together for some minutes. Marco picked up the metal coaster on his bedside table and threw it violently across the room. It hit the wall and left a dent in the plaster.

'Oh, don't Marco,' pleaded Verna, 'we'll get through this. We will, I promise.'

With venom Marco said, 'how could he treat you like that, the fucking bastard, who does he think he is? He's a selfish bastard who couldn't give a shit about anyone else.'

Verna had to allow her son to vent his anger and vitriol at his father. It was well-deserved, but she hated to see him in such pain. He sat beside her, put his arm around her shoulder and said, 'Amara is going to be devastated.'

Verna broke down and couldn't stop crying as he comforted her.

'I'll help you tell the girls; we'll say he's not well and has gone to Italy to sort his head out,' then through gritted teeth, 'the stupid fucking bastard.'

Verna nodded, saying she had already planned something similar, and for Joyce to be around as she already knew Leo was gone. 'You are more of a man than your father will ever be.'

Marco offered a resolute acknowledgement and pushed back his shoulders, 'it's not how you treat women, it's disrespectful. I've always been more like you than him.' Verna couldn't help but smile at her wonderful son.

Joyce had told Verna, Nigel said he would struggle seeing the children's grief, and may make the situation worse, but would call later if they wanted to see him. She understood Nigel's vulnerabilities. Verna brought the girls home from school, and gathered the children together. Joyce and Marco were waiting to share the bad news. Verna explained the situation about Leo simply and clearly.

'Dad isn't well, and he's gone back to Italy to—'

'Nooo!' Amara screamed in floods of tears before Verna had even got the words out. She knew, thought Verna, she knew, as she cradled her daughter, whose highly-tuned hypervigilance had come to fruition. Amara looked up at her mother with her father's dark brown eyes. 'When will he come back and see us?' she asked through uncontrollable hiccup-sobs as Verna wiped the abundant tears streaming down her pink sorrowful face.

'I can't say exactly, he isn't well sweetheart.'

'Can I ring him Mummy, please, now please!' Amara picked up Verna's phone, tapping it, but didn't know the passcode, and held it out to her, imploring her to ring Leo, 'I want to speak to him and tell him to come home now, I need to see him, please!'

'I'm sorry darling, so sorry.'

Joyce at this point intervened as Verna wasn't coping. She crouched in front of Amara, holding both of her hands, looking straight into her face, speaking softly, but firmly, 'your dad is safe darling, don't worry. He is staying with his father in Italy. I have an idea Amara,' maintaining eye contact, 'shall we make a card and you can write a message to him. Do some of your beautiful artwork and we can post it to him. I'm sure he'll love that.' With huge sniffs and slight nodding, Amara agreed. 'Come on, let's do it now,' Joyce encouraged her to go and get the craft box. 'I'll see if these rock buns and scones are ready.' Joyce was the master of distraction and comfort food, Verna thought, and worth her weight in priceless diamonds.

Verna looked at Marco who was upset at his little sister's response to the news. His youngest sister was sitting huddled up to him with tears rolling, making narrow tracks down her alabaster cheeks. 'We will see daddy again baby.'

Verna lifted up the full weight of her daughter and took her over to the tray of warm baked items fresh out of the oven. 'Smells like Joyce has made cinnamon rock buns, especially for you.' Izzy's bright blue eyes glistened with tears as she nestled into her mother's neck, 'which one do you want?' Verna stroked her ringleted blond hair, 'come on honey, choose one.'

Marco tucked into the scones. Amara was sorting through the bright sheets of card, glitter bottles, feathers and sequins in the craft box, her shoulders periodically lifted with sharp remnant sobs, as she wiped tears away.

They all dived into the warm reassuring scones and as the sniffles died down, Verna suggested, 'how about a Disney movie night. I'm sure Joyce will want to come over for that.'

'Ooh yes indeed I would! And mummy can take a long bath eh?' said Joyce into Verna's eyes, then brightly, 'shall we time how long it takes Nigel to cry, or worse, to join in with the songs, heaven forbid!' she dramatically rolled her eyes, which elicited a brief smile and sniffle from Amara.

'Marco, how about you contact Connor for a jamming session online, or invite a couple of friends over if you feel like it? You could have a marathon game session in your room, an all-nighter if you want ... and ... thanks son,' Verna patted his back, as she held a clinging Izzy close to her.

'Maybe, I'll see who's around.' He stuffed another buttery melting half scone into his mouth, with Rocco tucked under his other arm. Rocco had wandered to each family member individually, sniffing them, then nuzzling his face into their legs, until he received a pat or a scratch for reassurance. The family pet was attuned to the emotions of this family trauma, and sensed something major was occurring.

Joyce and Verna exchanged knowing glances. Life had to return to a stable, secure world as soon as possible. Marco, Amara and Izzy needed a safe space to grieve, within the comfort and familiarity of routine. Verna would offer them all of the positivity she could muster, even though her spirit was utterly shattered inside.

48

Hannah, May 2021

'They've split up?' Hannah repeated her sister-in-law Megan's news.

'So I believe,' said Megan, 'apparently Adrian has moved out to a rented flat, it's what I suspected, Gezza did want to have children and this seems to have been the issue. She's ten years younger than Adrian, and may well be looking for father material as she's only in her mid-thirties.'

Hannah replied genuinely, 'hope she finds him. Not that I want to gloat, but …'

'Gloat away, Adrian has proven to be the selfish sod we always knew he was. Good he has sons, maybe he won't die a lonely old man.'

'I am sad for him, he's not a totally terrible person, but you reap what you sow as the saying goes. Shame, I've always thought it would've been lovely to have some cute freckly, red-haired step-children.'

'Oh! almost forgot,' said Megan, 'Verna's took the children to see her brother in Bournemouth and Leo didn't go. She's taken them out of school too, most unlike her, being a stickler for rules. Apparently he ended up on a mental health ward during the summer, wonder what on earth has happened, there must be trouble afoot in that household too.'

'It must have been difficult running his business during the pandemic, he probably couldn't go on holiday for some reason?'

Megan didn't know anything about the kitchen argument between Hannah and Verna that fractured their friendship. Once Hannah had caught up with the local gossip, they engaged in chat about the children, parents, work, health, diet, food, clothes, you-name-it, and the inevitable discussion about perimenopause and other female-related uterine events.

Hannah recently had her cervical screening. 'My GP was in full PPE; mask, eye shield, scrubs and gloves, understandably so, she wouldn't want to either contract or pass on Covid, but it was like being probed by an alien.' After the call, Hannah was absolute in her motivation to make contact with Verna. However, wouldn't make any reference to Leo's infidelity, if indeed it was the case to prevent any underlying, I told you so, comment. A possible mental health intervention, Hannah pondered, whether that was true, she learnt long ago to take every morsel of Megan's gossip with a pinch of salt. Hannah was online looking at her steady stream of design requests.

'Coffee time!' Cam shouted upstairs. Hannah had set up a corner of the bedroom as a work station, but it was really cramped. She longed to move into The Willows, however wouldn't put any pressure on Cam. He had stuck to the plan of not doing much for some weeks, but she observed he was bored out of his brains, while she worked and the boys were in school.

'I'll do it,' said Hannah interfering with coffee-making, 'you go and sit down.'

'You've really got to stop this!' Cam said sharply, resting his hands on the kitchen worktop and sighed. Hannah looked at him perplexed and a little annoyed at his rebuff.

'Hannah, honestly, I'm fine. If there were any repercussions from the accident, it would have happened already. You're treating me with kid gloves and it's becoming annoying. I know you want to look after me,' his frustration spilled over, 'but you're making me feel like an invalid when there's nothing wrong, and I'm bored to hell. I can tell you're not as enthusiastic even when we're having sex in case I blow a gasket!'

Silence … then they both laughed.

'Okay, I get it, I'll back off,' Hannah looked seriously at him, 'but we have to be quiet during sex anyway, can you imagine the boys listening to moans, groans and grunts?' she grimaced.

'Yeah, you do need to stop making those noises.'

Hannah smacked his arm, 'it's not me making the racket!'

Cam grinned and suggested, 'how about we go to The Willows and see where we're at. Iain is sorted up at Laurel Trees, and he's doing a cracking job. For a skinny, wiry little fella, he's got the strength of ten men. He had an awful childhood you know and missed loads of school, but has come through it amazingly well, got a lot of time for the lad. A few more weeks and we'll be done.

They finished their coffees and went to The Willows. The sale was processed in record time as the vendors were days away from putting it up for auction, and keen to accept a cash offer. As soon as Hannah and Cam set foot through the door, it was like coming home. There was abundant partially renovated loft space, which Cam had begun to convert into a studio for Hannah, with a separate relaxation area for them in the evenings.

'It's an ambitious plan, but it can be done.' Cam paused, walked towards Hannah, wrapped his arms around her and said, 'I can't believe how my life is turning out. I'm so lucky to have met you,' he looked earnestly into Hannah's eyes and with a slightly nervous smile said, 'haven't got any bling yet, but will you marry me?'

'Of course I'll marry you! And I don't need you to give me a piece of ostentatious gorgeous white gold and diamond jewellery to cement the deal, but I wouldn't say no.' She smiled and kissed him. 'How about a traditional Scottish wedding at Laurel Tree House? Kilts and all!' Hannah surprised herself with her own inspiration, 'I'll speak to Jayne, she'll be great at helping me, em ... I mean, us, plan everything.'

Cam laughed, 'no problem, H, I'm happy to leave most of it up to you. But yeah, full kilt regalia sounds great. We need to tell your boys first of all, and I should ask Tommy for your hand in marriage, in keeping with tradition.'

'He'll snap up your offer, think he's been hoping someone would come along and take me off the shelf to stop him worrying … though I can't see him in a kilt.' Hannah burst out laughing at the thought of her father's sturdy bow legs on show.

Hannah and Cam announced the news to Evan and Ross who were supportive, though Ross had a quiet couple of hours. They then visited Martha and Tommy, and he officially asked for her hand in marriage, they were delighted.

'I'm thinking of asking Alisha over for tea if that's okay?' asked Evan, 'and can I invite a few others around later for takeaway too? Now restrictions are gone we can stay in the garden and use the back room for a games or movie night? And, can you keep Ross out of the way?'

Hannah replied, 'who is Alisha … and yes she can come for tea … and yes you can have friends around … but no, I'm not stopping your brother—'

'Don't want to be anywhere near you and your stupid girlfriend, and stupid mates anyway!' sneered Ross as he stomped away.

'Evan, why do you have to act like that, picking on your brother, it's bullying, have some respect for him!' Evan didn't seem bothered one bit; simply glad he got permission for the evening with friends.

'I'll sort something with Ross,' said Cam, 'could go bowling or to the cinema, something he wants to do.'

The evening was arranged and as Cam and Ross were leaving the house, Evan arrived with Alisha, who offered a polite greeting before heading into the back-room den. Hannah was impressed with Alisha's manners and her confidence as they engaged in conversation about school, friendships and her family. She was indeed a stunning girl. When Ross and Cam returned, the back-room party was in full swing with shouts of hilarity from the teenage gathering. Ross enjoyed the movie and the huge burger afterwards. He leapt straight upstairs to play on his new PS5, he had won the battle following Hannah's reasonable suggestion, that as Ross was always in receipt of Evans hand-me-downs, it was only fair he got something brand new. Ross never missed an opportunity to compare and gloat about the updated features of his console to Evan's outdated one.

Hannah was hiding away in the conservatory, glass of wine in hand, reading a book she'd been meaning to finish for ages, when Cam walked into the room and said disparagingly, 'well, she looks quite the heart-breaker.'

'Bit mean, are you implying my son isn't good enough or handsome enough for a pretty girl?'

'Not one bit, if anything he's probably too good for her.' He left to go upstairs and take a shower.

Hannah thought his comments were incredibly out of character, as Cam was one of the most amicable, gregarious men she had known. She didn't understand, he certainly was not racist, given Alisha's mother was Indian. Maybe it was unsettling having a young female in the house who would be visiting frequently, and perhaps staying over occasionally. Hannah understood those misgivings, but still, it was odd. She challenged him about it when he came into the conservatory, but he simply shrugged saying he'd hate to see Evan get hurt, as if it was inevitable. Cam helped Hannah clear the teenage debris and were thankful it was a successful night hosted by Evan. Alisha's mother picked her up, and she and Hannah exchanged pleasantries at the door.

Hours later, the penny dropped for Hannah as they lounged in bed, she turned to Cam and said, 'she reminds you of Delphine, doesn't she?' Cam glanced at Hannah and said nothing. 'It's tough, but our kids have to make their own mistakes. We can't protect them from everything, especially broken hearts.'

'True.'

'What happened with Delphine? And, what did happen in Ibiza?'

'Been having heart-to-hearts with my sister?'

'Indeed I have.'

'It's too long a story to tell you at midnight, but I was arrested … well … me and my mate, Stan-the-man, were arrested for nicking a boat and sailing it out to sea, had to be rescued by the coastguards and they were not happy! We left a bit of a trail of destruction behind us on that holiday.' Cam sniggered, then seriously said, 'the whole Delphine thing is way behind me now, Christ it would've been a big mistake if we'd got married.'

'Why did you separate?' Hannah knew the direct route would be more productive, 'had she met someone else?'

'Yep. A wealthy older guy who could keep her in the style she craved. Poor, literally poor, old Cam wasn't good enough.'

'If she hadn't dumped you, and Adrian hadn't left me, we wouldn't be lying here together in perfect happiness, so I'm glad she dumped you.'

'Well, if you look at it that way, Cam turned towards Hannah and slid his hand between her legs ... 'and keep a lid on it tonight, H, we don't want the lads overhearing.'

49

Hannah sat with her parents, Martha and Tommy, Cam with his parents, Fraser and Eileen, also Jayne and Martin around the large dining table at Laurel Tree House, discussing wedding plans. Jayne had escorted everyone around the building earlier, like a tour guide, pointing out its historical features. The external construction work was complete and the interior renovations were progressing, so far, without any hitches.

'Take it easy on the stairs Cam,' said Hannah as they headed to the cellar.

'Very funny H … very funny,' he replied.

Eileen was delighted with the house, which brought back her own childhood memories, as she chatted with Martha, 'the kitchen was called a scullery when I was a child, and we only had a pantry to keep fresh-food cool, no fridge-freezers in those days.'

'No, there wasn't,' Martha chipped in. 'I remember my nanna's bed-warming pans you filled with coal; and those heavy, pottery bottles filled with hot water to warm the bed. It was like sleeping between two sheets of ice getting into bed if you didn't warm it up. No central heating or electric blankets in those days, and scraping jack-frost off the windows on winter mornings.'

'Not forgetting the tin bath in front of the coal fire,' added Eileen, 'and the outside netty.'

'Oh yes, brass-monkeys in there, and creepy-crawlies,' confirmed Martha laughing. The women continued with the theme of days gone by, enjoying reminiscences like; hanging a line of terry towelling nappies out, flapping in a summer breeze, before disposable ones were common place, using a twin tub washing machine, and even before then hand-cranking a mangle to wring out the washing; also, how everyone thought microwaves were tools of the devil when they first went on sale.

'No idea why they are called the-good-old-days,' added Jayne dryly.

The families discussed wedding plans around the huge table with a glass of fizz or a whisky, which Jayne delicately sipped, everyone offered suggestions for the guest list, catering, and flowers. Final decisions would be made by the bride and groom of course.

'My list is easy,' said Hannah. 'I think my close family probably takes up half of the guest allocation.'

News was confirmed, restrictions eased, and after June 2021, one hundred guests could attend a wedding in Scotland, which was the maximum Laurel Trees could comfortably hold. Unless anything changed, they hoped to hold the ceremony in the grounds, weather permitting in September, with a contingency to use the largest reception room, if weather was poor. Whilst Jayne suggested all bells and whistles, Cam and Hannah insisted on keeping things uncomplicated. Hannah in particular wanted a simple tasteful affair, coordinating bronze and ivory colour schemes, with the men in traditional Wallace tartan kilts.

'It'll be more of a faff getting the fellas ready for this wedding,' she commented, 'can't wait to see Dad in his kilt,' she grinned at Tommy.

'I'll look like a right bobby-dazzler, I can assure you,' said Tommy.

'Aye, you will,' said Fraser, 'smart as a dart, and the cooling breeze is always welcome,' bouncing his eyebrows suggestively. He had the same crinkly, sparkly mischievous eyes as Cam. 'Our kid isn't daft getting wed on his fortieth birthday, at least he'll never forget his wedding anniversary.'

'Oh, so that was the ulterior motive,' suggested Hannah. Cam offered his own crinkly, sparkly mischievous grin.

Hannah resisted Jayne and Ellie's need to book a wedding-dress-try-on appointment and sip fizz while Hannah paraded around in fluffy meringues. It wasn't her style and social distancing still offered her reasons to deny them the opportunity. She gave them free rein regarding bridesmaid dresses to choose whatever they wanted within the colour scheme. Sara would have the final word on her flower-girl dress, but her mother Julia was waiting to tell her nearer the time as she'd have to scrape her off the ceiling for weeks.

Hannah ordered a semi-fitted simple ivory wedding dress from a boutique store online, which had a lace bodice and elbow length sleeves. She would wear a simple headpiece and no veil. She was thrilled when her mother-in-law-to-be, Eileen offered her a choice of Aunt Marie's necklaces to wear if she wished. She chose a modest silver chain pendant, set with diamonds, pale green peridot, and pink spinel stones. Hannah was overcome with joy when Jayne explained it was an, Edwardian Suffragette, pendant reflecting the colours of the movement.

'Excellent choice sis … can I call you that yet?' said Jayne as they hugged. She fastened the necklace around Hannah's neck.

'Of course you can, as long as you don't force me to drink whisky and dance the Highland Fling.'

'Looks lovely, it's yours,' said Eileen, checking with Fraser who nodded his consent.

Looking down, Hannah gently stroked the pendant, 'I love this, thank you so much.'

The couple agreed to no official wedding planner or master of ceremonies. They were pleased to discover humanist marriages, their choice of ceremony, were legal in Scotland. Hannah designed the invitations and guest placement cards and asked Eileen and Martha to sort out wedding flowers. Jayne and Ellie were in control of the practicalities and aesthetics of table placement, seating arrangements and helped Hannah with décor. Megan researched catering options to share with Cam and Hannah. Their photographer was a personal friend of Grant's, a keen amateur photographer who had completed wedding portfolios, and preferred contemporary, casual, candid shots. It was going to be a relaxed celebration. Cam appointed his brother-in-law Martin, to be his best man who would organise kilt hire.

Iain was the head groomsman, with Hannah's brothers as ushers. It all seemed to fall perfectly in place.

Hannah sat in the exclusive honeymoon suite on the four-poster bed with a glass of champagne, feeling emotionally exhausted after a busy planning day. It was only nine thirty but she needed to sleep. 'I hope we haven't upset anyone allocating specific roles and responsibilities,' seeking reassurance from Cam.

'Tough if they are. It's our day no one else's, we should have it exactly the way we want it.'

'I've been thinking a lot about Verna, I hope she's okay. If there's one friend I would want to have here, it's her.' Hannah couldn't help but spill a few tears, the glasses of champagne had prompted the tearful regrets. 'It's been over a year since I last spoke with her and I miss her.'

'Then invite her!' Cam sat beside her on the bed, held her close and asked, 'what's the worst that can happen? If she says no, then you know where you stand. To me it's been left up in the air and neither of you knows what to do. Plus, the pandemic has shifted everyone's thinking and behaviour. Someone has to make a move, are you worried she'll say no?'

Hannah nodded, 'maybe, because that would be final, the end of our friendship, but, I don't know … in some way I still feel a connection with her. After Megan's comments of her holiday without Leo, and the glimpses I've seen of her, I know something isn't right.'

'Perhaps she needs a good friend?' offered Cam.

'She should be here on the day. She'd love all this palaver.' Hannah smiled conjuring up images of Verna indulging in the glamour of it all.

50

Verna, July 2021

The Ravassio children became accustomed to the fact their father may not be around soon, and certainly not on a permanent basis. The adjustment wasn't too tough as they were used to functioning as a family without Leo when he was abroad on extended business trips their whole lives. There were moments of sorrow and longing for a perfect past, which the family had to work through. Verna, for one, felt like a grieving widow weighed down as if in heavy black clothing as befitted her mood. They were, in every sense, a bereaved family.

Verna continued to worry about Amara, from her exemplary behaviour and choice of language and expressions, Verna believed she may have, made a deal with God, to be as-good-as-gold so her dad would return. Verna wondered if she was saying prayers at night, though it could have been spells and incantations from, *Harry Potter* stories, which were the only thing keeping her going. She dearly wished Leo would reply to the card Amara sent, and tried to reassure her Leo was okay, and living quietly with his father; but the truth was, she had no clue where Leo was. Verna told Amara tales of her own time in Italy, showed her photos of the family home and the area around Sarnico, so Amara had some form of reference point.

'Might Daddy be in hospital in Italy Mummy?' Amara asked, curled up on Verna's knee on the sofa, her long legs dangling. Verna hoped she would revert to more age-appropriate dialogue and behaviour soon. Izzy was subdued, but was more expressive and understood her big sister wasn't feeling great; she often instigated games they could play together, or would simply hold Amara's hand, or hug her. Marco said little, and on the surface appeared to be getting on with his life as if nothing happened. Whilst Verna recognised this coping mechanism, it concerned her a deeper level of trauma was germinating within.

She had to make contact with, Antonio Ravassio, Leo's father to establish what was going on, there were also pressing legal matters to conclude. Verna worried each month child maintenance payments would cease and confessed her worries to her brother Simon, 'I have to assume Antonio is ensuring the funds are transferred into my bank account. I'm so grateful for your support looking over transactions, it's good to discuss the financial options with you and Jeremy.'

'If the funds stop, do let me know, it must be difficult when someone disappears and can't be easily tracked. At least you can contact his dad, or your solicitor can.' Simon moved the conversation on to something more positive. 'Are you still planning another trip here in the summer holidays?'

'Definitely, it's only a week until school breaks up, and the children are so excited.'

'So are ours, can't wait.'

'It'll be some time, if ever, before we're globe-trotting to the Florida Theme Parks, going on adventure breaks, or renting those audacious beach villas and city town houses in Europe. The annual skiing trips are done too, but honestly, Bournemouth was the best holiday we have had in years.'

'Pfft, course it was! How are you Verna … I mean, doing okay, really, okay?'

'I am Si, truly, I am. I'll feel better once the house move is settled of course.'

Verna made a point of the family sitting together for an evening meal at least twice a week, and a meal with Joyce, wine included, and Nigel at the weekend. A reluctant Marco usually gulped down his food to dash upstairs the instant he was excused; except on the Joyce and Nigel nights, as homemade apple pie, jam roly-poly, or sticky toffee pudding were on offer. One evening Verna asked the children, 'how are we all feeling about the new house, everyone okay with it?'

'Yea,' responded Marco, 'my bedroom seems bigger, or at least it'll be easier to arrange my PC desk, gaming chair and consoles.'

'And how about you two sharing until we get the alterations done for the fourth bedroom?'

'It's fine,' volunteered Amara, 'I'm happy as I'm going to have my new magical room set out exactly how I want it. Can I still have the Hogwarts theme we talked about?'

'Of course honey, but it's going to be smaller than your old room, you know that.'

'It's fine, Izzy needs more space for her ridiculous massive toys.' Amara rolled her eyes, so grown up, Verna was pleased to note.

Izzy was singing her favourite tune from the sensory group at school. Her assessment revealed she had, Developmental Co-ordination Disorder. It was easier for Verna to support her knowing what strategies she needed and school had been marvellous with their support. Izzy was learning touch typing methods as handwriting motor skills were difficult. Repetitive encouragement of other tasks was useful, and going through the calendar at the beginning of each day helped her focus. Whilst Izzy was hopeless, by her mother's admission, at any form of coordinated activity, she excelled in free-dance, and whilst she was a fidget during the after-school sessions, creating her own choreography, she could remember songs perfectly. Verna reflected Leo was missing out on the wonders of parenting her three fantastic children, his dismissiveness enraged her, 'his bloody loss,' she would often repeat.

Verna sold the cars, there was no regret or remorse about the pre-loved MGB as it left the driveway. She loved her brand-new SUV which catered for everything her family needed … and it was hers. She was amused thinking if Leo ever turned up, out of the blue, at their old house once they moved, he'd find a different family living there. Joyce and Nigel were relieved when Verna announced they were moving to a smaller house on the same estate. 'It's an exchange in effect,' Verna explained to them, 'the family wanted a larger house, so we did a sort of swap and the financial settlement fell in my favour.' Verna loved the idea of her own new home, the property had the location and attributes of their old house albeit on a smaller scale, therefore easier to manage.

Joyce called in to help out when Verna went to work; she accepted an offer as a beautician at the nearby exclusive leisure and golf complex. Though she held ambitions to run her own business, this work was easy and the location was perfect. She received quite a bit of attention from some of the male guests, and there was one chap in particular she was impressed with, however, that would wait. She couldn't contact Leo about a divorce and needed to focus on the children. Verna was enjoying the company and social aspect of working in a luxury environment, with lovely people.

'Are we popping to see Lena next week?' asked Joyce one day, 'I'll check with the care home to ensure the regulations still allow two visitors, if not I can go myself.'

'If you don't mind, I find it so depressing going on my own, and mum doesn't know who I am.'

'Don't mind at all, I can talk to her about things from the past. She's been such a glamorous lady, and she remembers all the designer clothes, popular perfumes and cosmetics. It's like a walk down memory lane, and she loves the old musicals too.'

'Bet you didn't think you'd end up singing a duet from South Pacific did you Joyce?'

'Indeed not, good fun though, plus it gives you a chance to speak with the staff about her care, she's not a well lady, is she?'

Verna shook her head. 'I should tell my father about the whole Loopy Leo scenario, and update him on Loony Lena, not that he'd concern himself about it.'

'If you don't mind me saying, I think he should take some responsibility.'

'Totally right Joyce. Haven't I've just ended up with the same type as my mother, funny, isn't it? But we've got you and Nigel as a far better surrogate family.'

Joyce smiled and swelled with pride as Nigel returned after walking Rocco. 'Keeping me fit is this little feller.' Nigel was besotted with Rocco and encouraged him to lick all over his face, the feeling seemed mutual. 'I'll come and walk him when you move, if you need me to?'

'Definitely, you're getting a key to the house and welcome anytime, there's no change, but for seven minutes extra walk away. Joyce needs to pop in to keep me company with the odd tipple too. Right Joyce?'

'Of course!' As they were leaving, Joyce shouted from the hallway, 'Post has arrived Verna!'

With a refreshing cup of tea in hand, Verna picked up the post and sat in the conservatory amongst boxes of stuff for the imminent move. Within the flyers and ominous official post, was a smooth vanilla coloured envelope, which gave her a start reminding her of Graziella's baby-reveal letter. It was addressed to both her and Leo.

There was another old-fashioned flimsy blue air mail envelope addressed to her in scratchy writing, not Leo's writing, and post-marked Italy. Verna remarked, 'not another bloody letter from Italy.' She wondered how it arrived as it was virtually illegible, also she thought pre-paid air mail letters were obsolete. Verna opened it and it was clear she was going to need internet translation and her best deciphering skills for this. At the end of the page, it was signed by Antonio Ravassio, Leo's father. Verna panicked in case anything had happened to Leo, separation was one thing but if he'd died, it would be devastating. She quickly scanned the letter for Leo's name and the word, morto, or anything similar, thankfully it wasn't written anywhere. Antonio referred to Leonardo using his full name, and from her sketchy Italian, she translated that he was living in the mountains. She would read it later.

Looking at the hand-written classy envelope, Verna recognised Hannah's handwriting. She was thrilled and had to stop herself from ripping it open. To her absolute delight it was a wedding invitation to Hannah and Cameron's wedding at somewhere called, Laurel Tree House, in Scotland.

'The lovely guy in the car park,' she whispered. Verna held it to her heart and a folded note dropped onto her lap, but she was interrupted by Izzy's loud distress and jumped up.

'Mummy! My hand's stuck.'

Izzy held out her hand. Colourful strings of wool were wrapped tightly around her hand and wrist. Sometimes she's a liability, Verna thought. 'Izzy darling, I've told you not to wind the wool around your hands, you only do that to help Joyce when she's knitting.'

'Please, take it off,' Izzy was in tears by now. Verna calmed Izzy and painstakingly unravelled the wool, making it into a game, then threw the remnants in the bin once Izzy went upstairs, making a mental note to put the craft box in a high place, out of her reach. It was quiet, at last. She topped up her tea and went into the conservatory opening the note from Hannah.

> *Dearest Verna,*
> *I sincerely hope this note finds you, Leo and the children well. As you can see, I'm getting married again. Who would've thought? Cam is a lovely guy, I'm lucky this time.*
>
> *I would be so grateful if you could find it in your heart to forgive me for the things I said. I wasn't happy with myself, but that's no excuse to take it out on a wonderful friend like you. Please accept my sincere apologies for being such a massive idiot! I'm so sorry.*
>
> *Whatever you decide to do with this invitation I will respect, but know that it is sent with the best intentions. We would both be so pleased if you could join us for our wedding celebrations. I've missed you Verna and would dearly love to see you soon. Much love to you, Hannah xx*

Verna immediately sent a text to Hannah; *Hi Hannah. Got the invite. Congrats! Thank you for thinking of me, of course I will come! So good to hear from you. Missed you. When are you free? Lots to tell!! Verna xx* Verna completed the stylish R.S.V.P. impressed with Hannah's gorgeous design, but expected nothing less. She gave a satisfied smile as the reply envelope rested neatly in her lap ready to post the next day, when her phone pinged.

51

Hannah, August 2021

It was moving day and whilst Cam, Hannah and the boys were excited to finally be moving to The Willows, it was a rush to do so before the wedding. 'Put the boxes in the rooms marked on the top!' Hannah reminded everyone. Most of her family, Cam's parents, his sister Jayne and husband Martin had volunteered to help out. Younger brother Grant was in charge of everything electrical; installing TVs and sound systems where needed and connecting everything to WIFI, including Hannah's work station in the loft. Ross was helping Nanna Martha in the kitchen making sandwiches and keeping everyone refreshed with rounds of cups of tea and biscuits. Martha had brought her ten-cup brown betty teapot along for that purpose and Megan had made huge catering size quiches, pies and sweet tray-bakes for lunch. All Evan was bothered about was getting his PC and consoles set up, with the help of Uncle Grant, until Grandad Tommy encouraged him to help in the garden. Pottering around outside was his domain, and Evan enjoyed helping him clear everything out of an old shed round the back of the house.

'Absolutely love this place,' said Ellie giving her sister a massive hug, 'totally suits both of you, and a perfect place to work.'

'Hey, you're welcome to work from here Ellie, there's plenty of space and it'll be good to have some company. I would love to have someone around to bounce artistic ideas off, and maybe do some joint ventures. I'm used to working in a team, and I've got loads of enquiries, could do with some expert help to be honest.'

'Good idea, I'd love to.' Ellie then grabbed Cam for a hug too. 'Everything is finished and packed for Laurel Trees, ready to be transported. I have an affinity with the paintings and other pieces, so I am actually going to ride in the back of the van with them to make sure my precious art-babies arrive safely.'

Cam laughed. 'You've done some cracking work Ellie. We are going to pay you for your time and expertise,' he held up a hand to her protestations. 'I know you've refused, but—'

'As long as I'm invited to stay regularly for mates' rates so I can tend to my art-babies, I'm happy.'

'The portrait of Aunt Marie from her photo is amazing,' said Hannah, 'you've really caught her strait-laced distinguished look, but softened it too. It's excellent, it'll take pride of place.'

Hannah's phone pinged. 'It's from Verna, it's Verna!' She read the message and replied immediately saying she was in the middle of moving and would call her later when she's free. The reply from Verna was brief saying how strange it was she would be moving soon too.

Cam gave Hannah a hug, a little on the smug side, 'see, bet you're glad I told you to invite her to the wedding.'

'That's great Hannah,' said Ellie, 'I do hope you and Verna sort things out. Wonder what's happened if she's moving house, maybe it has all gone tits-up. You may have been right about Leo.'

'Hmm she hasn't mentioned him, but she did write, I, not we, will come to the wedding, also, there's lots to tell.'

'Hey! Are you lot just going to stand about gassing? There's plenty of stuff to shift yet,' shouted Jake from the top of the stairs.

'Big brother really is watching us,' Ellie smirked. 'Thinks he's still in the army doing everything with military precision.'

'On my way,' said Cam as he leapt up the stairs to help.

Hannah and Cam spent their last night at Hannah's house. It seemed fitting for her to be speaking to Verna at a time when she was also going through transitions. Both women were heading for a new chapter in their lives.

52

Hannah and Verna, August 2021

Verna was excited about catching up with Hannah. Their emotional connection had been re-established, and both were at peace with each other. For now, though, she needed to make sense of Antonio's air mail letter as it may give some insight or information about Leo's whereabouts and wellbeing. The translation was difficult, as she was unsure of his scratchy lettering, however it made sense in the end;

> *Dear Verna*
>
> *I have the beautiful card and photos Amara sent to her father. I will give to him when he returns. It is sad we did not see the grandchildren. Claudia would have loved them. Amara looks like her, it made me cry. I would like to introduce myself as grandfather, get to know the children, and show them this beautiful place. I have plenty of space here. You may not want this, I understand. It is sad Leonardo and I did not have a good relationship, we are trying to improve this. I cannot tell you much about Leonardo, he*

is in the mountains, he seems healthy and at peace with his faith. Please tell the children they are in my heart. God bless you all. Antonio Ravassio

'Not sure about the, healthy, bit Antonio.' Verna remarked to herself. The loose translation of Antonio's letter evoked a simple message. It was regretful the estranged father and son relationship prevented him from knowing his grandchildren. Though it was never too late to repair the damage, Verna decided to hang fire on telling the children about the letter as she knew Amara would want to be on the next flight over there. She had to take it slowly, plus, they were moving soon, therefore little time to plan a trip. The thought crossed her mind, what would she do if they turned up in Italy and Leo was there, or worse if he didn't turn up to see the children. It was difficult, however she was inspired and relaxed knowing she could, run it by Hannah. 'Run it by Hannah,' she said aloud, she couldn't count the number of times she must have said that in her life. Her phone buzzed with a simple message: *Ready when you are x*

Verna replied: *Pouring the wine x*

A further reply read: *Way ahead of you!* Within seconds Hannah's phone rang. In a rush she said, 'Verna, how are you? Can't tell you how lovely it is to be in touch. Thrilled to bits you can come to the wedding.'

'Hi Hannah, so lovely to hear your voice. Let me apologise to you first of all, I was so out of order saying what I did, and—'

'Hey, I'll stop you there. We were both well out of sorts that day. It's done, no need to apologise.'

'Okay ... well I am sorry. We've already wasted lots of time not being in touch.'

'I'm sorry too, I've really missed you. Are you all keeping well? I'm intrigued by your message, what is there to tell?'

'Oh ... my ... God! How much time have you got?'

'The rest of my life,' Hannah said, and meant it. 'Hey shall we link up online? I'd love Cam to quickly say, hi, if you're okay with that.'

The women set up their devices and Cam made a brief appearance to introduce himself to Verna. He left the room saying, 'I think you two may be on for some time.'

'Ah, he seems lovely Hannah,' said Verna.

'Honestly, he is, fell on my feet this time.'

'Well, I've had the rug pulled out from under mine.'

Within minutes the two women were chatting, laughing and catching up on the intervening months. Hannah was horrified when she learnt about the Italian baby and the, Loopy Leo saga, as Verna referred to it. Hannah said, 'it's tough for the children when their dad goes out of their lives, especially suddenly like both our exes did. It's horrible, poor Marco, Amara and Izzy. I've missed them too, we should meet with the kids, I think garden visits are allowed, lost track of the restrictions if I'm honest. If your three see other children who have survived a separation, it may help. I can ask Evan to connect online with Marco too.'

'That would be superb, Marco has mentioned Evan a few times and I foolishly never got in touch. Then madness took over.' Verna was quiet.

'Honestly, the times I was about to ring you ... but didn't,' both women fell silent. 'Let's make a pact never to be so daft again.' said Hannah.

'Definitely, how stupid we've been, but the pandemic hasn't helped either. I'd love to see you, Evan and Ross and little Sara, she sounds an absolute peach.'

'She's gorgeous, it's exciting having a step-daughter, she's the same age as Izzy, they could play together, which would be lovely.'

'Oh, there's more to tell you about Izzy. You know she's always been a quirky little thing, forgot about that particular saga.'

'Another saga?' Hannah laughed. 'When can we meet up, we've missed so much?'

'I'll check with Joyce my babysitter and we'll sort something.'

'Come to my new house, you'll be like a first-footer.'

'Dunno about that, I haven't been so lucky lately.'

'Things can turn on a sixpence, I know that now.'

'Can't they just, our lives looked so different not so long ago.'

The two women looked at each other via their screens and smiled warmly. Over thirty years of friendship which had been broken, was fully repaired within thirty minutes. Later, Hannah crept into bed.

'Everything ok?' asked Cam. 'You've been chatting for nearly three hours, so I guess it is.'

With a huge yawn Hannah croaked, 'brilliant.' and was asleep within a minute.

A few days after the call, Hannah was squinting into dazzling August sunlight as she watered the thirsty floral hanging baskets adorning the front door of The Willows. Her loose-fitting tie-dye sundress and thong sandals helped to keep her body and feet cool. She put down the watering can, went in the house, emerging with hair scraped into a high pony tail, wearing huge sunglasses, so she could finish the task without being blinded. The sound of a car distracted her, she looked toward the road at the new silver SUV pulling up outside her gate. Verna got out, wearing a peacock-blue, corporate tunic and trousers from the salon, with her hair neatly gathered in a French plait, her bag slung over her shoulder. She held a small gift bag as she opened the gate smiling broadly at Hannah, who plonked the watering can down and hurried toward her. The two friends embraced.

'I can't tell you how good it is to see you,' said Verna.

'It's been far too long,' agreed Hannah, 'come in and cool off.'

'You haven't got a dress I could wear, have you? Came straight from work and forgot to bring one to change into.'

'Sure, got a couple of sundresses up here.' In Hannah's bedroom, she noticed a slight widening of Verna's waistline, and understood the problems of getting to a gym, or going for a run when you're a working single parent, plus there's age, and of course, wine.

'Here's some goodies from the salon, you'll have to come for a session.' Verna suggested.

'Lovely thank you, I definitely will.' Hannah looked at the gift bag, and didn't refer to the fizz-truffle episode in

Verna's kitchen, but smiled ruefully. 'Still thinking of setting up on your own? I'll do all of your publicity stuff.'

'That'd be great, but I'd struggle to pay the fees.'

'Would be on the house, it'll be good exposure for me. I seem to get industrial or construction type requests all the time, so it'll be lovely to create something glamorous for a change.'

'Thanks Hannah. Oh, I know!' Verna was inspired, 'I'd love to do hair and make-up for the wedding if you like?'

'That, is one excellent idea, as long as you make me look more beautiful than everyone else.'

'No problem, you gorgeous woman.' Verna was changed into the sundress when they both paused, looked into each other's eyes and fell into an emotional embrace.

'I've missed you so much Hannah Kay.'

'And I've really missed you too, Verna Stevens,'

Verna smiled hearing her maiden name. It was as if no hiatus had interrupted the two friends, who had their first awkward meeting at school all those years ago. They slid effortlessly into natural conversation as it had always been.

'Take a look at this.' Verna handed Graziella's letter to Hannah, who opened it gingerly.

'You sure you want me to see this?'

'Absolutely, I need you of all people to understand what I've been through.'

Hannah read the translated version of Graziella's letter Verna had placed in the envelope. 'My god Verna,' looking at the photographs, she stopped with instant recognition, 'Leo's yellow shirt ... Bellissima ... and the lake, and ...' The imagery was stark, tears welled up as Hannah looked into her friend's sapphire blue eyes, reflecting the stunning blue sky.

'You were right all along. Bellissima … hah! Is that what you called her?' Verna was amused. The women hugged again as Hannah grieved for the betrayal her good friend had suffered at the hands of her duplicitous, selfish, errant husband.

'If only I had listened to you.' Verna said as they lay on loungers, content in sweltering silence under the willow tree, with ice-cold drinks, nothing needed to be said. The missing piece of their life jigsaw has slotted back in its rightful place, and the picture was now complete.

'Is the salon in that huge mansion hotel near the lakeside? Isn't it part of an exclusive golf club or something? Is it really glam inside?' Hannah bolted upright, 'more importantly, are there any nice fellas?'

'Which question do you want me to answer first?' Verna smiled.

'The last one of course!'

'Well, there is this guy, Rod … Rodrigo, he's Portuguese, been living in the UK most of his life, divorced, adult kids—'

'Rodrigo, what is it with you and continental types?' Hannah laughed and asked flippantly, 'but is he rich and handsome?'

'Of course!' Verna replied with equal flippancy. 'I've clearly got a weakness, or maybe it's an illness. He is nice looking, not in a flashy way,' Verna's face relaxed. 'I couldn't care if he's wealthy or not, he seems considerate and polite, been a member of the club for years. The girls at the salon, and other staff tell me he seems a straightforward, honest guy, no skeletons as far as they know. I had a coffee with him after work one afternoon and he does seem genuine. But ... obviously, I'm wary. It'll take a lifetime for me to trust anyone.'

'Understandable, I nearly let Cam go at first. I was so unsure whether I wanted another long-term relationship that I, one hundred percent assumed, would fall apart and I'd be devastated again. Yet look at me now, glad I took the chance. Happy to report he's as sexy as anything too.'

'Great! Can't remember the last time I had a damn good romp, I'm about due anytime now surely.' Verna turned towards Hannah, lifted her sunglasses, squinting against the brightness, 'I'm so happy for you Hannah, Cam is great. You deserve it all, especially the business success. I told you Leo said he should've chosen your design for his company?'

'Don't tell me, he went for the pretty young thing instead?'

'Of course.' Verna nodded. Looking around the garden, 'this place is fantastic, what a find.'

'We'll do a tour in a bit. Anything new about Leo?'

'Nothing and it's been a while since he signed the house over. I'll send a note back to Antonio, as you suggested and will keep things quite loose. I don't know whether to consider the children meeting with Leo. If he's unreliable he may not turn up, which would traumatise Amara even more. I'm not sure about Marco either, he's inwardly furious and humiliated about it ... we'll see.'

Hannah turned to her, 'bloody hell what if he turned up in a cassock, like the sexy priest in, *Fleabag!* Now that would be traumatising.'

Verna burst out laughing and they both couldn't stop as their cheeks and sides ached.

Hannah reflected on her own experience after their hilarity waned. 'Seriously, it's bad enough for us, but horrible for the children. At least Marco and Evan have hooked up online, but we should get them together. In fact, the kids could stay over while you sort your new house, it'll be lovely to have them here, with little Sara of course, she's visiting soon.'

There was a pause, Hannah knew of the sensitivity of her next question. 'Will you tell the children about Gabriel?'

'Honestly Hannah, I don't know? It's not the baby's fault he was born as a result of an affair, and not Graziella's fault either, she thought Leo was divorced. Gabriel is their half-brother, and I know Amara would be thrilled to have an Italian sibling. She's definitely got an affinity with all things Italian, shows loads of curiosity about her origins, she's learning the language, and loves cooking Italian meals. It's all about her loss.' Verna for the first time looked dejected. 'Who knows, maybe over time me and Graziella could make contact. It's all so complicated. I'd hate for them to find out by accident, but telling them now, would be unsettling, and totally surreal. Plus, the virus transmission still worries me about travelling abroad, it's another complication.'

'Now is not the time Verna, you've enough on your plate with the move and new job, you need to focus on your children and getting your life back together. I thought Adrian was the ultimate arsehole, up and leaving me and the boys the way he did, but Leo having a baby with someone else.' Hannah shook her head.

'I know, I should write a book about it, but no-one would believe me,' said Verna.

'You've definitely trumped me in the selfish bastard ex-husband category.'

Both women laughed and shared knowing looks of how the betrayal feels.

'We should arrange a night out soon, now bars and restaurants are opening up,' said Verna.

'Agreed.' said Hannah as they clinked glasses of iced cloudy lemonade, smiling and relaxing in the shade of the gently swaying, golden shimmering, willow leaves.

53

Laurel Trees, Scotland, September 2021

'I pronounce Hannah and Cam, married!'

The guests erupted into applause and cheers when Cam and Hannah kissed. The celebrant completed a wonderful ceremony, tailor-made to include their vows, which included their children. Sara leapt up, hands in the air when her name was announced. Julia finally told Sara she would be a bridesmaid a few weeks before the wedding, so she had time to choose her fairytale flower-girl dress, shoes and hairband. She wanted to look like Hanny. Sara had made her own word up for Hannah, she said it was *"mixing Hannah with mummy."* Hannah adored her special name.

Cam's right-hand man Iain and brother-in-law Martin kept an eye on his whisky intake the previous night, staying in the nearest hotel with the chaps. They had organised kilt hire and ensured transport to Laurel Trees was in place for guests. Meanwhile, the women had Laurel Trees to themselves, and Verna did a sterling job of wedding hair and make-up. Sara was in her element, sitting patiently as her long dark hair was adorned with flowers, just like Hanny.

Ellie organised the chill-out music and kept everyone calm, topping up the fizz as they prepared for Hannah and Cam's big day. Hannah's sister-in-law Megan offered small exquisite light pastry treats for brunch too.

Hannah looked elegant in her wedding dress, dark hair loosely woven into her headpiece, holding a small spray of roses, peonies and dark green foliage. Ellie had expertly cleaned Aunt Marie's necklace which sparkled in the sunlight. Suppressing her nerves, Hannah walked down the aisle and met eyes with Cam as he turned toward her, looking resplendent in his kilt wedding outfit. She loved his shorter hair and neat goatee, in keeping with his handsome boho look. As she joined him for the start of the ceremony, handed over by an emotional Tommy, Cam gazed adoringly at her and said one word, 'stunning.'

Jayne and Ellie chose classy bridesmaids dresses which coordinated with the colour scheme. Evan and Ross agreed to wear kilts for the ceremony, they didn't have to, but once they got used to the idea from the men in the family, they were rather proud to wear them. They looked so grown up, Hannah reflected, as Evan now towered above her. Her mother, Martha, wore a beautiful diaphanous mother-of-the-bride outfit and Cam's mother Eileen wore a flowing maxi dress and silk shawl. They looked beautiful chatting together. The mix of contemporary décor, humanist service, and traditional Scots style, combined effortlessly. The weather remained fine, the food was lovely, the drinks flowed, the speeches were meaningful and hilarious, especially from Hannah's dad, Tommy. A wonderful time was had by all.

There was a moment after the marriage ceremony, held under a garland-strewn arch, when Hannah glided along the open-air aisle, arm entwined with her proud husband Cam. Evan and Ross followed holding hands with Sara in between. Hannah locked eyes with Verna; Marco and Amara sat either side, with Izzy perched on her knee. The friend she thought she'd lost forever, had returned to her. Verna mouthed, *beautiful*, with her broadest smile, and wiped tears from her face. Hannah Kay Wallace couldn't have been happier in her life.

Acknowledgements

The Letter from Italy was inspired by a podcast at the onset of the pandemic in February 2020. A situation arose where two lovers, in the early stages of an affair, had to make a decision as lockdown was ordered; both decided to leave their respective partners and move in together. Many scenarios in those remarkably unusual times got me thinking, and so, The Letter from Italy, was conceived. With those difficult times in mind, my first acknowledgment of deep gratitude goes to all health and key workers who risked so much to support the rest of us. Thank you.

Without the patience and kindness of three people, I would not be a writer; my sister Valerie, and my good friends Diane and June. I relied upon their wisdom, enthusiasm and advice to stick with me as I pursued my dream of becoming a writer, thank you. My appreciation also goes out to Deborah, in the USA, for your initial encouragement.

I thank my two adult sons, Daniel and Joel who most definitely inspired this book in the best possible way. Your consistent online chats when we couldn't be together were invaluable, remember those virtual family quizzes?! I hold every moment I now spend with you, Lauren and Jess as more precious than diamonds. Big thanks to my husband, John, we endured the Covid cabin-fever months together, but managed to enjoy our walks in a silent city.

This story is about separation, family, and friendship and how misunderstandings can grow into irreparable situations, causing estrangement. I have dedicated this book to the most wonderful, thoughtful, funny and compassionate friend I was privileged to have, Dawn. We lost Dawn too soon, but her legacy is her gift to our friendship group, gelling us back together. Thank you Dawn.

Finally, and most surely not last, is you lovely readers. I am eternally grateful and incredibly thrilled you chose to read this book. With all my heart, thank you! I do hope you've enjoyed Hannah and Verna's journey, and if you have a long-lost friend, why not give them a call.

About the Author

Mel was born and bred in Newcastle, the second of four children, she hails from a large extended family. She is married with two adult sons. She spent most of her career in Children's Social Care. When she is not writing, you will find Mel socialising with friends and family on Newcastle's Quayside, taking walks along the stunning north-east coastline, and has been known to take a dip in the North Sea! Say hello to Mel and find details of her books on her website at; melfrances.co.uk

DESTINATION MAISIE – *The Journey of a Lifetime*
Maisie's life begins with questions. Born illegitimately in 1960, she grows up in a children's home, then with a foster family. At seventeen, she finds a hidden letter from her birth mother, a revelation that changes everything. Determined to piece together her past, Maisie reunites with her mother, but her father remains a mystery. Decades later, a clue leads her to Crete, where she hopes to find her Greek family, but she uncovers a secret so devastating it shatters her. With a broken spirit the search for belonging becomes a battle to heal her emotional scars. Maisie's journey is raw, real, and unforgettable. A tale for anyone who's ever wondered where they belong.

THE IMPROBABLE THREE –
One death, three strangers, and a secret
Set in the heart of Newcastle City, journalist Maia Hewson navigates a new career, a tumultuous love-life, and a ten-year-old secret that threatens to unravel her world. When her close friend, Tom, meets a tragic end, Maia is drawn into the dangerous world of narcotics and child abuse. Together with two of Tom's friends from a children's home, they discover a sinister figure with a twisted past stretching back decades. The unlikely allies gather evidence for DS Chris Powell to investigate, but what must each of them risk to bring him to justice? A story of resilience, and how the most unlikely of friendships can triumph.

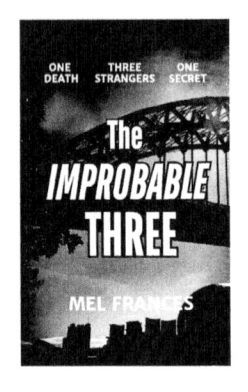

Printed in Great Britain
by Amazon